Molly swallowed. She felt like she had just stepped into the vortex of a new storm. The door opened and Carolyn stepped inside. She had taken off the robe. Molly could feel her blood percolate as she stared at Carolyn's breasts, the curve of her hips. She pulled Carolyn to her. Carolyn's lips were open, a sensuous invitation to what lay underneath.

This is what I wanted to do, Molly thought as her mouth explored Carolyn's. *I've wanted to taste her.*

"Come on." She had seen the sultry look in Carolyn's eyes and wanted more. She backed Carolyn up to the bed and bent over and took first one and then the other nipple in her mouth. Carolyn tasted salty from the seawater that had bathed her. "I've wanted to do this for so long," Molly murmured against her breast.

"Me too." Carolyn's voice was soft, almost inaudible. She touched Molly's neck and her hand traced a line down to her breasts. "I wanted to know how far these freckles went and now I know." Carolyn's mouth feasted on her breasts as if they were a banquet.

Molly closed her eyes. All the weeks of being near her and afraid to touch her erupted in her mind. She raised Carolyn's face to hers and knew from the look in Carolyn's eyes that she understood.

Molly pushed her onto the bed and stretched out on top of her. She pulled Carolyn's hips into hers and kissed her as powerfully as the storm that hammered the outside of her boat. Molly pictured the storm and could feel the boat rock underneath her.

I've got to make her happy. Molly's thoughts became a mantra as she listened to the change in Carolyn's breathing. The quick intake of breath as Molly's tongue swept over first one and then the other breast. The way Carolyn's hands gripped her shoulders as Molly's hand trailed down Carolyn's abdomen, resting just above that spot where she knew Carolyn's passion would come to fruition.

Visit

Bella Books

at

BellaBooks.com

or call our toll-free number

1-800-729-4992

Finest Kind of Love

Diana Tremain Braund

Bella
BOOKS

2004

Bella Books, Inc.
P.O. Box 10543
Tallahassee, FL 32302

Printed in the United States of America on acid-free paper
First Edition, Second Printing - January 2005

Editor: Christi Cassidy
Cover designer: Michelle L. Corby

ISBN 1-931513-68-6

This book is dedicated to Jean Symonds,
a consummate lobsterman and
spectacular woman

About the Author

Diana Tremain Braund continues to live on the coast of Maine in a house that overlooks the water. She and her dog, Bob, who is now six years old, take long walks on the beach. This is where she comes up with ideas for Bella Books.

You can e-mail the author at dtbtiger@yahoo.com.

Prologue

"We're going in," the boss said as he pulled the ski mask down over his face. "Lights are out, there's no one home." His voice gave off a hissing noise. "Pull that mask down," he ordered brutally, the words a command, not an invitation.

The spring night was tranquil. The spring peepers were singing a capella, the *peep-peep* sounds rhythmic and sonorous. The night was cool. The moon had slithered behind angry coal-black clouds. There was a murkiness to the night. No one was out on the street; they were waiting for the nor'easter that hung ominously offshore. The winds thumped against the side of the tiny Honda, which swayed as if it was doing a Vienna waltz. Soon the winds would redouble and multiply in ferocity and the car would move like it was in the throes of an epileptic fit.

The door on the aging Honda opened, then shut with the gentle *click* sound of a door being shut as quietly as possible.

Now they were on the sidewalk, heading to the house. Two masked shadows, slithering through the night.

He tugged at the ski mask, which stuck to his face. His sweat acted like Krazy Glue pulling the fabric tighter and tighter against his skin. He moved his mouth and the mask responded, moving like spandex on a bicyclist's taut thigh. There were tiny peepholes to look out, but his eyelashes kept scraping the top of the fabric, making his eyes tear. He pulled the mask up and away from his lashes so it didn't act like blinders on a jittery racehorse. His cheeks itched under the mask, but he was afraid to scratch, afraid to do anything more than put one foot in front of the other and follow the black-covered form that was in front of him. Was he following a shadow or simply a mirror of himself? They had selected black jackets and jeans. Why had they put the ski masks on so early? Wouldn't people looking out their windows wonder about two people wearing ski masks in May? Or were they really specters, spirits and spooks? Ahh, he thought, they had put the masks on early because it made them invisible. These were magic masks, he reasoned, that made them invisible to everyone but those who were also wearing masks. He giggled as he thought about his newfound anonymity. It felt like there was a vertiginous assault on his mind; he was spinning through the air like the May nor'easter. The pop he had taken earlier made him feel indomitable. The winds, like his thoughts, pushed him one way and then another. He liked it when his mind spun and his body felt buoyant.

"Quit bumping into me." The boss's words were a razor of reality.

How could he be bumping when he was flying with the wind? "Sorry," he mumbled.

"Wait here," the black shadow commanded.

He closed his eyes. He could feel himself floating above his skin. Like on a Ferris wheel that pushed higher and higher into the night. There were no boundaries to the night. No fences to hold his body in. No enclosure to control his floating thoughts. He heard the click, the front door opened.

"In." The voice mugged his thoughts. A hand grabbed his shoulder. "Stand here and watch the street. If a car even parks in front, let me know."

I can watch the street, he thought. *I can dance on the ceiling and pick flowers off the walls.* Where had he seen the flowers? He looked around. They were there on the wall. The light from the street lamp outside passed through the transom and cast a thin shadow on the wall. There were roses, thousands and thousands of roses. How nice, he thought, he was in a rose garden. Stop and smell the flowers. He giggled quietly. He reached out and he tried to pull a rose away from the wall. It eluded him. *If I tuck two fingers together,* he thought, *I can reach it.* He stared at one rose that seemed to demand his attention. *If I put my fingers here on the stem,* he thought, *I will own a rose.* He reached out and, using his thumb and forefinger, touched the flower. The flower pulled back. He stepped closer to the wall. Using three fingers, he eased his hand up to the wall. The flower pulled back. *Ahh,* he thought, *the flower wants to play cat and mouse.*

Opening his hand, he placed his palm against the wall and stretched his fingers toward the flower. His body swayed and his hip struck something hard. That something upended and clattered as it hit the floor. An upstairs light flicked on.

"What the fuck," a voice hissed from the other side of the room. "Get out of here." The breath was hot against his face. "Christ, she wasn't supposed to be home. Meet me at the house." The voice was ragged. "Here."

He felt something push against his chest. He wrapped his arms around it as if it was a football and he was a wide receiver and he jumped. His feet connected with the porch and he ran.

Sweat and dread mingled. He pulled the mask off his face and threw it aside. The winds were harsher and they jostled him as he ran. New rain beat his face. He opened his mouth to collect new breath, but a sharp pain pricked at his lungs. "Run," he muttered. *I've got to keep running.*

Chapter One

"Molly Bean, Molly Bean."

Molly located the source of the voice across the dock. "Hey, Auntie Em." Molly stood and waved.

"Goodness," an out-of-breath Aunt Em called as she hastened toward the boat. "I feared I was goin' to be late."

It was 5 a.m. and Molly was preparing to release the stern and bow ropes she had tethered the night before. Her thirty-eight-foot lobster boat was ready; she had lifted the provisions aboard an hour earlier. Barrels of bait sat nearby, the rotting fish smell hanging in the air like six-day-old road kill.

Molly's wooden vessel, the mahogany planking over white oak, was her baby. It had a specially built pilothouse with deck lights that glowed at night like tiny patio lights. Earlier Molly had removed the sidewall of the pilothouse, leaving it exposed to the ocean. On the gunwale there was a twelve-inch pot hauler hanging from a davit.

Part of the pot hauler was a large metal wheel, called a snatch block. Soon Molly would flip the rope around the snatch block and push a lever. The wheel would hum as it spun; it was the power that pulled the lobster rope from its watery home. The pot hauler and snatch block kept Molly from having to haul the lobster traps with her arms, something she had done for years. There were two hundred-gallon tanks just outside the pilothouse. They soon would hold the day's catch.

She watched as Auntie Em negotiated the bobbing deck of the pier. The marina had been built five years before and was nothing more than a narrow pier that jutted out into the bay. Off to one side were finger-piers secured by commercial Seaflex cords. The finger-piers moved with the swell of the waves.

The seventy-year-old woman seemed to float across the dock, her sea legs used to years of walking on water. That's how Auntie Em described her gait across the many docks and piers that were so much a part of Gin Cove, like floating on water.

"Right on time." Molly smiled.

"Phone kept me."

"You ready?"

"Ayuh."

Molly stepped into the pilothouse and started the engine. She let it idle in neutral. The 318-horsepower diesel engine growled. She turned on her VHF radio and the speaker crackled with lobstermen yakking as they headed toward their traps. The radio also kept her up on the weather, which could change rapidly on the ocean.

She checked her gauges; temperature, oil pressure, battery, everything seemed fine. She lifted the cover on her plotter and turned it on. The screen turned blue and green. It was a map of the surrounding area. She clicked to the second screen and the depth finder, and then to the global positioning system. She flipped on the radar unit and stepped back on deck.

Auntie Em reached down and untied the stern line, then tossed it to Molly, who carefully coiled it at her feet. She quickly untied the bowline and threw it to Molly's waiting hands. Then Auntie Em swung her right leg easily onto a crate and stepped aboard. Her legs weren't long enough to reach the deck of the boat.

"Ready?"

Auntie Em smiled her yes, face rugged, weather-worn by the years of sun. She tied a black bandanna around her iron-gray hair.

Molly stepped back into the pilothouse, slipped the gear lever into reverse and eased the throttle forward. The boat backed out of its slip. She maneuvered the boat up into the narrow inlet between the finger-piers, turning the wheel just enough to point the bow toward the sea. She moved the gearshift ahead and eased the throttle forward. The large diesel engine grumbled as the boat slid past the other boats. They were a fleet of forty-four lobster boats. Molly waved to Scott Miller, who was still carrying provisions to his boat. They chugged past her friend Allan Gray's high-performance pleasure boat, which rocked back and forth like a hammock in a breeze as the twirling propeller from Molly's boat created ripples along its underside.

Auntie Em stepped into the pilothouse and went down the steps into the cabin; she reached into the cupboard next to the head and pulled out a pair of orange slicks. She carried them back up the steps into the pilothouse. The two women didn't speak. In the morning there was an almost spiritual silence that years of being together had created. They were surrounded by the sounds of waves whipping the side of the boat and the disquiet of the engine.

Auntie Em shook out the oversized rubber pants. They would keep her dry. She tucked first one and then the other leg of her jeans into her socks and then stepped into the pants. They reminded her of the training pants she had put on so many children over the years. She tucked her oversized sweatshirt into the pants. She pulled the black suspenders over her shoulders and adjusted the legs so her jeans felt comfortable inside. The waist on the oversized slicks ballooned at her narrow sides. She braced her back against the wall as she slipped on a pair of black rubber boots.

She picked up a pair of gloves that Molly had placed on a crate next to the rotting fish. She ignored the smell of decay. Auntie Em knew that Molly had collected the eviscerated sardines from the co-op. All the lobstermen belonged to the co-op because it also was their gasoline/diesel station and convenience store. They bought their bait and diesel fuel from the co-op in the morning and at the end of the day, they dropped their catch off to be weighed. The amount was credited to their account. It was like a bank, you put lobster in one side and collected money on the other side.

Molly called the bait a lobster's gourmet delight. Auntie Em stood next to the bait box, the morning sun warm on her face. She pulled small mesh net bags from a box. With her other hand she reached into the barrel of rotting fish, grabbed a handful and stuffed them into the bag. She twisted the top and laid the bag on a crate. It was ready to go into the trap once the trap was hauled on board. It was repetitive motion, but Auntie Em enjoyed it. The smell of the rotting fish had long ceased being disagreeable.

Molly watched the screen on the depth finder; it was her underwater eyes that looked at the contour of the ocean bottom. She reached up and adjusted the picture. She was already in her orange slicks. A flannel shirt tucked inside, a white T-shirt underneath. She had a baseball cap pulled down tightly over her red hair. She watched the compass that was mounted just in front of the wheel.

Molly's eyes swept between her gauges, the debris floating in the water and the tourist boats. She slowed the boat to almost idle speed and searched for her first buoy. Each lobsterman had buoys of a distinct color. Molly's were orange and black, her lobster license number carved neatly on the side of each one. At one time, all the buoys were made of cedar, each handcarved from a block of wood, but now a more efficient, lighter and cheaper Styrofoam replaced the wood. Molly hated the Styrofoam buoys because they were ecologically harmful. When they broke loose from the rope the thrashing surf tossed them against the spiked rocks that broke them into small pieces, littering the shore. But she was forced to use them because wood buoys were no longer legal. Her buoys, like every other lobster fisherman's, were tied to lines that went hundreds of feet into the black ocean water. At the other end there was a green metal trap and inside, she hoped, lots of lobsters.

Gin Cove lobstermen were territorial, their sites either inherited or shared by family members. There were no deeds, just years of tradition that had marked areas for certain families. Newcomers had to slice out a part of the ocean where no one bothered to place their traps. If a newcomer happened to stray into an area claimed by another lobsterman, he might find his lines cut and his traps forever buried on the ocean bottom.

Gin Cove lobstermen hadn't gotten into battles like those that raged in southern Maine, where lobstermen actually had fistfights over a particular site. There even had been times where one lobsterman had fired a gun at another. No one was killed, but the message was clear: "Stay out of my territory."

The first string of Molly's two hundred traps was near Roger's Island, about thirty minutes from the marina. They were linked together in pairs. Her orange and black buoy was tied to a blue sink rope that reached down into the water more than fifteen fathoms to the main trap. There, a floating rope extended to a tailer trap. Lobstermen used a floating rope at the deepest depths because it kept the traps from getting hung up on the rocks. Environmentalists now were pushing to eliminate float ropes because of whale entanglements.

A second string of two hundred and fifty traps was near Pope's Folly, an island about thirty minutes west of the first strings. The third set was located off of Bailey's Mistake at the southern end of Gin Cove. Her father had lobstered in those spots and before that her grandfather. Then, as her father got older, he let her have some of the sites, finally retiring and turning the rest over to her.

Molly slipped the throttle into neutral and the boat glided across the water. She grabbed the gaff that was lying nearby. She pointed the hook at the water and snagged the rope on the buoy. She flipped the rope over the pulley and slipped it over the snatch block. The small engine whirred, the three-foot green wire trap bounced to the surface, Auntie Em reached for it and pulled it onto the gunwale. The tiny motor hissed and whirred again and Molly reached for the second trap that sprung to the surface. She rested it next to Auntie Em's trap. With the precision of assembly line workers, Molly followed Auntie Em and snapped open the cover. She flipped the smaller crabs and spiny sea urchins, called whores' eggs, back into the ocean; larger crabs went into a bucket. The undersized lobsters were tossed back.

They also turned each of the lobsters over. A female full of eggs would be tossed back and lobsters with notched tails were returned to their watery home. State law required that egg-bearing females or females that had just expelled their eggs had to be notched. Auntie Em held the large lobster up so Molly could see all the eggs on its underside. She handed the squirming crustacean to Molly, who reached into her jean pocket and pulled out a knife. Molly set the lobster on top of the crate. Its claws worked overtime as it tried to grab at the perpetrator who had pulled it from its icy home. She flipped open the blade and cut a triangular slice into the right flipper. She tossed the female lobster back into the water.

"Go and make lots of babies," Molly said as she watched the large mother float back to the bottom.

"Been a good year," Auntie Em said without looking up.

"Yeah, seem to be a lot of them moving down there."

When Auntie Em's husband, Ben, fished, lobstermen harvested anything that crawled into the trap. Lobsters were considered beggary food, something the locals didn't eat. In the 1950s and earlier, lobster was sold to the state and fed to prisoners. Sometimes they were traded to people from away, who didn't know any better. Then some enterprising lobstermen decided to turn the bottom feeder into a specialty food and it soon became a much coveted gourmet dinner served in some of the finer restaurants in America. And lobstering became a full-time business. The fear of a dwindling resource over the years forced the state to change the laws and impose size limits.

Finally in 1988, the state convinced the lobstermen that the smaller lobsters they were harvesting had not reproduced, and they imposed the 3.25-inch carapace length. The lobstermen agreed; they knew that their delicate resource needed breeders.

Molly and Auntie Em each laid a brass lobster gauge, which looked like a caliper without jaws, against the side of the lobster and measured from the eye socket to the base of the body. Molly knew at that length the lobster would weigh about a pound and a quarter.

They pitched the keepers into a bucket.

Molly didn't bother to examine the bait bag. The lobsters had torn through the steel-gray mesh with their large scissor claws. She tossed the torn bag into a nearby bucket, the remaining bait into the water. The seagulls that had been fluttering nearby dove straight down, grabbing the free food just as it slipped beneath the surface of the water, their task made more difficult because of the slight chop.

Molly and Auntie Em grabbed fresh bait bags, slipped the string through a metal eye on the bottom and pulled the string tight and twisted it around a plastic cleat at the top of the trap.

Molly balanced the trap on the gunwale with her right hand and with her left hand she pushed the gearshift forward and spun the wheel. She studied her depth finder. The trap would go into the water in the place it had come from.

Auntie Em also balanced her trap and waited. Molly nodded and Auntie Em pushed the trap into the water; the coiled line near her feet hissed as it sliced through the water. Molly pushed her trap in next. She kept one eye on the rope; she knew of sternmen who had gotten too close to the uncoiling rope and got a foot caught.

Although a few sternmen had lost a rubber boot, no one in Gin Cove had died. That was not true elsewhere. Just last year, a sternman in the southern part of the state had gotten his foot caught and was pulled overboard. He drowned before the captain could turn the boat around and rescue him.

She looked back at the bouncing buoy, once again the only sign that the lobster trap was even there.

Molly eased the boat toward the next rope in the string and the rhythm of pulling and tossing continued. The ten traps cleaned and rebaited, she smiled at Auntie Em. "Just one hundred and ninety more," she said with a laugh. Molly eased the throttle forward and pointed the boat toward the next string of ten traps.

Auntie Em picked up the banding tool that looked like a pair of reverse pliers and reached for one of the rubber bands. She slipped it over the pliers' jaws and, squeezing the handle, stretched the band wide. She picked up one of the squirming lobsters and grasped first one and then the other claw at the widest part. She slipped the rubber band over the pincers and tossed the lobster into a bucket. Once full, it would be placed inside the tank. Lobsters are carnivores and if they aren't banded, they eat one another.

The two women went from string to string pulling lobsters from their watery quarters and placing them into buckets.

At noon, Molly eased back on the throttle. They had had a good morning. Half the traps were pulled and most of the lobsters were banded. She cut the engine and let the boat just roll with the slight swells. She stepped out of the pilothouse and watched her aunt, who had been like a mother to her, finish the banding. Everyone called her Auntie Em, but as far as Molly knew she really wasn't an aunt to anyone.

Emma Richardson had been an only child and had grown up in Gin Cove. Molly knew she began working in the sardine factories when she was fourteen. The women who snipped off the heads of sardines and put them into the cans were called herring chokers. She was proud to call herself a herring choker.

Auntie Em worked for the same factory for forty years. That was where she met Molly's mother. Short on baby-sitters and with day-care centers not yet as far east as Gin Cove, Molly, like the other children in Gin Cove, grew up playing under the sardine tables. A horn on the factory roof sounded about one hour before the women were to report to work. Each sardine plant had a different horn so everyone in town knew who had fish that morning. The melancholy blast carried across the bay to houses still dark with the night's sleep. The women arrived at seven in the morning. Most of them walked, and others were picked up by the company bus. Their blue plastic aprons, hairnets and scissors were tucked into a bag next to their sandwiches.

At the plant they lined up two to a table, the morning chitchat leaping off the walls. Outside a giant vacuum cleaner sucked the herring from the boats onto a conveyer belt. The conveyer belt whined as it moved slowly past the women.

The herring chokers each scooped an armful of herring onto the table. A fish in one hand and the scissors in the other, the sharp blades snipped and snapped. The bloody fish heads tumbled onto the table and the bodies were tucked into a can. Piles of fish heads were dumped on the floor to be swept up by the night crew. A shift ended when the boat was empty and the fish were packed. During the large runs that at one time dominated the bay, women worked late into the night. At the end of the shift, their hands red and swollen, they walked or rode the company bus back to their houses. Auntie Em talked about those days with Molly not with pain but pride. Eventually, she was promoted to foreman, one of the first female foremen in Gin Cove. Then the factories closed.

She and Ben married late in life and hadn't had any children of their own, although half the children in Gin Cove had wandered through Auntie Em's house to get a piece of candy that was always in a bowl near the front door, or even to live there. Molly and her brother, Tommy, lived with Auntie Em and Ben after their mother died.

"How about lunch, Auntie Em?" Molly stepped inside the cabin, reached into her tiny refrigerator and pulled out two sandwiches.

She grabbed the thermos of coffee and tucked two cups under her arm. Although she had a small stove in the cabin, it was easier to bring the freshly ground morning coffee from home. She walked back up on deck and handed a sandwich to Auntie Em. Auntie Em flipped over a bucket and sat down.

Molly placed the thermos on one of the overturned buckets and handed Auntie Em a cup. She tipped over another bucket and sat down.

"So who called you so early that you were almost late?" Molly asked.

Auntie Em slid the sandwich out of the plastic wrap and took a bite. "Allan."

"Allan? At that hour? Why?"

"Wanted to talk."

"About?"

"You."

Molly made a guttural sound. "What about me?"

"Stop grunting—you used to do that when you was a kid." Auntie Em poured coffee from the thermos into the two cups. "I love this noon sun. It'll be winter soon enough and we'll be glad for these days."

"You're stalling." Molly picked up her sandwich and took a bite.

"Nope, I'm not stalling. I love the outside," Auntie Em said. "Allan said he invited you to his house tomorrow night for a get-together with a friend of Charlie's, said you turned him down."

"I didn't turn him down. I said I'd see."

"He knows you, that's as good as turning him down."

Molly sighed. "A friend of Charlie's is visiting and he wants to fix me up."

"No, he wants you to meet someone he thinks you'd like."

"Auntie Em, I've been through this. Allan's happy in a relationship and he figures everyone else should be too. I'm just not interested. Besides, why are you so interested? You've never evinced interest in who I was seeing. You weren't even crazy about my ex."

"Truth be known, I wasn't. I knew she'd hurt you and she did. Woman was just too spoiled and besides, you're thirty-five years old and you need to settle down. You need to find your soul mate."

Molly put her head back and laughed. "Soul mate? Boy, has he been doing a head job on you." Molly bit down on her sandwich like it was a tough piece of meat. "I have a new description of myself. I am a nonpracticing lesbian."

"What's that?"

"Following in the footsteps of our Catholic Church, Auntie Em. I can be gay as long as I don't do the deed. So since I ain't doing the deed, I'm a nonpracticing lesbian."

"That's nonsense."

Molly could see Auntie Em was earnest about discussing her lack of interest in women. "Just for the sake of argument," Molly said as she chewed. "Just what is a soul mate?"

"That's easy." Auntie Em took a sip of coffee. "Oh, that's some good. A soul mate," she said without missing a beat, "is your lover and your best friend. They are your breath of life. The person you want to be with first and always. A soul mate sees inside your soul, and loves you. It's like your lives are entwined and when you're not together it's as if part of your heart stops. You kiss a soul mate good night, regardless of how the day has worn on you. And when the passion subsides, as it does in all relationships, a soul mate stirs a passion in your heart." Molly watched as Auntie Em stared out at the sea. "A soul mate, Molly," she said very quietly, "is at one with who you are."

Molly sat unmoving. "Were you and Uncle soul mates?"

"Absolutely." Auntie Em set her sandwich down on the Ziploc bag. "When he died, part of me went with him. And when I die we'll be whole again."

"I don't think there is anyone out there like that for me. At least I've never met her."

"You will."

"How?" Molly scowled at her cup of coffee. "Okay, let's review my cycle of dates," she said acerbically. "The last one was the worst;

14

no, maybe the one before was the worst. Last year, one of my friends introduced me to a woman who couldn't breathe through her nose. She had some kind of rattle in her lungs from smoking and when she wasn't puffing on a cigarette and wheezing, she was talking. Talking all the time."

Auntie Em nodded.

Molly picked up her cup and set it down without taking a drink. "Allan introduced me to a woman who was so into herself, I don't think she even knew what I did for a living." Molly paused. "Wait, she did know and was totally unimpressed. Figured because I was a lobsterman I hadn't been ed-u-cated. That's what she liked to say. She was ed-u-cated." Molly dragged out the word. "She had a master's degree in sociology, but I think it was more in bragging." Molly paused and stared at the ocean. "The last one was the best. She lived and breathed shopping. I dated the woman for a month and all she wanted to talk about was driving to Bangor and shopping in the mall. I don't . . ." Molly took a deep breath. "Look, Auntie Em, it's not that there was anything wrong with the women, they just weren't right for me. I don't want to make another mistake. I'm sorry. I don't do relationships well." Finally she'd put into words what she had been thinking about for the past few months. "So I guess I'm taking my frustrations out on my friends."

"Why would you want to take your frustration out on Allan. He loves you. He wants you to be happy."

"I am."

"No," Auntie Em said. "No, you're not. Ever since you and Julie broke up, all you've been doing is working. That ain't happiness, that's forgetting."

"That's peace and quiet which equals happiness." Molly took a drink of her coffee.

"Molly Bean, it's been two years since that woman left you and you've had what, three dates?"

"I don't think I have to remind you, we live in Gin Cove, popula-tion somewhere around four thousand people. We have a small college and, I might add, the women professors are straight and married. We have a salmon plant and most the women who work there I grew up with. We have a bunch of stores, all run by women I've known most my life. Now, you tell me, where is the meat in that delicatessen?" Molly's voice had a note of surrender in it. "Look, Auntie Em, I want to fall in love again and I'd like to find a soul mate, but—"

"This one could be different," Auntie Em interrupted.

Molly stood up. "No." She held up her hands. "They are never different." Molly looked past Auntie Em. "Man, that boat is bearing down on us." She knocked over her bucket as she ran to the pilot-house.

Auntie Em stood up and looked in the direction Molly had been pointing. The boat exploded to life. The runaway boat was unrelenting as it bore down on them.

"Hold on," Molly yelled. Auntie Em grabbed the railing as Molly gunned the engine.

Molly's boat seemed to jump out of the way, but the wake from the speeding boat knocked Auntie Em against the railing. As the boat passed close by, a woman stepped out onto the deck and shrugged her shoulders in apology.

"Who the hell was that?" Molly said as she hung onto the doorway, her boat still rocking from the waves. "The boat damn near collided with us."

"Don't know," Auntie Em said as she let loose of the railing. "The captain must have gotten distracted or something. His wife or someone stepped out onto the deck and held her hands up like they'd made a mistake and was sorry."

"Mistake. I swear to God these tourists are going to kill us yet. They shoot through here like the ocean is their speedway," Molly fumed. She picked up her cup and looked inside; it was empty, its contents spilled on the deck. Auntie Em's sandwich also was on the deck soaking up the brown oily slime left behind by the traps. "Auntie Em, if you're still hungry I got another sandwich."

16

"Lord, no. I think my stomach's still boomeranging around down there. Funny, I couldn't move. I just kept watching that boat coming at me and I couldn't move."

"You okay?" Molly quashed the emotional response that was whirling inside her. If she got hold of that boat captain, she thought, she'd throttle him.

"Land, yes, just took my breath. Let's finish hauling." Auntie Em took a clean bucket off the deck and filled it with water. She took her cup and Molly's and swished them around inside and carried them to the galley.

Molly had left the boat idling. She stepped back into the pilot-house and pushed the throttle forward and headed toward the next string of traps.

They could talk later, Auntie Em thought as she watched Molly at the wheel. They would talk later.

Chapter Two

Molly eased back on the throttle, the engine humming as the boat glided through the narrows toward the marina. The late-day sun was resting just above the edge of the town. It had been a good day. They had hauled nearly three hundred traps and she still had time to drop her catch off at the co-op. She even managed to squirrel away a few smaller lobsters, all males of course. Illegal as all get-out, but Molly moderated her guilt by acknowledging that everybody did it and besides, she could taste them now in Auntie Em's lobster stew, the meat so tender you could divide it in half with a fork.

As she rounded the bend near the breakwater, Molly frowned. Auntie Em, who was standing next to Molly, saw the boat at the same moment.

"Isn't that the boat that nearly dumped us?" Auntie Em asked.

"Yes, and it is parked in our slip. Auntie Em, cover your ears, I am going to give this guy a piece of my mind."

Molly tucked her boat into the finger-pier next to where she always docked. She quickly reversed the engine and the boat seemed to hang in the water like a stalled airplane and then settle down in the water. She turned the engine off and walked on deck. She tossed a temporary line over a post to hold the boat in place. She looked over at the boat that now was an interloper in her space. The name painted on the side was the *Carolyn S.* Molly felt her jaws tightening as she tried to control her anger. This was a captain that deserved a dressing-down and she was just the person to do it.

"Yo, anyone aboard the *Carolyn S*?" Molly called, the anger unpronounced in her voice but there just slightly under the surface.

A woman stepped out of the cabin. "Can I help you?" She smiled. She had long blonde hair tied in the back with a scarf. Sunglasses covered her eyes. Her long angular figure was covered with white shorts and a tailored white shirt. The white contrasted sharply with her tanned skin.

"You got a captain aboard?" Molly asked.

"You got her, hon." The woman smiled again.

"You new at this, hon?" Molly answered back.

"I beg your pardon?"

"This boat, this a new toy or something? A gift from your boyfriend. Or how about your husband. This a gift from him?"

"No. You got a point to this sarcasm, or you just practicing?"

"We're the people you nearly ran into."

"Oh, my God, I'm sorry." The woman ran a hand through her hair. "Look, I apologize. My name's Carolyn Stanley and I am not usually that careless. The bay had been clear of boats all day and I was in just too big a hurry to get here. I had the throttle open and I turned around to get something to drink out of the refrigerator and I saw you at the last moment. Look, if anyone's hurt, please I will pay for it . . ." Carolyn paused, out of breath. "Look, I'm really, really sorry."

Molly felt her anger fading. "We're okay." She shrugged. "You just gave us a scare. You're not from around here?"

19

"Bar Harbor."

Molly suppressed a groan. Rich and opulent, she thought.

"I am an experienced seaman," Carolyn continued. "I take full responsibility for what happened. Honest, if there's anything I can do, I will."

Molly looked over at Auntie Em. Another flatlander, she thought. She knew Auntie Em was thinking the same thing. "You could start by moving your boat."

"I beg your pardon."

"Move your boat. You're parked in my slip. I pay money for that spot."

Carolyn raised her hands up in surrender. "Look, I really do seem to be doing everything to irritate you. I'm sorry. The harbor master said I could park on this side and I just picked this slip. I thought these were all temporary rentals. Sorry again."

"The tourists park over there." Molly pointed toward the end of the pier. Molly felt Auntie Em poke her in the side. Auntie Em nodded toward the end of the pier.

"Oh, no," Molly muttered under her breath. "Stall him," she said quietly to Auntie Em. Molly ducked inside the pilothouse.

"Afternoon, Joey," Auntie Em called.

"Hiya, Auntie Em." The marine patrol officer walked toward the two boats. He nodded to the two women.

"This here's Carolyn Stanley," Auntie Em said.

"Pleased to meet you, ma'am." Joey smiled at the woman. "Joe Barker." He held out his hand.

Carolyn stepped forward and shook hands with him. "Nice to meet you, officer."

"Where's Molly?" Joey asked Auntie Em.

"Right here, Joey. Just storing some last-minute gear."

"Not hiding any shorts are you?"

"You kidding? Not with you snooping around. I'm not about to pay a big fine for something like that."

"Mind if I take a look?"

20

Molly waved him aboard. She knew she couldn't say no. She looked over at Auntie Em. "Look all you want." Molly rolled her eyes and grinned. Auntie Em shook her head.

Joey stepped aboard Molly's boat and walked into the pilothouse. Molly stood just outside. She could hear him opening doors and poking inside cabinets. She looked over and saw Carolyn watching her. Joey stepped outside. "Looks clean, though you got a bucket in there has some seaweed and water in it. You weren't keeping some young lobster in there by chance?"

"Naw. The head's not working."

Joey nodded. "I'll just look inside." He pointed at the covered tanks.

"Have at it."

Just as Joey turned and walked to the tanks, Molly grabbed her leg and tried to stifle a cry. It came out a squeak.

Joey turned around. "Something wrong?"

"Not at all," Molly said. "I just tried to stifle a sneeze. Sorry."

Molly noticed the quizzical look on the marine patrol officer's face before he turned back to the tanks. He poked around at the lobsters, picking up first one and than another and measuring them, just as Auntie Em had done earlier in the day. Molly felt as though he was operating in deliberate slow speed.

"Take your time," Molly said through clenched teeth.

Auntie Em looked from Molly's face to her pants. The front was moving. Molly reached down and grabbed the inside of her thigh. She leaned against the railing and kept her hand on her thigh, the whole time watching the marine patrol officer as he looked through the day's catch.

Molly could read the expression on Auntie Em's face. She watched as Auntie Em put a hand to her mouth and choked back a laugh.

"You all right, Auntie Em?" The patrol officer stopped measuring and turned to ask.

21

"Sure, just a tickle in my throat." Auntie Em put her hand against her mouth and coughed.

They had taken the small lobsters in the last set of traps and Auntie Em had not bothered to band them because they were going to be tonight's supper. Molly looked over at Carolyn and saw that she too had seen the movement in Molly's pants. Molly held her breath. If the woman said something, Molly knew she would be in trouble.

As Joey stood up, Auntie Em moved from the railing to stand in front of Molly. "Everything okay, Joey?"

"Seems fine." He smiled at the older woman. "You guys going to the town meeting tonight?"

Auntie Em shrugged.

"Gotta settle the school budget," he said.

"Don't think I'll be going," Molly said. It felt as though her jaw had locked shut. One of the lobsters had latched on to the inside of her thigh.

"I have to—got a kid in school. Bunch of folks want to make some major cuts to the budget, they—"

"Gosh, Joey." Molly feigned interest in her wristwatch. "I gotta get my catch turned in before the co-op closes." Molly could feel the rest of the lobsters begin to follow the others up her leg, their tiny claws digging into her skin as they pulled themselves claw after claw up toward her thigh. Her jeans were no longer a barrier. Molly couldn't believe what was happening. The tiny lobsters had hardly moved after they had been put in the bucket and now they seemed determined to compete in some kind of race. Boy, she thought, sticking them inside her pants had really ticked them off. "They close, I got a mess on my hands." Molly stopped. She could feel sweat under her arms. The lobsters were almost at the top of her thigh. She didn't want to think about what they might grab on to next.

"That's right, officer," Carolyn said. She smiled warmly him. "I'm afraid I parked in her slip and I was just getting ready to move. Maybe you could help?"

"That's for the harbor master," Joey said.

"No, I know where I have to dock, but I might need some help securing the lines over there." Carolyn pointed toward the end of the dock. "I'd sure appreciate some help." Her voice was soft, coaxing.

"Sure." He smiled at Carolyn. "We'll talk later," he called over his shoulder to Molly.

Molly's smile felt as if it had been glued to the sides of her face. "Sure thing."

The boat swayed slightly as Joey stepped back onto the pier.

Molly walked stiff-legged into the pilothouse and wiped her forehead against her sleeve. "Ready to cast off," she called to Auntie Em, her voice barely above a squeak.

Joey tossed Auntie Em the lines and turned to Carolyn, his back to Auntie Em.

Molly watched as Auntie Em mouthed a thank-you to the woman. Carolyn smiled.

Molly eased the throttle back and reversed the engine. She pushed the throttle forward and the boat floated away from the slip. She couldn't remove the lobsters from her pants because she had to travel in front of the pier, past Joey, to reach the co-op. She eased the throttle forward, motoring slowly. She looked over to where Carolyn had berthed her boat and noticed that the woman had engaged the marine patrol officer in conversation; he had his back to Molly.

Molly let go of the throttle and pulled her suspenders down, pushed the rubber slicks over her thighs and looked down at her legs as Auntie Em entered the pilothouse.

"My God, Molly, whatever possessed you to put the lobsters in your pants?" Auntie Em also was looking at Molly's legs. There were lobsters hanging from her thighs to her calves. She looked like a Christmas tree with long brownish red ornaments.

"God, get them off of me," Molly yelled, giving in to the pain. "I couldn't think of anywhere else to hide them." Molly tried to pull the one that had climbed highest on the inside of her thigh, but when she bent over she felt lightheaded.

Auntie Em kneeled and forcing open their tiny pincers, pulling first one and then the other lobster away from Molly's thigh. She then reached down and pried open the claw of a lobster that had latched on to Molly's calf. A fourth lobster had a grip on the side of her ankle.

Molly watched as Auntie Em removed them one by one. When Auntie Em reached for the lobster that was hanging from Molly's left calf, Molly could feel her hands and shoulders shake as she made her way down Molly's legs.

"You're laughing. I'm in pain, and you're laughing," Molly ranted.

Auntie Em sat back on her heels and tears squirted from her eyes. She wiped her eyes on the back of her sleeve. "You looked like a Christmas tree." She laughed, wiping at her eyes again. "A lobster tree." She opened the pincers on the last lobster that had been clinging to Molly's left ankle and dropped it into the bucket, but she could not stop laughing. "The way your pants were moving, I thought I was about to take a heart attack." Auntie Em sat down on a chair and held her sides. "And then I thought that woman was going to blow the whistle on you. You should have seen the expression on her face when your pants started moving. It looked like you had Ping-Pong balls in your pants." Auntie Em stopped to catch her breath.

Now that the last lobster was removed, Molly also started to laugh. She reached down and rubbed the insides of her legs. She pulled up her pant leg and studied her calves. "God, I am going to have black and blue marks where no woman should have black and blue marks. Thank God they didn't break the skin," she said between breaths.

Unloading had taken some time, and now Molly and Auntie Em were back at the pier. Molly filled two pails with water. Auntie Em pulled two brooms and some washing soap out of the closet in the galley. She dumped the soap in the pails and swished the mop around inside.

The two women worked side by side as they scrubbed the top of the deck. While Auntie Em swept the seaweed and other debris overboard, Molly pressed hard on the broom as she scoured the oil that had soaked into the deck.

"I'm almost through here, Auntie. Why don't you go up to the house and start the lobster stew?"

"You sure you want to eat them now that you sort of bonded with them?" Auntie Em teased.

Molly frowned. "Cook 'em all up. I want to eat the little buggers," Molly said as she helped Auntie Em up onto the dock. Auntie Em followed Molly's gaze across the finger-piers to where the *Carolyn S.* was tied up. There were no lights on inside the pilothouse.

"Y'know, you ought to thank her."

"For what?"

"She saw the lobsters in your pants and distracted Joey, so you owe her that."

Molly shrugged. "Maybe, and maybe the commotion over her tying up in my slip attracted Joey's attention."

"Molly Bean, you know better than that. Joey has a big territory. There are a lot of piers and he is here just enough times to keep us all honest. So don't blame that girl for us nearly getting caught."

"Maybe you're right," Molly mumbled.

"God, you're stubborn. You know I'm right. Now go over there and tell her thank you. You don't have to tell her what you had crawling around in your pants. Land, she'd never believe it."

"All right, I'll go, but I don't think she's there. Cabin's dark."

"So, she hasn't turned the lights on yet. Go." Auntie Em pushed at Molly's shoulder.

"I'm goin', I'm goin'."

Molly walked toward the *Carolyn S.* and leaned over and knocked on the top of the cabin door. She straightened up and waited. She turned back to where Auntie Em was standing and waved the back of her hand at her.

"Go, go," the hand silently told her aunt.

"I'm going, girl, I'm going," Auntie Em said.

Just then the cabin door opened and Carolyn stepped onto the deck. She had on long white pants and a blue sweatshirt over a white blouse.

"Hi," Molly said. "I came to thank you."

"For what? I mean, it's nice of you to thank me." Carolyn's smile was luminous. "If anything, I should apologize to you again for nearly throwing you and your aunt into the water and then pulling into your slip. I'd say I acted like the proverbial naughty tourist."

Molly shrugged. "Auntie Em said you kinda helped out with that situation . . . um, before."

"Oh, you mean the lobsters in your pants." Carolyn laughed. "That was quite a sight. I expect they were shorts."

"Well, sort of." Molly knew that her face had turned as red as her hair.

"Don't worry, I won't say anything. Remember, I live in Bar Harbor. We have an occasional lobsterman who gets caught with a few shorts on board. Although I must tell them in the future about your ingenious way of handling them. I expect no marine patrol officer would think to search inside a man's or a woman's pants."

"No, I don't expect they would. Actually, I couldn't figure out where else to put them. I knew he'd look inside everything on the boat."

"By the way, you did have them banded. Right?"

"Well . . ." Molly flushed again.

Carolyn put her hand over her mouth and laughed. "You mean to tell me they were using their claws to climb up your leg. Oh, my."

Molly joined in the laughter. "Oh, yeah, and believe me I am going to have the bruises to prove it. No one is going to believe this one."

"Well. I hope you haven't suffered any permanent damage."

"Just to my dignity once this story gets out."

"Don't worry, I won't tell anyone."

"Don't matter. There are no secrets in Gin Cove," Molly said with a laugh.

"It's like any other small town in Maine."

"By the way, we didn't meet properly back there." Molly pointed at her slip. "My name's Molly Bean. The woman with me is my sternman—everybody calls her Auntie Em." Molly held out her hand.

"Carolyn Stanley." Carolyn's warm and soft hand slipped easily into Molly's. "Nice to meet you."

"I expect you're visiting around here." Molly's hand still felt warm from Carolyn's touch.

"Yes, I have a friend that lives here, actually an old college buddy. We reconnected over the Internet." Carolyn paused. "This is my first visit to Gin Cove."

"You need a ride or something?"

"Thank you, no. He said he would pick me up here. I was just freshening up."

"Well." Molly backed away from Carolyn's boat. "Again thank you."

"You're very welcome."

"You or your friend need lobster for a dinner while you're here, just look me up. If I'm not on my boat, I got a house out of town, but everybody knows me, so just ask. I go out every day except Sundays and I'd happily tuck some away for you. Regulars, not shorts," Molly said with a grin.

"Thank you. I might mention that to my friend."

"Good enough. Well, see ya around," Molly said.

"Hope so." Carolyn smiled.

Chapter Three

Carolyn opened the door on the first knock. "Oh, it is so good to see you." She hugged her friend Charlie tightly to her.

"You look great." Charlie stood back and looked at his old friend. "Man, you haven't aged."

"Ah, always the kind word. I feel older. You look great," Carolyn effused.

Charlie rubbed his hand over the top of his head. "A little less hair maybe, otherwise fine." He linked his arm through Carolyn's. "Where's your bag?"

"I just thought I'd stay on board. I didn't want to be the bothersome houseguest."

"Nonsense, you are spending the weekend with us. I won't have it any other way. Now get your bag, woman. There are two people who are going to wine and dine you and spoil you rotten."

Carolyn smiled. "Come on." She motioned for Charlie to follow her inside. "We can talk while I throw a few clothes into an overnight bag."

Charlie followed Carolyn down into her sleeping quarters. "Very nice," he said. "Larger than I expected."

Carolyn's bed was off to one side; dark mahogany cupboards on either side and overhead framed the bed. There was a small porthole on the wall next to the bed. A table and two chairs were on the opposite wall. A small stove, sink and refrigerator stood nearby. Carolyn pulled pants and a blouse out of a closet, shorts and shirts from the cupboards. She tucked them into her black bag.

"Give me a second to get my toiletry items," she said as she opened the door near the galley and stepped into the head.

"We're going to have a great time while you're here," Charlie said through the closed door. "We're going to take you to Campobello Island in Canada. You're going to love it—they have some wonderful hiking trails. On Sunday, we are going to picnic on St. Andrews. It's a great spot. There are all these wonderful shops, nothing like what you get here in the States. Everything is imported from some exotic place."

"Sounds like fun," Carolyn said as she opened the door, a small makeup bag in her hand. "But I want to spend time with you, playing catch-up." She paused. "Charlie, it's been too many years. I don't know what happened."

"Life. We got busy with our careers, but let's face it, we can make up all kinds of reasons why we didn't stay in touch with each other, but none of that matters. What matters is that you're here, and we can catch up on all the years." Charlie picked up Carolyn's bag. "You ready?"

"Absolutely."

"Good. I'm taking you home, and I'm not letting you out of my sight for the next few days," Charlie said as they walked across the pier.

He tossed Carolyn's overnight bag in the back of his truck.

≈≫

"Carolyn, you look great," he said as he drove.

"Thanks." Carolyn smiled with ease. They traveled through a small downtown area made up of tiny shops and white spiral churches. It so reminded her of Bar Harbor. "I've missed you."

"Me too. I don't know what happened." Charlie scowled at the road. "We just seemed to float apart."

"Careers, life plans. Running through life," Carolyn said. "Pick any of the above. I'd write, you wouldn't." She smirked at him.

"I guess." Charlie turned on his blinker to turn right and now the small downtown area they had passed through was left behind. "I hated to write letters. I love writing e-mails, go figure." They were on a country road. On either side the white birch trees with their black trademark spots seemed to float past. Carolyn could see tiny sections of the ocean off to her right.

"I'm so glad you reconnected with me. It rekindled that sense of safety I always had with you." Carolyn looked at Charlie. They had grown up in Bar Harbor, and although they knew each other in elementary and high school, they hadn't really been friends. Charlie had chosen Boston College. Carolyn won a scholarship to the same school. They had connected in college, two Mainers who had become best friends. Just before graduation, Carolyn had applied to the University of Southern Maine's law school; Charlie had applied to its M.B.A. program. She looked over at her friend. Yes, his hair was a little thinner, she thought, and there were a few more lines in his face, but other than that he was the same man she had known in college. His lean six-foot-two frame still held the heart of an angel. "And I ain't goin' to let you go this time, mister."

"Same here." He reached over and took her hand. "I couldn't believe it when I saw your name in the *Bar Harbor Times.* Mom sends me a copy every week. I thought, how many Carolyn Stanleys could be living in our hometown?"

"And I couldn't believe it when you said you'd moved back here."

"After I got my M.B.A., I went back to Boston. Met Allan there," Charlie said with a laugh. "He hated it there. Kept talking about returning to Maine. After a while it seemed like a good idea. I wasn't really happy in Boston."

"That world out there isn't all that kind," Carolyn mused.

Charlie nodded. "This is a kind world. I love it here. Funny, when I was growing up all I could think about was getting out. I wanted to go to the city, make it as a big-time advertising executive. Lots of money and lots of loves. I hated Boston. I hated my job," he said with a smile. "Now I look around and I think about how blessed I am. I'm the public relations man for a small hospital in rural Maine and I love it."

"Me too. I stayed in California way too long." Carolyn stopped. "I should've come home sooner, but lassitude got me and it was easier to just put one foot in front of the other and keep going down that path. Then, after the breakup, I thought, what the hell am I doing here? I packed everything up, moved back home and hung out my shingle."

"Was it difficult?"

"The breakup or hanging out my shingle?"

"Both."

"Actually, the breakup seemed harder at the beginning. Now I'm glad it's over. As I told you on the telephone, Christine was . . ." Carolyn hesitated. "Let's just say she wasn't the person I thought I had fallen in love with. Things changed. She had a lot of secrets and I had a lot of questions." Carolyn shrugged. "Afterwards, she told me she was never fully committed to me. Said she'd always loved someone else."

"I'm sorry, love. I should have been there for you," Charlie said softly.

"I'm sorry you weren't there either, mostly because I could always trust you to tell me the truth about my life." Carolyn smiled.

"And you about mine. Well, here we are," he said as he turned onto the driveway.

"I love it," Carolyn said. The captain's house, painted yellow with black trim, stood on a small hill. Carolyn looked at the wraparound porch on the front of the house that seemed to go on endlessly, the double wooden front door with the beveled glass. Large windows seemed stacked on top of one another moving from the first floor to the third, and on the third floor, a small door and a smaller porch mirrored the one below. "Widow's walk, right?" Carolyn said, pointing at the top. When shipping was Gin Cove's economic mainstay, homes were built with their eyes to the ocean. Each had a widow's walk as a place to wait for the returning captain.

"You bet. That's our favorite place. We have breakfast up there most mornings in the summer. It means carrying the food up three flights of stairs, but hey, we don't care. Actually, I've gotten smarter over the years. We used to get up there and find the salt and pepper was back in the kitchen. So I had some cupboards built next to the railing and I keep extra everything in there." Charlie got out of the truck. "Come on."

Carolyn was still looking at the house when the front door opened. A man with blond hair and a large barrel chest strode toward them. He was shorter than Charlie and rounder. A neatly trimmed beard reached from ear to ear. He gave Charlie a quick kiss and held his arms open to Carolyn. "All new friends get a hug in this house," he said warmly.

She stepped into his arms and felt the comfort of his hug.

"I'm Allan."

"I guessed." Carolyn laughed and stepped back. "I'm so glad to meet you," she said to Allan's Viking blue eyes.

"Come on. We have your room ready for you. As you can see, we have tons of them." Allan put his arm around Charlie's shoulder. "Have you eaten?" he asked Carolyn.

"No, the man here rescued me before I had to eat my own cooking."

"Great," Allan said as he held the door open for her.

"Wow," Carolyn said. A large wooden spiral staircase seemed to reach to the sky.

"Look up," Charlie said.

Carolyn followed his gaze. The stairs stretched to the third floor, and above the landing was a magnificent stained glass window. "Wow." Carolyn laughed. "I seem to be stuck on one word. This is beautiful, Charlie, Allan, just gorgeous."

"That's what sold us on the house," Allan said. "In the morning the sun casts this wonderful tapestry of colors on the floor. You feel like you are stepping on every color in the rainbow."

"I bet it's magnificent." Carolyn stared at the window. "How many rooms?"

"Twelve. A living room, dining room, kitchen, study and library on the first floor. Five bedrooms on the second floor, and two on the third floor. The master bedroom has the widow's walk," Allan said. He smiled self-consciously. "It seems almost decadent for two guys to live in such a big house, but when I was a kid I used to dream about living in this house." He paused. "It's nice when dreams come true." He slipped his hand into Charlie's.

"Come on," Charlie said, taking Carolyn's bag from Allan. "While my man here gets supper on the table, I'll show you your room."

Carolyn followed him up the stairs.

"Your room is right next to the bathroom. It also has a view looking out over the ocean. It is the second-best bedroom in this house," he said as he opened the door to the room.

Carolyn laughed. "I feel like I just stepped into the middle of a dollhouse." The furniture was vintage American colonial. The bed sat in the middle of the room; the large pink canopy overhead matched the comforter on the bed. "I'm never going to leave here." Carolyn looked around the room. A fireplace was on one side, a large dresser on the other. A settee was next to the large windows that looked out over the ocean.

"Good, you can stay here forever." Charlie gave her a hug. "Go ahead and freshen up, sweetie, and I'll meet you downstairs."

"Charlie." Carolyn turned toward her friend. "Thanks," she said quietly. "Thanks for finding me. I feel like I've come home."

"Good, that's how we want you to feel." Charlie held Carolyn's hands. "You know, I misplaced my best friend once. It's not going to happen again. Now freshen up."

Carolyn could hear voices as she walked down the long oak staircase to the first floor. She followed the voices past the living room and into the dining room. Allan was placing bowls of food on the table. Charlie was standing next to an antique desk that held numerous bottles.

"Find everything you needed?" Allan asked.

"Yes, thank you."

Charlie gestured toward the desk. "I found this at a yard sale if you can imagine. It was in pretty bad shape, but Allan and I sanded it with lots of love and now it's our liquor cabinet."

"I like it." Carolyn walked over and ran her fingers over the smooth cherry wood.

Charlie held up a bottle of nice sauvignon blanc. "This satisfactory?"

"Perfect," Carolyn said.

"Carolyn, you sit there." Allan pointed as he sat down.

Charlie finished pouring the wine and sat down. He picked up his wineglass. "To old friends found again."

"Hear, hear," Allan said.

"And, I might add," Carolyn said, tipping her glass toward Allan, "let's also drink to new and wonderful friends."

"I'll really drink to that," Charlie said.

"Thank you, Carolyn. Now eat, eat," Allan said as he handed her a platter.

During rest of the dinner Carolyn and Charlie reminisced about old college friends.

✑∿✑

Carolyn pushed her chair back from the table. "I couldn't eat another bite," she said. "It was delicious. My compliments to the chef," she said, looking from Charlie to Allan.

"Allan," Charlie said. "He's the cook in this house."

"Nonsense," Allan interrupted. "We each have our favorites and so we really do take turns cooking. Charlie wields a mean spatula when it comes to barbecuing. In fact, he is in charge of dinner tomorrow night."

"I'm looking forward to it. Charlie said you work at the college?"

Allan nodded. "I feed from the public trough."

"Nonsense. He's the dean of finance and he gives more hours than he gets paid for."

"How about you, Carolyn?" Allan said as he sipped his wine. "Charlie tells me you have your own practice."

"I do," she said. "It isn't as romantic as it sounds. The first couple of years I was back in Bar Harbor, it was tough. I took a lot of court appointments—you know, representing drunk drivers and people who were either clamming or lobstering illegally. It paid forty dollars an hour and kept food on the table." Carolyn laughed. "I hated it. I hate criminal work. After a few years, I got into real estate law, estate planning, those kinds of things. Now I handle mostly that. I love it. My mom was getting older so I moved in with her. I'd come full circle from child to adult child." Carolyn paused. "Actually, I'm making it sound more difficult than it was, because it really did help those first few years while I was getting established in my law practice. But it sounds silly when I talk about it, moving in with my mother as an adult. In the end it worked out well, because she eventually needed help and I was there for her. She died two years ago." Carolyn paused. "Now I live there alone. I sleep in the same room I slept in as a child."

"I was sorry when you told me your mom had died. I liked her," Charlie said quietly.

"Thank you." Carolyn shook her head as if to sweep out the memories. Her father had died while she was in college. Charlie had been her steel beam during those weeks and months after his death. "How about you?" she said to Allan. "You like here better than Boston?"

"Absolutely. The money isn't as good as Boston, but then you don't spend as much to live either. After September eleventh, we just couldn't live there any longer. We'd talked about moving back to Maine, but we had our careers and we liked the money. It was really weird after September eleventh, so we applied for jobs here and in Bar Harbor. I don't think it mattered to either of us which community we would live in. I had visited Bar Harbor with Charlie and he had visited here with me. So Charlie and I sent résumés to everyone. The hospital called to offer him the public relations job, and while we were trying to decide if we could live off of one salary until I found a job, the dean of finance announced she was retiring and I was hired. Within weeks we bought the house and were packing. I do miss some of the cultural things, the theater, the symphony, but I love it here."

"I know what you mean. The whole time I was in California, I just knew someday I would return home. Then after the breakup it just seemed logical to make the move rather than wait."

"Come on." Charlie grabbed Carolyn's hand. "We'll have dessert on the balcony."

"Good idea." Allan stood up. "You two go upstairs and I'll bring the dessert up."

"Let me help clean up," Carolyn said, picking up her plate.

"Don't be silly. This may be an old house, but it has a very modern kitchen with a dishwasher, so you two just go and sit and I'll be up in a few minutes." Allan gently pushed them toward the door.

"I like him," Carolyn said as they settled into the lounge chairs.

"I'm glad because he was the best thing that ever happened to me." Charlie looked toward the door as if Allan was standing there. "I never thought I would ever be in a long-term relationship, and I don't think Allan thought so either, but he was different," Charlie said quietly. "I knew almost immediately I wanted to spend the rest of my life with him, and we have a good start."

"You said it's been five years?"

"Hard to believe, isn't it."

"No, not really."

"Well." Charlie shrugged. "It's just that gay guys have this tomming around reputation, and I'll admit I did all that, but once I met him I didn't want another person in my life." Charlie paused. "Thank God we were both careful."

"I was worried about that," Carolyn said, thinking about several friends who had died of AIDS. "I was afraid to ask."

"I saw a lot of friends die, not now so much with all the new drugs, but before."

"I thought of you often over the years," Carolyn said quietly.

"Me, you."

"Whenever something happened, not just the bad stuff, but the good stuff, I missed telling you about it," she said. "I missed the dormitories." Carolyn laughed. "I never thought I'd say that. Not so much the room, but the sitting around in our pajamas and talking about life. That was an easier time back then."

"I don't remember it as being that easy." Charlie chuckled. "I seem to remember a lot of groaning and griping about exams, grades, you name it."

Carolyn laughed. "I guess the past always seems like it was more fun."

"How are you doing?" Charlie said, changing the subject.

"Fine, really."

"Anyone in your life of interest?"

Carolyn scratched her ear. "No, and there won't be. I'm just not looking right now."

"Are you even dating?"

"Not really." Carolyn shifted in the chair.

"I'm sorry. I'm prying."

"Not at all," Carolyn protested. "It's just that it's more complicated than I'd thought. It's not easy to meet women, and I'm still practice-building, so I'm consumed with that. Plus, I just don't want to go through the pain again." Carolyn held up her hands. "Believe me, the breakup is not as nice as the start."

"It never is."

"And this one was particularly messy. We had commingled everything. It was like the divorce from hell. In fact, we had to hire attorneys. In the end, we weren't even talking to each other." Carolyn paused. "I just don't want to ever go through that again. I think what hurt most was the loss of trust. That bothered me more than the separation of property. She kept the house in California and bought out my half. After that I just didn't want to move into an apartment, so I came back here." Carolyn looked up as the double doors opened.

"Here we go," Allan said, carrying a tray. "Charlie said your favorite dessert was warm pecan pie with ice cream." He set the tray on the table. "And my boy there makes a mean pecan pie."

"Oh, wow." She turned to her friend. "You remembered."

"Of course I remembered." He smiled affectionately at her. "We were . . . we are best friends."

"Come on, you two, stop with the near-tear confessions." Allan grinned as he handed Carolyn a plate and fork.

She dipped her fork in the pie and swirled it around the ice cream. "Oh, this is delicious," she said as she grabbed for a napkin to wipe some of the ice cream that had dripped on her chin.

Allan handed a piece to Charlie just as the telephone rang. "Here, love. I'll get it."

"I'm jealous," Carolyn said. "A good kind of jealous. Charlie, you look so happy."

"I am." He shook his head. "That's the part I don't understand. I dated men that I was bored with after only just hours. With Allan it was so different. It was . . ." Charlie looked up as Allan stepped back onto the porch.

Carolyn noticed the grim expression on Allan's face.

"What's the matter, hon?" Charlie asked.

"There's been a death at the university. Laura Davenport?"

"What, the new art professor?" Charlie frowned. "How?"

"Don't know. All I know is she's been dead for a few days. Everyone thought she was at a conference. She said she'd be back on campus today for some kind of faculty meeting. When she didn't show up one of the other faculty members went to her house, found her dead. Maine State Police are investigating. Look—" He paused and glanced at Carolyn. "I don't wish to be rude, but I've got to go over to the campus. The president wants administrative staff there."

"Don't worry about us." Charlie stood up. "If there's anything I can do . . ."

Carolyn also got up. "Maybe I should go back to the boat."

"Don't be silly. You two enjoy yourselves. I'll be fine. I just have to go over there." Allan leaned over and kissed Charlie. "Don't wait up. This could go late."

"Of course I'll wait up." Charlie hugged him. "Be careful."

They watched as Allan left. "Look, Charlie, why don't I go back to the boat?"

"Allan's right. It seems silly you sitting on the boat, me sitting here. We can keep each other company as we wonder what the hell's going on. Come on, let me freshen up your coffee," he said as he reached for the pot.

Chapter Four

Molly could hear the faraway ring. She tried to bury herself deeper in sleep. The ringing was unrelenting. She reached out and slapped at her alarm clock. The ringing continued. Molly raised her head, her eyes still closed, and reached for the telephone.

"Yeah?"

"Molly, it's Billy."

"What's wrong?" Molly rubbed her eyes, hoping to force them open. She and Billy Welch had gone to school together; he was also Gin Cove's police chief. The only other time he had ever called her was when some teens had vandalized several boats at the marina, Molly's being one of them. "Has something happened to my boat?"

"No, your boat's fine. It's your brother. We have him here."

Molly sat up in bed. "What do you mean you have him there? Has he been in an accident?"

"We broke up a party. Tommy was there."

"Is he drunk?" Molly looked at the green numbers on her clock. It was three o'clock in the morning.

"Molly," Billy said, "he's high."

"You mean drugs?" Molly swung her legs over the side of the bed. Her feet searched for the slippers she knew she had left there when she went to sleep. Somehow they had gotten all twisted in the night. "Tommy doesn't use drugs."

"Look, I think you need to come down here. He's in no condition to drive and someone needs to take him home."

"I'm on my way."

Molly pulled a pair of jeans off the chair and slid them over her pajama shorts. She reached in the drawer and took out a shirt and pulled it on over her nightshirt. She grabbed her tennis shoes and put them on, then headed out.

She backed her Ford Explorer out of the shed and onto the road. She hadn't been out of bed at three o'clock in the morning since she was in her twenties and was coming home from a party. She thought back to those days. She and Tommy were living with Auntie Em. Those late nights she would pull in the driveway with her car lights off. Then she would put just enough downward pressure on the back door to keep it from squeaking when she eased it open. She had practiced the quiet assault on the door for years, but somehow the moment her foot touched the kitchen floor Auntie Em would yell, "Glad you're home. Good night, dear."

Molly frowned as she thought about some of those nights when she never should have driven home. She had been lucky and never was stopped by a cop. But Auntie Em seemed to know and would talk to her about making the mistake that could change her life. Molly shivered now as she thought about how different her life would be if she had been drunk and in an accident. Lately, it seemed, Tommy was not as lucky.

He was eight years old when their mother had died. Molly was eighteen. Her mother had told her that she had wanted to have one child almost grown before she had to deal with a second one going

41

through adolescence. Molly knew that what really had happened was that Tommy had been an accident.

One quick look at the plump pink thing in the little blue blanket produced immediate hate. Tommy Bean got all the attention and for a time, Molly thought, all of her mother's love.

Molly, who was ten, felt lumpish and clumsy in her body. A body she tried to hide by wearing oversized flannel shirts. Her dislike for her brother carried over to his toddler years. If she wanted to play baseball with her friends on Saturday, she had the choice to take him along or stay home and baby-sit while her mother was at the sardine factory. Molly would take him along, but then he would wander off and she would have to look for him, and somehow the baseball game never finished.

One Saturday she tied him to a tree. She told him they were play-ing cowboys and he was the bad guy and she was the sheriff and that was why he had to be tied up. The baseball game had lasted longer than expected and when she got back to the tree he had cried himself to sleep. Even though she bought him his favorite candy to buy his silence, he still told their mother and she was punished.

Then their mother had been killed in an automobile accident. Their father, who spent days lobstering and nights drinking, was never home. Molly remembered those first few weeks after her mother had died . . . it was like searching through fog.

Years later, after she inherited her father's boat and took up lob-ster fishing, she went out in what seemed like a light morning fog, but hours later the fog had hardened around her and the world dis-appeared. That was what the days and nights felt like after her mother died. Auntie Em had understood, and she had packed up Molly and Tommy's clothes and moved them into her farmhouse. It was supposed to be temporary, but Molly lived there while she attended college and that was where Tommy grew up.

Molly turned right onto the Gleason Cove Road. Her car sped past the Wal-Mart store and the city's animal shelter and into the downtown. If she had kept going she would have been at the marina.

She pulled up in front of the police station. The stores on either side of the station that were usually busy with daytime customers were soundless. The whole world seemed to be asleep except for Molly and the people inside the police station. The last time she had been here was for a fund-raising effort put on by the Lobstermen's Association to raise money for the eighth-grade class trip. The Jail and Bail fund-raiser had netted the association $1,000 and had landed Molly in jail three times. People who wanted to have friends jailed donated money and the police would arrest the individuals, take them to the police station where they were allowed to make telephone calls to raise money for their bail. If friends didn't come through with the fifty-dollar bail, then the arrestee had to sit in jail for a half-hour. Of course the cell door was open, and Dunkin Donuts had provided the munchies to prisoners, who laughed and joked while they waited to be sprung. Each time, Molly was able to call enough friends who donated enough to pay her fine. Then it had been fun; now somehow she didn't think her brother was having much fun.

Molly pushed open the wooden doors and stepped in front of the counter. The woman at the desk looked up.

"Julie, hi." Molly couldn't keep the surprise out of her voice. "I didn't know you were back."

"You're about the only one." Julie smiled. "I've been back about six months. I've seen you around town, but you're always rushing someplace. I guess I have to arrest you to get your attention."

Molly blushed.

Julie looked at her appraisingly. "I remember, the red blush goes nicely with your red hair." Julie had that self-satisfied smile that Molly had come to detest. "I thought about stopping by."

"I . . ." Molly paused as the door opened.

Billy nodded to her as he closed the door behind him. "Glad you're here. I'd like to talk to you before I release him." He gestured toward his office. "It's been busier than hell around here. The murder at the college this morning and now the party."

"What murder? My brother wasn't involved with that," Molly said quickly as the questions spilled out of her mouth.

"A professor at the college was found dead this morning. The staties are handling it. I don't imagine your brother was involved. He was too busy getting high. Don't really know much about it. College called the police, but as soon as my guys got over there they saw it was a homicide and the state police have been handling it ever since. I haven't spoken with them, so don't really know what's been going on, except I understand she got to the campus last September. People said they liked her, a bit eccentric, but most of those college professors are."

"I didn't know."

"Been on the radio, television."

"I was lobstering all day, had dinner with Auntie Em, went back to my house and I was sound asleep when you called. Didn't even turn on the radio. But what about my brother? Has he been charged with anything?" Molly asked as she followed Billy. He opened the door to his office and nodded for Molly to sit down.

Billy sat down behind his desk. "Not yet, but he is going to be charged with possession of OxyContin. The state charge is a little more formal, but essentially that's what it is."

"OxyContin?" Molly gripped the sides of the chair. "Tommy isn't into that crap."

"It looks like he is," Billy said quietly. "He's been seen at a local drug dealer's house a lot."

"Who?"

"Robbie Olson."

"Robbie Olson? That's crazy, Robbie and Tommy went to school together. They're best friends. Have been since grade school. If Tommy was there, it wasn't to buy drugs. Beer maybe. A party, probably. Not drugs, Billy."

"Yeah, it was. He had them on him. Not enough to charge him with anything more than possession, but I think he was just lucky this time."

Molly stood up and paced around Billy's office. She looked at the large poster on the wall of a police officer helping a child. A large wooden frame had police patches from other police departments that Billy had collected over the years. Many of the departments Molly noticed were in-state, a few were from out of state.

"I think I would know if my brother was high."

"How often do you see him?"

Molly paused. "Not a lot, lately. He worked as my sternman last summer, but he got a full-time job at the college last winter in their maintenance department. A job he said he liked."

"Cleaning up after students?"

"No, it was more than that. Fixing things—he was always good at things like that."

"Well, he's not there anymore. He said they laid him off several weeks ago."

Molly sat back down. "I didn't know. I wonder if Auntie Em knew?"

"I doubt it." Billy stopped. "Look, Molly, you and I have been friends for a long time so I am going to lay this out for you. I think he has been supporting himself lately by dealing. He's been hanging tight with Olson and another suspected drug dealer."

"Who?"

Billy paused. "We haven't arrested him yet so I'd rather not say."

"Tim Carnes?"

"How'd you know?"

Molly shrugged. "You hear." She looked down at her hands. "Although I hear stuff about everyone else, but not about my brother," she said ruefully.

"People aren't going to tell you, Molly. No one's going to look you in the eye and tell you your brother's dealing drugs. This is a small town that thrives on gossip, but they'll never tell you when it's someone close to you even though everyone's talking about it."

"Yeah." Molly pondered his words. "I know. How long have you known?"

"We arrested a guy a few weeks ago. We flipped him to get at his dealer. He gave us Olson. Neighbors called to complain about the loud Friday night party, and when we got there, people ran out the doors, windows. Those we didn't catch, we know who they are and they'll be arrested. Tommy was asleep in a chair in the living room, more than likely passed out. When we searched him we found this—" Billy showed her the blue pillbox in the palm of his hand. He reached over and flipped open the top. "These two pills were inside. Oxy."

"Maybe somebody planted them on him as they ran out."

Billy scowled at Molly. "They're his."

"Look . . ." Molly hesitated as she tried to put into words the years that separated her and her brother. When they were younger he had looked to her for protection. As a girl, being a redhead led to insulting remarks and silly rhymes, but not as nasty as what Tommy got from some of the students. She remembered the time she had found him behind the school crying. Some older boys had held him down and had used a dirty rag to try and scrub the freckles off his face. His face was blood-red and scraped. He was six years old. He told Molly who they were and when she found them alone, she yanked each one up by the collar and threatened to castrate him. She was sixteen at the time and frightening in her anger. She shook her head, reminding herself she was at the police station and her brother was in serious trouble. "He . . . I can't say," she said feebly.

"Molly, I think there may be a solution."

"Jail?"

"How much do you know about Oxy?"

"Just what I've read in the newspapers. It's a prescription drug. Doctors prescribe it for severe pain related to something like cancer. I know that it's become some kind of street drug. I'll tell you honestly, I just haven't been paying that much attention. I've heard down at the dock someone say this kid or that kid's using, but I really wasn't interested," Molly said weakly. "I guess I should've been."

"It's this county's cancer, and it is eating our young. It popped up about four years ago. A little here, a little there. Now, it's pervasive. We know it's in the middle school. We've arrested kids as young as twelve, not selling but using, who're now in the juvenile system. It's in the high schools. We suspect some of the athletes are using, although we haven't been able to catch them. Boys, girls, they all are using. Mostly they get turned on at parties like the one at Robbie's. It's friends doing friends."

"Tommy's twenty-five. He's not a kid. I can't believe he would get sucked into something like that."

"Age don't matter. We've arrested people in their twenties, thirties, forties. I arrested a guy two weeks ago, he was in his seventies. He had a legitimate prescription for it. Trouble was he was keeping some for himself and selling the rest."

"I knew Tommy was drinking. He liked to party, but drugs?"

"It doesn't take much to get hooked on this stuff. I had addicts tell me that they tried it once and were hooked. It's not like cocaine or heroin where it takes using to end up abusing."

"I don't get it. If it's a painkiller, do people who take it with a prescription also get hooked on it?"

"No. It has a time-release coat on it. When used right, it's absorbed into the system. Addicts suck the coating off and they either crush and snort it, or they inject it."

"Inject? Like heroin?"

"Like heroin, only more addictive."

Molly clenched her hands together and rested them against her chin. "Is he—" She paused. "Is he high right now?"

"No. He slept most of it off. Molly, I want Tommy to help us."

"How?"

"I want Robbie's supplier, and I think Tommy knows."

"He's not talking," Molly said. "They're probably Robbie's." She knew it wasn't a question.

"We want the guy who's higher up the food chain. The one supplying Robbie and Tommy. Neither he nor Robbie is saying much."

"I'm not surprised. He and Robbie are like brothers. They were always together. They probably have one of those men's blood-oath things," Molly said contemptuously.

"How about if you talk to him?"

"I don't think he'd tell me."

Billy looked down at the papers on his desk. "What about Auntie Em?"

"He might tell her. They're close." Molly gestured helplessly. "When we were young we'd fight like brother and sister. Poor Auntie Em, she'd have to break it up. Tell us we should hang together 'cause we were all we had. My being ten years older didn't help. Then I went to college and it seemed we just found different lives. I thought it had gotten better. Last year he worked as my sternman. We never talked about anything, though," Molly said reflectively. "He's a good person, has a great sense of humor. I love him; I just don't know him as an adult. After he quit—" Molly held up her hands, trying to explain. "Not because of any problem between us, just that the college offered him a year-round job and he took it. I don't blame him. After that we really didn't see much of each other, except on the occasion he was staying at Auntie Em's and I dropped in for a visit. We don't confide in each other, that's all."

"Maybe Auntie Em can help." Billy reached for a paper on his desk and handed it to her. "I have something else here. I'd like Tommy to think about. I think Tommy is a good candidate for drug court, and it could keep him out of jail."

"How?"

"It's been around just a few years. He has to attend drug court once a week and report his activities to the judge. The judge here is high—" Billy stopped. "Sorry, no pun intended. He's keen on the program. Donates lots of his own time. Basically, a group of people—a social worker, counselor, probation officer—kinda closes ranks around Tommy. He has to confront his problem and deal with it. He has to find a job and every week prove to the judge that he's not hanging with his old crowd and that he's on track."

"Did you tell Tommy about this?"

48

"Don't want no part of it."

"You're kidding."

"Said he'd rather go to jail and get it over with. Said he can handle the problem himself."

Molly shook her head. "I don't believe it. He'd rather go to jail?"

"Frankly, Molly, most of them do."

Molly put her head in her hands and rubbed her fingers against her temples. "Billy, this is a lot to take in. I just learned my brother is a drug addict, that he may be dealing and that he refuses to be helped. I don't know what to say." Molly stopped and swallowed. She could feel the tears. She clenched her teeth together. It was a trick she had learned as a child. If she clenched her teeth hard enough, the tears would stop.

I'm not going to cry, she thought. *I am not going to cry.*

"You want me to talk to him?"

Billy cleared his throat. "Maybe it'd be better if it was Auntie Em."

Molly stood up. "I'd like to argue and say no, but I think she'd have more sway," she said dejectedly. "What now?"

"Bail is five hundred dollars, cash. He said he didn't have that much."

"I'll pay it."

"Pay his bail, we'll release him to your custody. I'd like him back here Monday to talk."

"He'll be here."

"Can you bring Auntie Em?"

"Yeah." Molly rubbed her head. "What's tomorrow—I mean today—Saturday? I'll talk with her. I know she'll do whatever to help him."

Billy stood up. "Look, I'm really sorry about this, Molly."

"I know, Billy." She turned toward the door. "You know what's strange about this?"

"Yeah, you never expect it to happen in your family. I hear that all the time from family members."

"You're right. I never paid attention to the drug problem because I figured it was happening to someone out there." Her hand swept the air. "I tried pot in college, never liked it. I figured Tommy was experimenting with alcohol, maybe a little pot. But not this."

"This stuff wasn't around when you and I were going to school. If it had been, who knows what our lives would have been like. Most of them try it just to say they tried it. They just don't realize how easily they're hooked. Come on." He took Molly by the arm and opened the door. "Wait out there at the desk and we'll finish processing him."

Molly looked at the desk; Julie had her back to her.

"Could I just wait here?"

Billy followed her gaze. "Sure. Once he's processed I'll let you know. Sorry." He nodded toward Julie. "I didn't even think about that."

"It's okay."

"Everything okay between you two?"

"I didn't even know she was back. Last I knew she'd transferred to a police department in Castine."

"She did, then about six weeks ago she asked for her old job back." Billy paused. "She's a good cop."

Molly squeezed Billy's hand. "I know. What happened between us is ancient history, but right now I'm just not in the mood for ancient history." Molly's smile was tight.

Chapter Five

Carolyn stepped out onto the widow's walk. Allan and Charlie were still in bed. It was six o'clock in the morning. Charlie had set the clock on the coffee maker for that hour and now Carolyn stood looking at the ocean, a fresh cup of coffee in her hand.

Getting up at six was something she did during the week, not on weekends, especially not on weekend mornings, but something was different here. She had awakened early and could not go back to sleep. She had slipped out of her bed and quietly gone in search of the coffee Charlie had promised. The house was serene, almost virtuous in its quiet. She could smell the coffee brewing even as she walked down the stairs.

Then, feeling the enticement of the widow's walk, she quietly went to the third floor. Charlie had shown her a side door that led onto the balcony. She did not wish to disturb her sleeping friends. She had heard Allan come in. When she looked at the clock it was two in the morning.

She stood watching the ocean; the morning sun pranced on the waves. How many women had stood here wondering if their husbands would return from the sea? Carolyn wondered if she would ever feel that same fear, that wonderment at loss.

When California Christine had said that there was another woman and their relationship was over, Carolyn had cried, but she had not felt lost. Now she wondered about that. Why hadn't she fought to keep the relationship going? Why was she so willing to give up?

Carolyn sensed a connection with the women who had stood on the walk. Had they stood here night after night, praying for the safe return of their husbands? If Christine had been a sailor instead of a lawyer, would she, Carolyn, have been out here praying for her safe return? Carolyn didn't know.

"Hi, sweets." The words were soft.

"Hi, Charlie." Carolyn gave her friend a hug, his unshaven cheek rough against her face.

"I almost hated to disturb you. Where were you?"

"I was thinking about the women who stood here waiting for their husbands to return and I was thinking . . ." Carolyn laughed. "I was just thinking foolish thoughts. You're up early."

"Not really. I like to come out here and just sit. What were you thinking, hon?" he persisted.

Carolyn pulled one of the chaise lounges closer to the railing and patted for Charlie to sit down. "I was just wondering what it must have been like for those women to stand out here, night after night, wondering if their husbands would return, worried that they wouldn't." Carolyn paused. "And then I was wondering if there ever had been anybody in my life that I would worry about like that." She hesitated. "I came to the conclusion, probably not."

"I would." Charlie pulled his robe close across his chest. "If Allan was out there, I would be worried to the point of hysteria."

"I know I loved Christine, but I—"

"Didn't mourn the passing of your relationship," Charlie finished for her.

"That's right. How did you know?"

"You haven't talked about her much since you've been here, and you broke up how long ago?"

"A year ago after three years together, but maybe I get over lost love faster than other people."

Charlie smiled. "I doubt it. Don't get me wrong, I think you loved her, but she wasn't your soul mate."

"Is Allan your soul mate?"

"Absolutely."

"How'd you know?"

"Because." Charlie reached for Carolyn's coffee cup. He took a sip and grimaced. "I forgot you like sugar in yours."

"Serves you right." Carolyn laughed. "How did you know?"

Charlie looked down at the green stripes on the chaise lounge. "You're going to laugh."

"No, I won't laugh."

"You know that poem about footprints in the sand?"

"Sure."

"Well, a soul mate leaves footprints in your heart." Charlie's long fingers traced the lines on the green stripes. "I knew because one night we were here and we had had this wonderful dinner. Afterwards, we made love and he was holding me in his arms and I got this strong, eerie feeling." Charlie stopped.

"Strong, eerie feeling?"

"It was in my heart, yet it was tactile, like I could almost touch the emotion I was feeling." Charlie paused. "At that moment I knew that I couldn't live without him. I knew that if he died first, I would die. So I made him promise that I would die first. It's so silly." Carolyn could hear the embarrassment in Charlie's voice. "If he died, then I would die, yet I wanted to die first."

Carolyn touched Charlie's hand. "I understand. I've never felt that before for any woman."

"Then you haven't experienced the adventures of a soul mate, my love," Charlie said quietly.

"Probably not," she agreed.

"You will."

"How? I am thirty-two years old and I have yet to regret a lost love. What does that say about me?"

"You haven't found love," Charlie said matter-of-factly. "Allan was hopeful. He wanted to introduce you to his dearest friend. He even talked to her aunt about getting her to come to dinner tonight."

Carolyn frowned. "A fix-up? Here in Gin Cove?"

Charlie beamed. "Here in Gin Cove," he said intensely.

"Tell me." Intrigued, Carolyn sat forward in the chair.

"She's a lobster fisherman, she and Allan have been friends since grade school—"

"Please don't tell me," Carolyn interrupted. "Is she about five-foot-seven, very lean-looking with flaming red hair?"

"Yes, that's Molly Bean."

Carolyn groaned. "Tell Allan he needn't worry about fixing us up. I almost drowned the woman." She then told Charlie about her near mishap at sea and Molly's smuggling efforts at the marina.

Charlie put his head back and laughed. "That's Molly. I bet she told you Auntie Em was making lobster stew."

"She did."

"Lobster fishermen around here are probably the most conservation-minded people in the world, except when it comes to lobster stew, and then they have this preposterous need to break the law and hide a few undersized lobsters to stuff into that stew."

"Well, that was what she was doing. Imagine my surprise when I looked over at those orange rubber pants she was wearing and they started to move." Carolyn laughed. "Do you know what it reminded me of?"

"No, what?"

Carolyn used the sleeve of her pajamas to wipe her eyes. "My mother's fudge. I used to stand and watch it bubble as it cooked. First one large bubble would pop to the surface and then another. Well, that was what happened with Molly. First there was this one bubble as a lobster moved up her pants, then another and then another. At one point she had to grab her thigh. I think that one of the little critters was ready to grab on to her you-know-what." Carolyn put her head back and laughed.

Charlie joined in the laughter. "That must have been something to see."

"It was."

"Did she say anything afterwards?"

"She did." Carolyn kept wiping her eyes. "She actually apologized."

"For the lobsters in her pants?"

"Sort of, mostly because I'd helped her break the law by distracting the marine patrol officer. And of course I apologized to her for almost dumping her and her companion in the water."

"Auntie Em." Charlie paused. "Gray hair, about seventy years old."

"That was her. I felt badly about her, I really hoped she hadn't broken a leg or something—but not too much about the redhead. I figured she deserved it. She really is quite full of herself."

"Truly, she is very nice."

"Really?"

"How do I describe Molly?" Charlie said, and then laughed. "I feel like I should burst into song. She loves adventure and is not afraid of anything. She is kind, thoughtful and a true friend. I met her through Allan and I love her to death."

"Well, I expect I blew it, and you know, Charlie, I knew better. I had the boat wide open, anxious to get here, and I had gone into the galley for just a few minutes and when I came out, there they were. I thought we were going to crash."

"What happened?"

"It was Molly, not me. I was paralyzed. I just stood there. Molly got the engine on her boat started and pulled away within inches of a collision."

"Well, now you've met our Molly."

"Probably the one and only time. Believe me, she was not happy with me."

"Happy with who?" Allan said as he stepped out onto the deck. He leaned over and gave Charlie a kiss. "Good morning." Allan ran his hand through Charlie's hair.

"Good morning." Charlie smiled at him.

"With me. I was just telling Charlie about my meeting with Molly. Little did I know that she was a friend of yours." Carolyn then related the near mishap with the boats.

"Ahh," Allan said. "I thought you two might like each other."

"Too late, I broke a cardinal rule of the sea, and I can tell you that lady's face was as red as her hair. It was only the noise of our engines that kept me from hearing what she said. I think her words would've embarrassed not only me, but her."

Allan nodded in agreement. "Molly can be pretty . . . how do I say it." He paused. "Expressive at times."

"A challenge," Charlie added. He stood up.

"How'd it go at the college?" Carolyn asked quietly. She figured that Charlie and Allan had already talked about the death when he came home.

"Police are investigating. They think she was killed either Tuesday night or sometime Wednesday. They aren't saying much, but I think it was some kind of robbery gone wrong. Professor Davenport was supposed to be at a four-day conference." Allan shrugged. "She was to leave Tuesday during the day. She called friends and said she had the flu and was going to spend the next few days in bed. What I gather, friends and colleagues didn't think much about it until she missed the Friday faculty meeting. They called, then one of her friends went over and found her."

"Was she a friend?"

"I wouldn't say that. We're a small campus, course everyone knows everyone else. I knew her, but I wouldn't say we were anything more than colleagues. As dean of finance I don't have that much interaction with the professors. But it's so sad. It's the first murder ever on the campus."

"Really?"

"Really." Allan slipped his arm through Charlie's. "Let's talk about something else. There's nothing I can do right now. The president sent us all home and told us not to say anything if the media should call. So I would rather have some breakfast, tell you more about Molly and then head out."

"You guys go ahead. I'll be in in a minute. I'll finish my coffee and then take my shower." Carolyn waited until Charlie and Allan had gone back inside, then she turned to the railing.

A soul mate? She thought about Charlie's words. *What would it be like to have a soul mate?*

Chapter Six

Molly dropped Tommy off at his apartment. "I'll be back in two hours to pick you up. I need to shower."

"And talk to Auntie Em," Tommy said as he stepped out of the car.

"And talk to Auntie Em," Molly said quietly. Tommy had been detached after they left the jail. She had tried to talk to him, but he would only grunt his answers. Tommy turned back to the car. "Molly, it's too late."

"For what?"

"To battle the drugs. I've lost this one." Molly could see the despair in her brother's eyes. "I—" Tommy slammed the door.

She watched him walk up the steps to the apartment complex. He looked so much like their father. Their father was only five feet nine inches, but he had arms like a gorilla from the years of pulling traps and a belly as soft as a beach ball from all the years of drinking. Even when he was in his fifties, his red hair had not taken on the auburn cast so many redheads acquire but was the same bright red it had been when he was younger. Tommy's was just the same.

Molly rested her head against the steering wheel. They had grown up strangers, she thought. In college she was so preoccupied with her own life and finding her way as a lesbian that she had not been concerned about his adolescent problems, his teenage challenges. She had not understood him, and at some point he had accepted the fact that his older sister didn't really care. Molly put the car in gear. Now more than ever, they both needed Auntie Em.

Molly parked the car in the driveway; Auntie Em was waiting for her at the kitchen door. Molly listened to the squeak as she closed the door behind her.

"I know."

"How?"

"What do you think? I've had several telephone calls telling me Tommy was in jail. That he was at a drug dealer's house partying."

Molly lowered her head. "I'm sorry, Auntie Em. I wanted to tell you myself."

Auntie Em shrugged. "The town drums beat you to it. People love the telling. Every single telephone call began with 'I'm so sorry to break the news to you, Auntie Em, but I heard on the radio this morning that Tommy's been arrested. He was at some kind of drug party,'" she mimicked. "Course they do relish telling me. Otherwise, what's the fun of gossip. They also mentioned something about a murder. Tommy isn't connected to that?"

"Absolutely not. Some professor at the college. The chief said the state police are handling it." Molly took her jacket off and laid it on the back of a chair. "I'm sorry. I should have called you, but I didn't want to wake you up."

"No matter," Auntie Em said. She waved Molly toward a kitchen chair. "Sit. Where's Tommy?"

"I dropped him off at his apartment. I told him I wanted to

shower. He knew I wanted to talk to you. I'm supposed to pick him up later."

"How bad is it?"

"Well, the people-babble was right on line. He was arrested last night at Robbie's house. Billy says they've suspected Robbie was a drug dealer. Last night they raided the house. Made a bunch of arrests including Tommy. They found him with two OxyContin pills." Molly paused. "Do you know what they are?"

"Land, yes, been all over the newspaper about the drug problem. They call it Down East heroin. OxyContin, Dilaudid—you name it, we got it, and the kids have been experimenting with it."

Molly smiled. Her aunt may be seventy but there wasn't much that did not come up on her radar screen. "That's right. They're going to charge him with possession. Billy wants him to go to drug court. I expect you know about that."

"I do. How does Tommy feel about it?"

"He doesn't want drug court, wants to go to jail, says he can handle it himself." Molly didn't want to tell Auntie Em what Tommy said about it being too late.

Auntie Em nodded. "Sounds like him, sounds like you for that matter."

"I never used those kinds of drugs," Molly protested.

"That's because they weren't available. Otherwise you'd have experimented."

Molly scratched her head. "How'd you know?"

"That you'd experimented with marijuana? I smelled it on your clothes when you'd come home late at night. I wasn't worried much because after a while, I didn't smell it."

Molly smiled. "That's right. I stopped using, didn't like the way it made me feel. Made me sleepy, lethargic."

"That's good." Auntie Em sighed. "Tommy was different. He liked the stuff. Drank too much. The smell of marijuana was always on his clothes. I prayed that it wouldn't happen, but I ain't surprised he's gotten into this other stuff." Auntie Em shook her head. "I tried to talk to him, but he just pulled deeper inside."

60

"I'm surprised. I knew he liked his drink. Why not? Pa did too." Molly stopped. "But when Billy said he was on that stuff, I didn't want to believe it."

"Why?"

"What Billy says, the addiction is bad, really bad."

"We're not going to abandon him. He needs help." Auntie Em paused. Molly could see her mind click into the fix-it mode. Whenever there was a problem, Auntie Em could always fix it. Molly wasn't so certain this time. "He can move back here," Auntie Em continued. "I'll feed him. He needs to see a counselor, get some help, but I know we can help that boy."

Molly shook her head. "I don't know, Auntie Em. From what Billy said this is real potent stuff. This junk unleashes a whole menagerie of demons. Billy seems to think he's going to get into worse trouble if he doesn't get help."

"Well, Billy doesn't know Tommy like we do."

"Do we know him, Auntie?" Molly asked. "Do we really know him? I don't think we do."

"Of course we do. I raised that boy since he was eight years old. I know him as well as I know myself. I know he ain't got a bad bone in his body. This is just a phase. We got to help him get through it and then he'll be better, much better."

"I don't know, Auntie Em." Molly could hear the worry in her own voice. "I hope so, but if he's like Pa, he isn't going to want help. He drank himself to death."

Auntie Em reached over and took Molly's hand. "We got to help," she said quietly. "He's our family."

Showered and feeling just a bit more like she was alive, Molly turned onto Water Street toward Billy's apartment. She had thought about what Auntie Em said and she still was anxious. She pulled up in front of Tommy's apartment. She looked at the dark windows at the front of the house. Two different couples lived downstairs. Tommy lived upstairs. Molly had only been there once before when she had to pick Tommy up to take him to work. Now there was an eerie silence as she studied the windows. There was no light on in Tommy's upstairs studio apartment. And the overcast day demanded some kind of light.

Molly got out of the car. The front door on the three-apartment complex was open, but then she knew it would be—this was Gin Cove. Molly took the stairs to the studio apartment two at a time. She knocked on Tommy's door and waited. There was no voice inviting her in. She knocked again. All she could hear was silence. She tried the handle on the door and it opened. Molly stepped inside the apartment. The smell was suffocating. A cat rubbed against her leg.

"Hello there." Molly reached down and picked up the cat. She rested it against her shoulder and stroked its back. The cat purred. Molly identified the smell; it was the acrid smell of an unclean litter box. The living/bedroom was a mess. Tommy's wall bed was open, the bed unmade. Clothes were strewn across the floor. Molly kicked a shoe as she walked toward the kitchen.

A month's worth of dishes were piled high in the sink. A line of ants walked between the window and the unscraped dishes. Molly shuddered. Styrofoam boxes with half-eaten food were strewn all over the kitchen. Empty pizza boxes were stuffed in the trash. Molly set the cat down and it immediately ran to its food dish. The dish was empty of both food and water. She looked through the cupboards and found a can of tuna. She picked up the dish and scrubbed it clean with paper toweling. She filled one side with water and emptied the can of tuna into the other. She set the dish on the floor. The cat started to lap up the food. She took off her shoe and, balancing on one foot, she used the shoe to smack the ants.

Molly picked up a pair of yellow rubber kitchen gloves and put them on. They looked as though they had never been used. She stacked the dishes in the sink on the sideboard. She opened several drawers and found some trash bags, then stuffed empty food containers inside. She ran the hot water in the sink and began washing the dishes. Sweat beaded under her arms as she washed dish after dish. Finally, the last one was dunked and washed clean. She emptied the dirty water and wiped the counters and table clean. Molly inspected her work. At least it was clean, she thought.

The cat, finished with its meal, had been rubbing against her legs. "Well, little—" Molly held the cat up and looked. "Girl. I guess you're going to need a home for a while." She carried it into the living room. Clothes were tossed everywhere. She didn't bother to pick them up. She was willing to clean her brother's kitchen, but not pick up his clothes. She couldn't tell if he had packed anything to leave because she couldn't remember what clothes he liked to wear.

She walked over to the table next to the bed and pushed aside discarded beer cans. The telephone was under a pair of her brother's boxer shorts. At least she thought they were. She picked the receiver up with two fingers and dialed her aunt's number. Auntie Em picked up on the first ring.

"He's gone."

"Not a surprise."

"Didn't leave a note, nothing."

"What are you going to do next?"

"Call Billy, then go home and go to bed. I've been up since three o'clock this morning."

"You going to come here, go home or go to the boat?"

"I haven't thought about it. Probably the boat." Molly paused. "Did you know Tommy had a cat?"

"No, he never said anything to me."

"Well, he does. A cat. I'll take it to the boat, till he comes home."

"He didn't leave a note?" her aunt said again. Molly could hear the apprehension in her voice.

"I don't think so. Not in plain sight at least." She looked around. "Hard to tell, though. The place is a mess."

"Well, your brother never was much into cleaning up after himself. I had to clean his room all the time." Her aunt paused. "And pick up after him."

"Well, it's still happening. Someone is cleaning up after him now," Molly said sarcastically.

Auntie Em was quiet on the other line. "He couldn't have gone far. Probably staying with friends, I expect," she said.

"Probably. Anyway, I'll call Billy and tell him he's missing and then I'm going to be on the boat, hopefully sleeping."

"Okay, dear," Auntie Em said quietly. "Get some rest." She paused. "And Molly, don't give up on your brother. I expect he just didn't want to face me and tell me what he's been doing. He'll come around by and by, I believe that."

"I hope so. Otherwise Billy's going to find him and put him in jail."

Molly put the cat in the truck. It immediately sniffed the seats and floor.

"You're not going to find anything exciting in here," Molly said to the cat. "You're the first animal to take a ride." Finished with its inspection, the cat jumped up on the dash and lay down. Molly could hear her purr.

She drove through the downtown, past the police station. Her thoughts turned to Julie and the years they had lived together. Funny, she thought, how easy it was to hate the person you once loved.

"Believe that, cat," Molly said to the sleeping fur ball curled up on her dash. It was hard to remember when they had stopped loving each other. She did remember that the passion they had felt that first year had lessened. Heck, all the books said that would happen. The real problem, Molly thought, came later. She felt it in her bones but didn't know how to address it. Thinking back to her conversation with Auntie Em, she realized that Julie had never been her soul mate because they felt so comfortable spending time apart.

Julie couldn't talk about her work because of the confidentiality of it, and she seemed uninterested in what Molly did. The first year they were together, on her days off, Julie would go with Molly. But the hour was early and soon, Julie would roll over and go back to sleep. She said she would rather roll in the mud with a crook than stand at the side of a rail watching lobsters trying to escape their traps. Their schedules also didn't help. Julie had to work different shifts, while Molly's life was dictated by the run of the lobster.

When she suspected Julie was seeing someone else, Julie denied it. As a cop working the night shift she had plenty of excuses for why she wasn't home immediately after her shift ended. When Molly tried to talk about it Julie got angry and said she was trying to pick a fight. In the end, Molly realized they had become bored with each other, bored with their lives and bored with their lovemaking.

Then one Sunday, they were sitting outside enjoying the July sun and Julie announced she had applied to a police department down south and was moving. Within weeks of moving to Castine she and Becky Wilson were living together. Becky had been a nurse at Gin Cove Hospital.

"Never believe a woman when she tells you she's not having an affair," Molly said to the cat. The cat opened one sleepy eye and then settled back down in the sun.

Molly drove into the parking lot by the marina. She reached over and picked up the sleeping cat. "Come on, little girl, I have a whole new world for you to sniff." The cat rested against Molly's shoulder. Its sun-warmed fur was cozy against her chin.

She noticed that Allan's boat was gone. Good, she thought, her two friends were enjoying a Saturday morning on the water. She knew Allan and Charlie liked to go out early. She would call Allan Monday. She had to talk to him about Tommy.

Molly also looked over to see if the *Carolyn S.* was still in its slip. It was. Interesting woman, she thought. Molly had been so preoccupied with her brother's problems that she hadn't even thought about the lady who had nearly turned her boat upside down.

She stepped onto the deck of her boat and opened the door to the pilothouse. "Here ya go, cat. Have at it," Molly said as she set the cat down. The cat immediately jumped up near the depth finder and the radio. Molly closed the door behind them. She didn't want to spend the day chasing after cats. No wonder people owned pets, Molly thought. You can talk out loud and no one will think you're crazy, although Molly still felt silly talking to the cat.

She watched the cat for a few minutes. "Well, little girl, I'm going to bed." Molly stepped down two steps and opened the door to her cabin. She walked past the galley and into her sleeping quarters. She dropped curtains over the porthole near the table and lay down on her bunk. She dropped the curtains on the porthole next to her bunk. She rolled over on her side.

She felt a slight movement on the mattress and turned her head to look. The cat stared at her.

"I'm going to sleep, you can cat around all you want," Molly said. She closed her eyes. The cat sniffed the length of her body and then lay down against her back. She wasn't worried about outside noises. On Saturdays most of the fishermen were already out to sea, and the tourists were relegated to the end of the pier so their noises wouldn't disturb the fishermen. Molly slept.

When she awoke, she felt cold. The cat was gone. She lifted the curtain on the porthole and looked out. She could see the afternoon sun setting and felt the chill in the air. She stretched. If she didn't get up now, she wouldn't sleep tonight. She swung her legs off the bunk, grabbed a sweatshirt and put it on.

In the galley she reached into the refrigerator and took out a bottle of Poland Springs water. She took off the cap and drank. Her mouth was dry. She walked up the two steps to the pilothouse to find the cat was asleep near the gauges. It lifted its head when she walked past. Molly reached over and rubbed its ears. She picked up her cell phone and dialed Aunt Em's number.

Auntie Em answered on the first ring. "Hello?"

"Hi, Auntie, I just woke up. Have you heard from Tommy?"

"No, not a word. Billy called. They haven't seen him around

town. He said that if Tommy violates any conditions of his bail, he goes directly to jail."

"One of his conditions was that he not hang out with Robbie, but somehow I feel like he's already violated the condition," Molly said.

"That's what Billy said. They're watching Robbie's house. Right now no one's home there. Listen, I want you to come to supper tonight. I don't think either one of us should be alone. If you want, you can sleep here."

"I'll come for dinner, but I think I'll come back here and sleep. I got this cat to deal with," Molly said. The cat now was rubbing up against her legs. "What time is it?"

"Four."

"I'll be there around six. I got to go to the store and buy some cat food and litter. Then I'll be over."

"Good," Auntie Em said.

Molly stepped out on the deck and closed the door to the pilot-house behind her, the cat inside.

"Hey, you." She turned to see Allan walking toward her. The blond hair on his legs glistening in the afternoon sun; a sweeping smile on his face. He hopped on deck and gave her a big hug. He pulled back and looked at her. "What's wrong?"

"It's Tommy." She had resisted the urge to cry earlier; now she could feel the tears. She turned away.

"Hey, come here." Allan held her in his arms. "What's wrong, kitten?"

"He was arrested last night," she said against his chest.

"For what?"

Molly stepped back and wiped the tears on her sweatshirt. "Possession of OxyContin. You're about the only one in town doesn't know. Poor Auntie Em learned it from the rank and file gossipers."

"Sorry, hon. We had that murder on campus, and I've been preoccupied with it."

"Oh, I'm so sorry, Allan. I didn't even think about what you must be going through." Molly bit her bottom lip, fresh tears spilling down her cheek.

"Come here." Allan held her tightly. "This is your brother. I understand. I didn't think he was into that stuff."

"He is. Least that's what Billy said. Tommy was at Robbie's house last night, at some kind of party. When they arrested Tommy, he had two pills on him. I made his bail for him. I dropped him off at his apartment, he was going to clean up and then we were going to go to Auntie Em's. He's disappeared."

"As in left the state?"

Molly shook her head. "I don't think so. He's around here, just hiding. Billy said if he was caught violating any part of his bail conditions, he'd go to jail. Somehow I think he's with Robbie, and I also think Billy's going to find him."

"Me too." Allan looked up and Molly followed his gaze. She was surprised to see Carolyn walking next to Charlie.

"Do you know her?"

"Yes, that's the woman I wanted you to meet."

Molly groaned. "She thinks I'm a criminal. I was smuggling shorts," Molly said, quickly slipping her sunglasses on to cover her red eyes.

Charlie set the chairs and cooler they were carrying on the dock and stepped on board. "We've been looking for you," he said as he gave Molly a hug. "I understand you've met my friend Carolyn."

Carolyn smiled.

"By chance." Molly smiled, but she still could feel the tears just below the smile.

"More than by chance," Carolyn added. "I tried to drown you and your aunt. Hardly an auspicious way to meet someone."

"But memorable," Charlie said with a laugh. "Listen," he said, turning to Molly, "we're just going up to the house to have dinner.

Why don't you join us? Allan invited you earlier, even talked to Auntie Em."

Molly remembered her reluctance to meet someone new. Now, with the problems surrounding her brother, she knew it was impossible. "I'd love to." Molly feigned enthusiasm. "Really. But I'm going to the store and after that I promised Auntie Em we would have dinner. She's making it right now."

"Too bad," Charlie said, looking behind her.

She smiled. "That's why I'm going to the store." Relieved that she could turn away from Carolyn's penetrating eyes, she pointed at the cat that was now standing on the table looking out at them.

"I thought you hated animals on a boat," Charlie said. "Dogs, cats—you said they get in the way."

"It's just temporary. Cat belongs to my brother, so I'm taking care of it for a few days. I have to get some cat food and some litter. I'm afraid to let her roam because she might get taken by a fox."

"What's its name?" Carolyn asked.

Molly paused. She didn't have a clue. "Cat. I just call her Cat."

Allan, Charlie and Carolyn laughed.

"Simple, but nice," Carolyn said.

"Listen, we have to get home." Allan turned to the others. "I want to get dinner started."

"Sorry you can't join us." Carolyn smiled at Molly.

"Me too," Molly said softly.

"That's easily remedied. I coerced Carolyn into spending Memorial Day weekend here. She thinks she can get an extra day and turn it into a four-day weekend, so you are just going to have to spend a day with us." Allan grinned triumphantly.

"This time of year, a day's kinda hard to promise," Molly hedged. "I'll be pulling lobsters."

"But not on Sunday. You take Sunday off because the law says you can't pull traps on Sunday until June, so no excuse. I insist," Charlie said. "We will plan a Sunday around the four of us."

"Well, that's three weeks away," Allan interrupted. "We'll check with you before then," he said to Molly. "Come on, troops," he said to the others. "We have dinner to make."

Carolyn stuck out her hand to Molly. "Nice meeting you, again," she said softly.

"Same here."

Carolyn and Charlie stepped off the boat and picked up their stuff. "I'll be right along," Allan said. "Sorry about that," he said after the others started up the dock.

"Don't worry about it. Charlie doesn't know what's going on in my life right now," she said. "Do me a favor and tell him when you're alone. I'd rather not have everyone know our problems."

"Of course." Allan held out his arms and Molly stepped into them. "You going to be all right?"

"Absolutely. We Beans are survivors."

"I know, kitten," Allan said. "I'm going to call you tonight. Where you going to be?"

"After I have dinner with Auntie Em, I'm coming back here. I have to take care of that cat."

Allan grinned. "I think you like that cat."

"It's a nuisance," Molly huffed.

"Not so much a nuisance," Allan countered, "as a distraction."

"Probably."

"I'll call you around ten o'clock. Carolyn and Charlie sat up and talked for hours. I conked off and went to bed. I expect they both are tired. I'll call you then," Allan said. He gave Molly another hug and stepped off the boat. "Molly," he said, "things are going to work out."

"I know. It's strange, but last night when I got the call from Billy and I was driving to the police station, I realized just how far apart Tommy and I are. I knew he was hanging out with Robbie, but I just thought it was because they were lifelong friends. I didn't even think about the drugs. Then when Billy said he was into that stuff, I just couldn't believe it."

"I know. We have it at the college and it's a serious problem."

70

"Oh, God, I haven't been supportive of you and your mess. Did you know the professor?"

"Not well. She'd only been here since September."

"What happened?"

"Don't know. All I know is we were called into a meeting last night where the president told us not to talk to the press. Funny, I wouldn't have anything to say, because I don't know squat."

"It must be crazy over at the college."

"It is, and tomorrow's going to be crazy dealing with the students, especially those who knew her and took classes from her. We've set up counseling. I talked with the president today and he said some of the students were already on campus. I offered to go in, but he said they were handling it. Mostly, I think everyone is in a state of shock."

"Shocked and probably scared. We just don't have murders here."

"It's scary and sad." Allan reached across and took Molly's hand. "I'll call you later. You're not alone in this, kitten. You got friends, good friends who are going to be by your side."

"I know, and believe me that makes me feel good." She watched as Allan walked away from the boat.

She turned back to the pilothouse. The cat was grooming its paws.

"I bet you're hungry," Molly said as she stepped inside the pilot-house. She picked up her car keys. "I'll be back to feed you before I go to dinner." Molly closed the door to the pilothouse. She chuckled to herself. She was talking to that animal again. Yet somehow, Molly thought, the cat knew everything she was saying.

Molly pulled into the familiar driveway to the house where she and Tommy had spent so many years. Auntie Em's white Cape Cod was a mirror image of all the other two-story white cottages that filled the landscape of Maine. Auntie Em had inherited the house from her mother, and except for an occasional coat of paint, little had changed from when she had grown up there.

71

The second-floor bedrooms had slant ceilings that required you to duck your head when standing next to the exterior wall. People from away, as the locals called them, who bought some of the Cape Cods in Gin Cove had attempted to modernize them by adding dormers to increase the space in the bedrooms, but not Auntie Em.

Every room in Auntie Em's house had been wallpapered. Auntie Em said it was the cheapest way to clean the walls, so her mother had just kept adding new wallpaper every few years when she did her spring housecleaning.

The upstairs bedrooms were mirror images of the rooms downstairs. Small rooms with lots of doors. After Molly and Tommy moved in, Auntie Em had told them to do what they wanted to make their bedrooms feel more like their own, so one summer she painted hers white. She had tried to peel off the old paper, but each strip revealed a new layer, so she had just painted over it. Where the wallpaper was overlapped, there were long white humps, a constant reminder that the wallpaper was just below the surface.

Tommy had filled his with posters. He thumbtacked them over the wallpaper. And now, all these years later, the bedrooms remained the same.

The rooms downstairs were tiny little squares with old wooden doors that were shut in winter to keep the heat in. No one seemed to open them in the summer because the rooms were rarely used. Two double glass doors led to the parlor, but those doors too remained closed. Auntie Em's bedroom was downstairs, the door was open.

The kitchen was the grand room in the house. A large round table sat in the middle of the floor. A fireplace was on one wall; a woodstove insert had been added to make it more efficient. Two rocking chairs sat in front of the hearth. Auntie Em had kept the white porcelain cookstove that her mother and grandmother had used, but she also had installed a gas stove nearby. Windows that provided striking views of the ocean were on either side of the fireplace. People never strayed beyond the kitchen. You just seemed to sit down in one of the rocking chairs as soon as you walked in.

Auntie Em was waiting for her on the porch. Molly hugged her. "Has Tommy called?"

"No." Molly followed Auntie Em into the kitchen. She could smell the chicken soup.

"Oh, Auntie Em, it smells wonderful in here."

"Well, I just thought we needed some chicken soup. Plus, if Tommy had called . . ." She paused. "Well, it's always been his favorite. I thought he might come home if he knew I was cooking it."

Molly smiled. "You know"—she picked up the cover on the pot and smelled—"there are kids who today think that chicken soup is something that only comes out of a can with a red label. They all need Auntie Ems to teach them that this is what chicken soup is supposed to smell like." She put the lid back on the simmering soup. "When I was driving over here, I went to some of the places I thought he might be. I didn't see his truck." Molly sighed. "The chief said Robbie made bail. I drove past Robbie's house, but there were no cars there. Billy wanted to talk with Tommy on Monday. But he said the only real date he has to be concerned about is in two weeks when he has to make his first appearance in court. Unless he violates his bail and they catch him; then they're going to put him in jail."

"I'm worried . . ." Auntie Em shrugged.

"Me too." Molly sat down at the table. "I never expected this."

Auntie Em picked up the bowl in front of Molly and filled it with soup. She did the same with her bowl. She took a plate covered with a cloth off the top of the stove and handed it to Molly.

"Oh, wow, homemade buns." Molly could smell the yeast.

"I cook when I'm worried." Auntie Em sat down.

Molly reached over and took her hand. "I remember Tommy and I caused you to cook a lot while we were growing up."

"You weren't that bad." Clearly embarrassed, Auntie Em pulled her hand away. She started to butter a bun. "A handful at times, but not that bad," she mumbled.

Molly lifted the spoon to her mouth. "This is wonderful," she said. "I'm glad you didn't add any carrots."

"I know you hate cooked carrots," Auntie Em said as she tasted the soup. "Could use a little more salt."

"It's fine." Molly swished her spoon around in the soup to help cool it. "We were a handful. We weren't even family and you were so willing to take us on. I know I was a brat. Now I regret all the mean things I used to do to Tommy."

"You weren't any different than any other brother and sister who'd squabbled. It's just there was such an age difference between you two. You never got the chance to be close."

"I know. I was the older one, and I should have tried." Molly paused. "Anything I say now will sound like an excuse."

"Can't go back. Now we just got to go forward," Auntie Em said quietly. "We'll get there by and by."

Molly smiled. "You always say that."

"Well, it's kind of my form of faith in believing good things will happen. That's why I say it. Like people who knock on wood or go to church, something like that."

"I am so grateful that you and Uncle Ben took us in." Molly smiled affectionately at her. "I just don't say that enough."

"Your ma and I were friends," Auntie Em said matter-of-factly. "That day we was standing at the table cutting those herring heads off and all of a sudden your mom stopped. It was real funny. She just said, 'Auntie Em, if something happens to me, see to the children.' I told her I would. A promise is a promise."

Molly had heard the story many times before, but she knew Auntie Em liked to tell it.

"She didn't want you to live with your dad's family . . ."

"Too much drinking. Pa was good for a while. Then it even got him," Molly said. "I told you before, I used to worry about my drinking. At one point I wondered if I would be able to stop. I did, but for a time I think I liked it a little too much."

"You're different. You got more of your mother in you. Tommy, he's your dad, through and through. Your dad worked hard, but at night he liked to have fun. Even being married didn't stop him from going out and getting in his cups."

"And Mama just put up with it. I'd have kicked him out."

"It was a different time, Molly. Don't be too hard on her. All your mom knew was working in the factory and raising you two kids. There weren't all these . . . what do you call them?"

"Support groups."

"Right. None of those shelters. Her mom and dad had passed away. Her two sisters had moved to Massachusetts and were raising families of their own. She had few choices."

"They got out." Molly thought about her aunts.

"Molly." Auntie Em looked at her. "Your mom did the best she could. She stayed here, just like you, because she wanted to. You could have gone anywhere, but you chose to stay here."

"I did." Molly looked down at her empty soup bowl.

Auntie Em followed her gaze. "You need more soup."

"Just a half a bowl." Molly leaned back against the chair. "It would have been easier if I'd left."

"Probably." Auntie Em set the nearly full bowl in front of her. "I think it would have been better for Tommy if he had moved somewhere else. There's just not anything for him here. You were different. From the time you were little, you wanted to fish lobster. Tommy never knew what he wanted to do. Maybe if he'd gone to college, he'd live somewhere else."

"Tommy barely made it through high school."

"True, but it don't hurt to think about what might have been."

"No, it doesn't." Molly stopped when she heard the first ring of the telephone.

Auntie Em picked up the receiver. "Oh hi, Billy. No we ain't. You?" Auntie Em listened. "No, no luck either, huh? Molly's here. She went looking for him, couldn't find him." Molly could hear Billy's voice, but not the words he was saying. "If he comes here, I promise you I'll call. It's the only thing going to help him. Thanks,

Billy. Good night." She hung up the telephone and sat down at the table. "You heard?"

"Yes."

"They still haven't found him. He was wondering how we were holding up."

Molly picked up her bowl and carried it to the sink. She filled the plastic wash pan with soap and hot water. She dumped her bowl and silverware inside. "You finish eating and I'll do the dishes."

About an hour later, Molly was back on her boat. She had fed the cat and found an old square pan that she had dumped the litter in. The cat was curled up on some maps sound asleep. Molly was in her bunk reading. She jumped up when she heard the knock on the cabin door.

"Coming," she said as she put on her robe. It might be Tommy, she thought, looking for his cat. She looked through the glass in the door and gaped. She had not expected Carolyn. "Come in," she said.

Carolyn laughed. "Look, this was an impulse visit. I saw your light and I just decided to come over."

"I thought you were spending the night at Allan and Charlie's."

"I begged off after dinner since I have to start out early tomorrow. I have an early morning appointment on Monday." She paused. "They understood. They weren't happy, but they understood. Plus I think Allan is more preoccupied with that event at the college. There were a lot of telephone calls from students. I left because I thought it'd be easier."

Molly gestured toward her cabin. "I . . ." She looked down at her naked chest partially hidden by the robe. "I was reading. Would you like something to drink? Coffee, tea, bottled water? I don't have anything stronger." Molly stopped. She sounded like one continuous run-on sentence.

"Bottled water would be fine. Since you were mostly the topic of conversation tonight, I thought it might be nice to get to know each other."

"Allan, right?"

"Mostly. Charlie did his part too. You almost reached sainthood tonight, to hear those two talk. You are a fabulous lobsterman, one of only a handful in the state. You are a great friend . . ." Carolyn paused. "Let's see, you are concerned about the natural resources and are an environmentalist, yet you are opposed to big government rules. Sort of a hybrid Republican-Democrat."

Molly put her head back and laughed. "You've been talking to my friends," she said emphatically. "But you have me at a disadvantage. You know a lot about me, and I know very little about you except that you are from Bar Harbor and you like to open up the throttle and mow unsuspecting locals down," she teased.

Now it was Carolyn's turn to laugh and be embarrassed. "Somehow I don't think you're going to let me forget that."

"Nope. It's too juicy a tale to forget."

Carolyn groaned. "There's really not much to tell. I grew up in Bar Harbor. I was an only child and my parents are deceased. My mom died not too long ago."

"Oh, I'm sorry."

"Don't be. The last four months of her life was a blur of pain. I think that's why I attach so much importance to friends. To replace lost family."

Molly liked the way Carolyn's eyes held hers while she talked. The way she used her hands to punctuate her sentences. She sat with her legs crossed, her body relaxed.

Molly also looked at her long neck and wondered what it would be like to start kissing it just above the collarbone. Molly gave her brain cells a mental smack and jumped up. "I have just the thing that will go with that bottled water."

She could feel the heat in her body. She needed distraction. She reached into the small refrigerator and pulled out half a pie. She frowned. She was thirty-five years old and she was having her first hot flash.

"My Auntie Em's apple pie." Molly held it up in mock reverence.

"This is by far the best apple pie in America, actually the world. You've got to have a piece."

"Just a small one." Carolyn held her thumb and forefinger close together, indicating the size of the piece she wanted.

Molly ignored Carolyn's measurement gesture and cut off nearly a third of the pie. She put it in the microwave and heated it. From the refrigerator she pulled out the can of whipped cream Auntie Em had given her and shook it up and down. She sprayed it onto the pie, mounding it at the top. "How's that?" Molly asked as she also handed her a fork.

Carolyn's eyes grew wide. "I'd hate to see what you would serve if someone asked for a large piece." She took the plate and sat down in the chair near the kitchen table.

Molly scratched her head. "No one ever does. They always say a little piece." She picked up her own plate and sat down on her bed. She curled her legs under her.

"Oh, wow, this is good," Carolyn enthused. "Give your aunt my compliments."

"I will. So are you enjoying your visit?"

"Absolutely. I love Allan."

Cat got up from her nap and walked onto the table. She rubbed her head against Carolyn's hand. Molly watched as Carolyn absent-mindedly petted the cat. Molly felt Carolyn's gaze stray to where the folds on her robe covered her chest. She quickly looked away.

"He's special," Molly said as she watched the cat rub up against Carolyn's hand. She wondered what that hand would be like rubbing against her chest, down her stomach. Molly swallowed. *This is demented*, she thought. *The woman wants to be friendly, that's all.*

"Charlie thinks so too." Carolyn smiled. "They make a great couple."

"They do," Molly said agreeably. "It almost restores your faith in coupledom."

"Ouch." Carolyn stopped petting the cat. "That woman must have really bit you."

"What about you?" Molly countered. "Do you believe in coupledom?"

"Very good. Answer a question with a question and then you don't have to answer the question."

"Stop, that's just too complicated."

"Let's move on to safer ground." Carolyn picked up her fork and ate some more pie. "Allan said you were born to lobster."

"*Born* may be too strong a word." Molly wondered who had broken their half of Carolyn's coupledom? Carolyn clearly did not want to talk about it. "More like it was just something I had to do." Molly talked about her father and how she had inherited his boat and used it to build a business until she could afford to buy an even bigger boat. Carolyn asked her questions ranging from the market price for lobsters to the cost of replacing gear. Molly liked the way Carolyn listened.

"I noticed you named it *Finest Kind*."

"It was a favorite expression of my mother's."

"I like that." Carolyn set her empty plate down on the table. "I couldn't think of anything so I named mine after me. It sounds like such a head-trip. It was more or less a gift to myself after . . ." Carolyn paused. "Just a gift to myself."

"Good a reason as any. It has nice lines. It's made for speed rather than work, but it's a beauty. A thoroughbred next to a plow horse. That's what lobster boats are—dependable, seaworthy boats that expect to work every day." Molly hesitated. "Look, I've spent a lot of time boring you with stories about lobster fishing. It's your turn."

Carolyn looked at her watch. "Oh, wow, it's ten o'clock. Next time. I've got to get going. I really do have to get up early." She held up her hand. "Don't get up. I'll see myself out."

Molly got up off the bed and adjusted her robe. "You really don't want to talk about yourself." She raised her eyebrow.

"Really, I do have to go. I promised myself I would be in bed early." She held out her hand to Molly. "Next time, we can talk about who we really are," she said invitingly.

Molly took her hand. "I'd like that." She wanted to lean over and kiss her. Instead she adjusted the tie on her robe; it felt like a cinch around her waist. "Funny, I hadn't wanted to spend the evening alone, yet I didn't want to go anywhere. I enjoyed this. Thanks for knocking."

"Now that you mention it, me neither." Carolyn's smile sparkled. "And I'm glad I knocked."

"I'd offer to walk you home, but as you can see—" Molly gestured toward her robe.

"Don't be silly. What do I have, all of ten slips to walk past?" Carolyn turned to her. "Well, good night then," she said softly.

"Good night."

Carolyn turned to walk across the deck of Molly's boat. "I'll be back for Memorial Day, so maybe we can do this again?"

"I hope so. I—" Molly's cell phone interrupted. "Excuse me."

"Get your phone. I'll see you in a few weeks."

"Promise."

"Promise."

Molly watched Carolyn as she walked across the deck. "Hi, sweetheart," she said to the telephone. Carolyn turned around and waved, her face luminous in the overhead lights. Molly quietly closed the door to her cabin. "Glad you called, Allan," she said. "No, I haven't heard from him."

Chapter Seven

Molly spent her days pulling traps, her nights sleeping on the boat. Tonight was no exception. She had had dinner with Auntie Em, checked to see if the chief had heard anything about Tommy, and then returned to the boat. She was fixing an overhead light on the cabin when she heard the familiar voices.

"Hi darlin'," Allan said as he hugged her.

Charlie did the same. "You up for company or would you rather be alone?" he asked.

"I'm not in the mood for company, but I am in the mood for good friends." Molly smiled and hugged them again.

"I don't imagine you've heard anything," Allan said about her brother.

"Not a thing. The waiting is the hardest." She sighed. "I was never good at waiting."

"Few people are."

"How about at the college? I've been out of touch with news. Anything new on the professor?"

"Not a word. The police are saying very little. We had a memorial service for her at the college. Her family was there, clearly saddened. Lots of tears." Allan stopped.

Molly watched as Charlie reached over and took Allan's hand. *That's what a soul mate is*, she thought. Charlie had instinctively reached out to soothe his partner's pain.

Allan went on. "It was so sad. I don't think there was a soul there who wasn't crying, even people who didn't know her well."

"How old was she?"

"Forty-four."

"Married?"

"Not now. Her mother and father were there and her two sisters. She apparently asked to be cremated. The family is going to take her ashes back to Michigan. That's where she was born."

"I'm so sorry, Allan. I hate to think what you've been through these past few weeks."

"Not as bad as what you're going through, sweetie, with your brother."

Molly shrugged. "Well, at least he's alive."

"Come on, you two, we're here to have a picnic. Let's go out on deck," Charlie suggested.

"Good idea." Molly smiled. "We have so few great nights in Maine, it's a gift when we can have a picnic."

"Besides, I brought something to munch on and Allan brought a really nice wine." Molly smiled at her friend. Charlie so contrasted Allan in personality and looks.

Charlie was tall. He had wonderful dark curly hair that when it got a little long curled around his ears. His eyes were chocolate brown to Allan's teal blue. Charlie was intense. Allan was calm. They were like a stormy day and the sunshine. She needed both in her life.

Allan rubbed his hands together. "We thought we'd have a wine and cheese picnic."

Molly smiled. "Sounds wonderful."

"I heard from Carolyn," Charlie said as Allan poured them each a glass of wine. Charlie handed Molly a paper plate and napkin. He opened a blanket and set it on the deck. From an ice chest he unloaded plates of cheese and crackers.

"How many people are coming tonight?" Molly said with a laugh.

"You know me, the overachiever." He joined in the laugher.

"You heard from Carolyn?" Molly coaxed.

Charlie beamed. "Yes, she'll be here next weekend, Memorial Day weekend. Remember? Said she might be able to stretch it into a couple of extra days."

Molly felt a tingling in the middle of her stomach. Julie had made her tingle only after they had gone to bed the first time. This was something new.

"That's nice." Molly feigned disinterest.

Allan sat down on the blanket next to her. "She asked about you," he taunted.

"She did," Charlie said enthusiastically, "both on the telephone and in her e-mails."

"She mentioned she visited with you here on the boat before she left."

Molly knew they were trying to torment her into revealing what she had felt. "For a short visit." Molly bit into the cheese. "This is wonderful. What is it?"

"Cheddar," Allan answered. "Now quit stalling and tell us what happened."

"Nothing." She looked from Charlie to Allan. "Honest."

Charlie scowled. "That's what she said."

"No attraction?" Allan stopped. "No 'I'd like to take you to bed and screw my brains out'?"

"God." Molly laughed. "Would you two stop. She was here about maybe forty-five minutes. We talked mostly about lobstering. She told me a little about her life. We talked about our boats and how they were different." Molly shrugged to cover her embarrassment. "Then I fed her pie."

"Pie!" Allan repeated the word as if she had hurled an insult. "Pie."

"She fed her pie," he said to Charlie. "That must be some kind of lesbian romance thing we don't know anything about. First pie and then bed."

"No." Molly smirked. "That's not 'some kind of lesbian romance thing,'" she mimicked. "It just felt right."

"It felt right." Allan shook his head in disbelief.

"What did you expect me to do?" Molly asked.

"Oh, I could think of a few things." Allan winked at Charlie.

"You two are so bad."

"Anyway," Charlie said as he passed a plate of cheese and crackers to Molly, "I told her that we'd spend all of Sunday together. We were wondering if you'd like to spend Saturday night at our house. We could have breakfast the next morning on the deck. Then we thought about picnicking at Roger's Island." Charlie frowned. "That of course depends on the weather cooperating."

"I'd love to, but you guys know that now, with my brother, I'm not planning that far ahead."

"Memorial Day weekend is a week away," Charlie said in exasperation.

"Look, kitten," Allan said softly, "we know you want to help him, but don't close the trap door." He held up his hand to stop her protestations. "No pressure, but remember you can help Tommy, and you can be with your friends."

"I'll see." Molly thought about Carolyn. She wanted to see her again. Spend time with her. "No promises, just we'll see."

"We haven't told her about your problems with your brother," Allan said. "We felt that was up to you."

"Thanks. I don't need the whole world knowing. I'm glad the media hounds have dropped it. It hasn't been in the paper or on the news in a while." Molly frowned.

"They're focused on the murder." Charlie stopped. "She's an attorney, you know."

"No, I didn't know. She didn't talk a lot about herself."

"And a very good one," Charlie added.

"Has she been out of a relationship long?" Molly's curiosity got the best of her.

"About three years." Charlie sipped his wine. "How'd you know?"

"I just sensed she didn't want to talk about that side of her life."

"Let's just say it was a nasty divorce. The woman is still in California. Carolyn came back here." Charlie grinned. "Hooray for our side. Now she'll get to know you, you two will fall in love and live happily ever after."

Molly's brows knitted so tightly they felt like they were connected. "What Harlequin romance novel has he been reading?" she asked Allan.

"He just wants you to be happy. Like me. How's Auntie Em doing?"

"Good," Molly said thoughtfully. "Better than me. But then, she's not carrying around the guilt I am." Her brother's problems continued to dance just at the edge of her consciousness.

"Not guilt," Allan said delicately. "Molly, you're ten years apart. It's difficult under the best of circumstances to be close to some family members. This just made it doubly hard."

Molly stood up and walked to the end of the boat, her back to her friends. "I just didn't try. Last year was good. It seemed like we were connecting. Then he got the job at the college and we went our separate ways again."

"But think about what you said." Allan came up behind her. "You connected last summer. That means you two like each other. You can connect again," he said kindly.

"Allan's right, Molly. He's your brother and no matter how much space separates you, well—" Charlie stopped, clearly grasping for words. "He's your brother."

"I keep saying that over and over like a mantra." Tears burned the corners of her eyes. "I just don't want to screw this up again."

Allan wrapped his arms around her and held her to him. "You won't, kitten. You won't. This is your chance."

"If it's not too late." Her words were muffled against Allan's shirt. "This is a bad one."

"Yes, it is." He took the corner of his T-shirt and wiped her face.

"God, this crying gives me a headache."

After Allan and Charlie left, Molly slept better than she had in weeks.

The morning fog had rolled out early and Molly was ready to cast off. Auntie Em was standing at the bait tub, stuffing herring parts into small bags. The cat had become so accustomed to the boat that as soon as they cleared the marina, Molly let her out on deck. This morning was no exception.

"She's got sea legs just like you," Molly said, pointing at the cat who was walking across the deck to the pilothouse. Now that Cat was on-board the seagulls that used to flutter almost on top of their heads in search of spent bait kept a respectable distant from the boat.

Cat had taken on the role of sentry and lookout. The first few days Molly had worried that the animal might topple overboard, but Cat seemed to know just how close to the edge she could get and was doubly careful not to jump up on the railing—all things she had taught herself.

"You're not going to want to give her up," Auntie Em called over the noise of the engine.

Molly shrugged. She thought about her brother. "If I have to, I will." Molly glanced at the boat that was going slowly past them. The captain had seen Molly's boat in plenty of time and had slowed so the wake from his boat wouldn't upset hers. A man joined a woman on deck and they waved. Molly and Auntie Em waved back.

"That's the third time in the past week that you've stopped to see whose boat that is. You're hoping to see her."

"Who?" Molly groused.

"Who?" Auntie Em mimicked. "Carolyn. The woman who has you thinking about women again."

"Ridiculous."

"Really?" Auntie Em turned toward Molly and put her hands on her hips. "Then why all of a sudden are you so interested in boats that are going past us. You've never before given a rat's ass about them."

"Listen to you. 'Rat's ass'?"

"That's right. You've irritated me."

Molly put her head back and laughed. "Come on," she said as she stepped into the pilothouse. "We have more traps to pull."

"You just hold up."

Molly stopped. Auntie Em was using her talking-to-a-child voice.

"I want to know what's going on in your head."

"Nothing, Auntie Em."

"You like her."

"Yeah, I like her. But I would like it more if you'd stop using that voice."

"What voice?"

"The one you used to use when I was a kid. It sort of goes up a little higher."

"I'm sorry," Auntie Em said in a quieter voice. "Now, before you bury our conversation in the noise of the engine of this boat, just answer me this. Do you like her?"

"I do."

"Does she make you tingle?"

"Tingle?" Molly laughed. "Where do you come up with this stuff?"

"It's nothing new. Your Uncle Ben used to make me tingle. It happens between people."

"She does, Auntie Em. I find her to be quite interesting. Her last night in town she stopped at the boat."

"You didn't tell me."

"No." Molly paused. Except for Allan and Charlie she hadn't told anyone. She was still trying to figure that night out. "But she did."

"What happened?"

"We talked."

"Here?"

"On the boat," Molly confirmed.

"Where?"

"What is this, some kind of official inquiry?"

"Well, if you would just talk I wouldn't have to work so hard."

"Okay." Molly sat down on the captain's chair next to the wheel. "I'll talk. It was her last night in Gin Cove. I was here. Actually, I had gotten ready for bed and I was reading. There was a knock. I thought it was Billy coming to tell me they'd found Tommy. It was her. She came in and we sat and talked."

"What did you talk about?"

"That's the funny part. I can't really remember. Somehow what we talked about seems quite unimportant now. All I know is that I just kept looking at her." Molly smiled. "Then I offered her a piece of your pie. Which, by the way, she raved about."

"Have you called her up, e-mailed her?"

"No." Molly laughed. "I don't have her telephone number and I don't know her e-mail address."

"You ask Allan for them?"

Molly thought back to the night before and the gentle teasing she had taken from her friends. She hadn't thought to ask Allan or Charlie for Carolyn's telephone number or e-mail address. They told her about Carolyn's breakup, her move to Bar Harbor. Charlie talked about the years they had spent in college together. "No. I haven't done anything."

"I liked her," Auntie Em said matter-of-factly. "I think you should call her up."

"And what would I say?"

"Start with hi. Everything else will follow."

"This is crazy." Molly got up and paced around the pilothouse. "My seventy-year-old Auntie Em is giving me advice on women."

"No different—men, women. It's all the same."

"Not quite, Auntie Em." Molly stopped her pacing.

"When it comes to courting, it's all the same."

"Courting!" Molly's voice squeaked. "Haven't you skipped a few parts in between, like getting to know each other, dating?"

"It's all the same."

"You've got to stop watching that daytime television."

"You know what I liked about her?"

"No, but I got a feeling you're going to tell me."

"She was confident, not cocky. Julie's cocky, not confident. There's a difference."

"You really liked her."

"I did."

"Well, I did too and she's coming for a visit Memorial Day. She, Allan, Charlie and I are going to spend that Sunday together."

"Why didn't you tell me?"

"Because if it doesn't happen, or if she doesn't come, then I didn't want two people unhappy."

"She's gonna come. I know it. Now, we'd better get back to lobstering or we're going to lose our light," Auntie Em said, looking at the sun.

"I agree," Molly said as she started the engine. She looked over at her aunt, who was staring out the window. "I love you, Auntie Em."

"I know."

Molly turned the boat toward Pope's Folly Island. She looked at her watch. They might not get all three hundred traps pulled today, but somehow she felt better now that she had put into words what she had been thinking about Carolyn. That night on the boat, she knew Carolyn had been looking at her. Molly had wanted to get up off the bed and take her in her arms and kiss her. Instead she fed her pie.

Two hundred traps later, Molly slowed the boat as she came in sight of the marina. She could see Julie standing on the dock near her slip.

"Auntie Em." Molly nodded toward the dock.

"That's not going to be good news." Auntie Em said aloud what Molly had been thinking.

"I don't expect." Molly maneuvered the boat between the finger-piers, then reversed the gear and the boat just floated into the slip. She slipped the gearshift into neutral and let the engine idle. She tossed Julie the bowline.

"Just like old times." Julie smiled at Molly. "Auntie Em, I've missed you."

Auntie Em snorted and tossed her the stern line. "You here for a reason or just slumming?"

Molly suppressed a smile at *slumming*. It was the first time she'd ever heard Auntie Em use that word.

"For a reason."

Molly waited.

"We picked Tommy up last night. He was staying in Cutler with some people."

"Where is he?" Molly asked.

"Jail. He violated his probation. He was high when we found him." Julie paused. "Very high."

"When can we see him?" Auntie Em asked.

Julie hesitated. "I think you might want to wait. He's not in too good a shape."

"What do you mean?" Molly asked.

"He's coming down. He's sick."

"Don't matter," Auntie Em said. "When he was sick as a kid, I tended him. I'll do it again."

"This is different." Julie looked at Molly. "Chief said you could see him tomorrow after his court appearance if you'd like."

"I want to see him tonight," Auntie Em said. "After we scrub down this boat, we're coming over to the jail."

"Can't, Auntie Em. Visiting hours are only during certain times and you're already an hour beyond. Billy was real clear on that."

Molly looked from Julie to Auntie Em. "Maybe it's better if we do wait. Tommy may not want us to see him like this."

"How come he isn't in a hospital?" Auntie Em demanded. "If he's so sick."

"Can't, Auntie Em. If he were in a big city jail, yeah, then maybe. We don't have the money for that. If he got real sick then the chief would have him hospitalized. Otherwise, he just does—" Julie stopped.

"He stays in a cell," Auntie Em fumed. "Well, I'm going over there." She swung her leg onto the pier.

"Auntie Em, wait. I'll go with you," Molly said, shutting down the engine.

"You take care of your catch," Auntie Em said over her shoulder. "You can meet me at the jail when you're done."

Molly watched as Auntie Em walked up the ramp. She resisted the urge to run after her. For too many years she'd seen Auntie Em when she was determined to make something happen, and she knew that Billy was about to be knocked down by an aircraft carrier going at full speed.

"Look, I'm off duty, could you use some help?" Julie asked.

"I'm fine." Molly continued to watch her aunt.

"Hey, I just want to help," Julie said as she cast the lines back into the boat and stepped on board.

Molly shrugged and eased the boat out of the slip toward the co-op.

"Have a good day?"

Molly knew she was asking about the day's catch. "It's been a good spring so far. Lobsters are really running." She could smell Julie's perfume as she stood next to her in the pilothouse. Cat was sitting on the table.

"When you get it?" Julie asked, pointing at the cat.

"Belongs to my brother. She's been on board for a few days now," Molly said, looking at Cat. "She seems to like it."

"Will it be hard to give it up?"

Molly shrugged. "Probably." Molly was surprised at the sense of loss she felt, knowing she would have to give Cat back to her brother.

She slowed the boat as she approached the co-op. Julie tossed the stern line to Clayton Johnson, the owner, and then jumped onto the dock with the bowline in her hand. She tied it to the cleat.

"Hey, Molly, sorry to hear about your brother," he said.

"Thanks." Molly grabbed a crate and handed it to him. She did not want to talk about her brother.

"Heard they picked him up last night in Cutler," Johnson said.

"You probably know more about it than I do, Clay," Molly said, handing him another crate. She looked at Julie and shrugged. "I been out on the water all day."

The town's talking drums had been hard at work and there was nothing she could do about it. She and Julie continued to hand him crates and waited as he weighed the day's catch.

Molly filled two buckets with water while Julie pulled the mops out of the closet. How many times they had worked together like this in the past, Molly couldn't remember. But she was grateful that Julie had been quiet after they left the lobster pound. The two women worked side by side scrubbing the deck.

Julie wrung out the mops and set them on the deck to dry. "Molly, look. I know Auntie Em is determined to get in to see Tommy right now, but that's a bad idea."

"I know. But I can't stop her when she's that determined."

"You don't have to. The chief left orders with the corrections officers to be nice to her but to not let her in. Your brother doesn't want to see her. Tomorrow will be soon enough. He's still going to be sick tomorrow, and for the next few days."

Molly shook her head. "How bad is it?"

"Terrible to watch. Like everything you see on television."

"It's so cruel."

"I agree." Julie leaned against the railing of the boat. "There's just no money for treatment. And the treatment centers in Bangor and Portland are full. The chief's been screaming about this since prescription drugs became the albatross around this city's neck. But there just isn't any money."

"Then someone needs to do something about it. Someone needs to get money to help people."

"And who is that someone?" Julie stared at her. "Look, it's people like you who learn that their family members are hooked into this trash. But you're usually so preoccupied with trying to help your relative that you don't focus on the real problem." Julie held up her hand to forestall Molly's reaction. "This is not to assign blame. I'm just saying, people in this community have not gotten mad. And because they haven't gotten mad, they're not doing anything about the problem."

"I'm mad," Molly said.

"For now, but once your brother is dealt with, you'll stop being mad and then someone else's brother or sister or husband or wife or child will get hooked. There's no collective voice. So when it comes to local and state budgets, money is not put aside to start treatment centers. And the federal dollars are shrinking. Besides"—Molly could hear the frustration in Julie's voice—"the state has one and a half million people in it. There's not a lot of money to take on this new problem."

"That sounds so miserly, when it comes to someone's life."

"Miserly maybe, but no one listens. We need a treatment program here, at least an outpatient clinic. Everyone's tried—the chief, the medical community. They went after a million-dollar grant, but the federal government gave the money to another state. I can't even remember which one."

"So we do nothing."

"I wouldn't say that. We're trying. We have drug court. It's helped. We have some outpatient counseling groups, but there's not enough of them."

"I want to do something," Molly said quietly.

"Let's see if you feel the same way once you're brother's case has been dealt with. Look, I hear what your saying. You just don't know how tough this battle is. Or how time-consuming," Julie said.

"Maybe not, but I can learn." Molly could hear the determination in her own voice. "Now I have to go get Auntie Em, before she tears up the jail."

"I doubt she's at the jail. I imagine they sent her home. Hang on." Julie flipped open her cell phone and dialed. "Hi, Barney. Auntie Em still there? I didn't think so." Julie paused, listening to the words on the other end, then she laughed. "Thanks, Barney." Julie put the cell phone back in her pocket. "Auntie Em threatened to spank Barney if he didn't let her in." Julie laughed again. "I'm sorry, it'd be funny if it wasn't—"

"My brother." Molly finished the sentence for her. "I can imagine the tongue-lashing she gave him. Barney's my age. He probably spent time at her house."

"Didn't we all." Julie looked at Molly. "How are you doing?"

"Okay, all things considered."

"I've thought about you often."

Molly tossed the orange slicks she had been holding into a bag; she was going to have to wash them tonight. "I don't want to hear that."

"Molly, wait." Julie put her hand on her shoulder.

Molly turned and stared at her.

Julie dropped her hand. "I remember that look. I want to say I'm sorry. That other thing . . ." Julie gestured as if trying to grab the right words. "I made a mistake. I'm sorry. I'd like to have dinner some night, no pressure."

"Julie, that's not going to happen. Look, I have a shoulder full of problems right now, and I don't need this act-three scene where the

94

two brokenhearted lovers fall into each other's arms." She picked up the bag with the dirty slicks inside. "I've got to go find my aunt."

"Sorry." Julie looked down at her hands. "I know my timing sucks. But I'm sorry. I screwed up princely and I regret it. Look, once this thing with your brother settles down, can we talk?"

"And when will it settle down, Julie? After he's in jail? Throw away the key and forget he's my brother?"

"Wait, I'm not the enemy here when it comes to your brother. In fact, I want to help."

Molly bit down on her lip. "I'm sorry. I am taking all kinds of anger out on you. Anger over the way you dumped me, anger over my brother, anger—"

"Hey, I get it. Right now let me just help." Molly could hear the concern in her voice.

Molly shook her head in agreement. "What happens next to him?"

"He makes an appearance tomorrow on a bail violation. The assistant district attorney will probably argue that he should stay in jail. I don't think you know him—he's only been on deck a few weeks." Julie stopped. "By the way, have you hired an attorney?"

"No, I didn't even think to do that." Molly thought about what Charlie and Allan had said about Carolyn being an attorney. She quickly rejected the idea, not wanting to drag Carolyn into the middle of her family problems.

"I'd give Joe Matthews a call. He's pretty decent. If you can get him, he'll argue that this was your brother's first offense, first time he ever violated bail. Ask that bail be set at the same amount. If the judge agrees, which I expect he will, because our jails are full of people who have committed worse crimes, he'll turn him loose. Then he'll set a date for him to be arraigned on the possession charge. After that he goes back to the jail where he is processed for release. Then he goes home with you."

"Billy mentioned something about drug court. What about getting him into that?"

"It's a real possibility, but the chief said Tommy wasn't interested."

"That was before, this is now. He's been in jail and he's been coming down. Maybe he'll see it as a chance."

"It's possible, but you need to know . . ." Julie hesitated. "The success rate is not very good."

"What's 'not very good' mean?"

"Of the ten or so that join a class, only one or two graduate. The rest backslide."

Molly hesitated. "Are all those who are in drug court, are they all Oxy users?"

"No."

"How many of them have graduated?"

"One."

Oh, great, Molly thought. "And drug court has been going on for how long?"

"About a year." Julie stepped toward Molly. "But you can't look at that. We certainly don't. We don't have that many things going for us here that will help fight the problem of addiction, rather than just locking it up. One is a good number—that's someone who got off and has remained clean. That's a win, Molly, a real win."

"What do you think Tommy's chances are?"

"Look, I could lie and say great, but honestly I don't know."

"I don't think he's been using that long."

"Funny, unlike heroin, that doesn't seem to matter. This stuff starts squeezing you the minute you start using."

"I've got to go find Auntie Em. I imagine she's gone home, but I need to be with her."

"Molly, I do want to help, and I do want to see you again, personally. I screwed up. I'm still in love with you. I don't think I ever stopped being in love with you."

Molly backed away from her. "Julie, I can't think about that now. I really can't, and it's unfair of you to make me think about that now."

"I'm sorry." Julie stopped. "I keep saying that."

96

"I gotta go."

"Okay. Look, I'm on duty tomorrow. Anything I can do to help, I will."

"Thanks."

"Come on," Julie said, stepping onto the deck. She reached out a hand to help Molly. "I'll walk you to your truck."

Molly ignored the hand and stepped onto the deck. "Thanks. I'll accept your help when it comes to Tommy. I can't think about anything else beyond that."

"Well, that gives me hope," Julie said softly.

Molly threw the bag she was carrying in the back of the truck and got in. "Not a lot of hope," Molly said as she looked Julie in the eyes. "It's not a lifeline, Julie. There's not a lot of hope."

"It's okay. You can't stop me from thinking there might be some hope."

Molly could see Julie in her rearview mirror as she turned to get into her own car.

Chapter Eight

Auntie Em was standing in the driveway. She had on a black skirt and a floral blouse. *All dressed up and no place nice to go*, Molly thought. She smiled as Auntie Em opened the truck door. It was a quarter to eight. Tommy was to be arraigned at eight o'clock.

"You sleep much last night?" Molly asked as Auntie Em got in and slammed the door behind her.

"No." Auntie Em ran her hand through her coarse gray hair. "I just kept thinking about him. I've seen how those actors do it on television when they pretend they're coming down, grabbing their stomach and throwing up. Do you think it's that way?" Auntie Em turned in the seat to look at Molly.

"It is, Auntie Em, it is. Julie told me yesterday that it's bad."

"That poor boy, suffering. They got to do something." Worry weighed in Auntie Em's voice.

"They have some kind of drug they give them—it helps, but it doesn't make it all go away."

"Have they given it to him?"

"I expect."

"Do we know what's going to happen today?"

"Julie said that they'd arraign him on the probation violation. The district attorney will argue that he should stay in jail because he violated his bail conditions by being high again." Molly shook her head. "I called Joe Matthews at home last night. He's going to represent him. Julie said he'd probably argue that Tommy's never done anything like this before and the judge should give him a second chance. She seems to think he'll go home with us today."

"Well, I don't like her." Auntie Em's voice felt like a cold steel scalpel. "But at least she knows what's going on."

"True. I think we should go right to your house," Molly said. "I think he's going to want to sleep. I thought I'd stay there too. It means that Cat stays on the boat alone tonight, but I'll feed her right before I come over. I'm out so early, she'll hardly know I'm gone." Molly looked over at Auntie Em, who was as still as a leaf. "I got to work, but I arranged for one of Clayton's boys to help me the next few days as my sternman." Molly looked at her aunt. "I think you should stay with him."

"Me too. I'm glad you arranged it."

"Tommy needs you right now, and for however long it takes, you stay with him."

Auntie Em reached over and patted Molly's hand. Molly turned onto State Street. The courthouse was behind the police department and right next to the jail. *One-stop shopping*, Molly thought bitterly. She had only been to court once before and that was when one of her friends was getting a divorce. Molly had gone along for moral support. Dark mahogany wood stretched from the floor to the white ceiling. The judge sat on a raised platform at the front, flanked by the American and Maine flags. The court clerk sat in front of him, the court reporter to her side. Two tables, one on either side, faced the bench. The district attorney would be at one, Tommy and his attorney at the other. A dark mahogany rail separated the court officers from the public. The seats at the back of the courtroom reminded Molly of church, the long expanse of wood benches, one right behind the other. That's where they would sit. Julie had told her to sit behind Tommy, so they could hear everything he said.

Molly was surprised to see all the cars in the parking lot. She drove up one aisle and down another, finally finding parking at the very back of the lot. "You want me to drop you off at the door and come back?"

"Heavens, no," Auntie Em said. "By the time you get back here, the space will be gone. Others are just as late as we are. Wonder why there's so many cars here today?"

Molly parked and they walked to the courthouse.

"Don't know. I can't imagine there'd be that many people in court." Molly held the door open for her aunt and followed her up the stairs. Julie was standing in the hallway. Molly was surprised, but also a little relieved.

"Molly, Auntie Em. It'll be just a few minutes and they will open the courtroom. You can go in and sit down."

"Who are all these people?" Auntie Em asked in her church voice.

"People to be arraigned today, or they are making their first appearance. It's the call of the calendar."

"All these people do something wrong?" Auntie Em looked around. She nudged Molly. "Isn't that Ed Stewart over there? Look, there's Matt Cline. Oh, my God, there's Mary Stanton. What they here for?"

Julie looked down at her paperwork. "Matt Cline was clamming in a closed area. Mary Stanton's here on a charge of assault." She flipped pages. "Ed Stewart is here for drunk driving."

"Who'd she assault?" Auntie Em asked in a whisper.

"Don't know," Julie answered back just as quietly. "But you'll know soon enough once the charge is read."

"Bet it's her husband." Auntie Em nodded to Mary. "If she assaulted him, he deserves it. She guilty?"

"Most are." Julie chuckled. "Although they'll all tell you no, but about ninety-nine percent will end up entering a guilty plea."

"Today?" Auntie Em asked.

"Those that are to be arraigned will be read the charge, and most will say they're not guilty. Gives them a few extra months out of jail. Judge will set a trial date. Mostly what will happen, their attorney will negotiate some kind of plea in between today and when they are going to trial." Julie stopped. "Most will take it. Other people are making their first appearance today. They don't enter a plea, but a judge will appoint an attorney if they can't afford to hire one, and others will tell the judge they can hire their own. Judge then sets a date for them to be arraigned."

"There more people here than at the Fourth of July parade," Auntie Em said as she looked around. "It ain't like this on *Law and Order*."

"No, not like that at all." Julie chuckled quietly.

"What the rest of them here for?"

"All kinds of charges. Assault, arson, clamming in a closed area. Some more serious—murder, rape. Although"—Julie looked down at the neatly typed pages she had in her hand—"those last two not today."

"You arrest all these people?"

"No. I'm good, but not that good." Julie glanced quickly at Molly and then turned away. A kink in their relationship had been Julie's constant arrogance. "People are from all over the county. They may have been arrested by the Maine State Police, the Jefferson County Sheriff's Department or some of the other smaller police departments, Warden Service, marine patrol. Some by us, but mostly they come from all over," Julie said.

"Speaking of murder, they find anything out yet about that poor professor?" Auntie Em asked.

"Couldn't tell you, state police is mum," Julie answered. "They may be using our facility, but they're about as tight-lipped as a closed door."

"Seems such a shame," Auntie Em said, looking around. "We just don't have murders here." She nudged Molly and nodded toward Mary Stanton. "I know she assaulted her husband. Serves him right."

Molly noticed that Auntie Em was as wide-eyed as a youngster on Christmas morning.

Molly saw Allan before he saw her. She pushed through the crowd. "I'm so glad you're here." Her thoughts were a jumble.

"I wouldn't be anywhere else." Allan hugged her.

"I knew you'd come," Auntie Em said.

"Morning, Julie." Allan nodded.

"Allan, nice to see you."

Molly looked quizzically at Auntie Em. "You invited him?"

"She didn't." Allan had his arm around Molly's shoulder. "I called her this morning and asked if I could be with you today. Auntie Em said she thought it'd be good. I had to arrange some things on my calendar, and once I did that I came over here. I'm just glad I'm not late."

"Thanks," Molly whispered to him.

Allan winked at her. "I—"

"Superior court is now open," the court officer yelled as he opened the door. People began to file through the door two at a time.

"Come on." Julie grabbed Auntie Em and Molly by the arm. Allan was by Molly's side. Julie led them down a side aisle to seats near the railing. Molly watched as people sat down all around them, some chatting with their neighbors.

"There must be a hundred people here," Auntie Em said, looking around.

"Actually more. I think there's something like one hundred and twelve," Julie said.

Molly frowned. "Do we have to sit through all of these?"

"Quite a few." Julie looked through the sheets, flipping page after page. "Tommy was arrested yesterday. Other people already been on the list for a while. Names are added as the paperwork is turned in. Here he is," she said, pointing at the page.

Molly looked at where she was pointing and saw her brother's name. Next to his name it said Bail Violation. "Why'd we have to get here so early then, if he's so far down on the list?"

"Some people don't show up. Other times an attorney will ask the judge to pass on a case because he's in negotiations with the district attorney. It could take anywhere from an hour to three hours before we get to Tommy's case."

Molly sensed Auntie Em stiffen. She looked to where she was looking. A door next to where the judge sat was open and several men and two women walked in. They sat on chairs away from everyone else. "Who are they?" Molly asked.

"People who were jailed over the weekend. Most are making their first appearance."

The door opened again and a second group filed in. Molly saw Tommy's red hair first. She knew Auntie Em had seen it also. The person in front of him was blocking their view, but as soon as he sat down, Molly heard Auntie Em gasp.

"Oh, my God, look at him," Auntie Em whispered. Tommy looked like a disembodied spirit. His freckles seemed to hover over his bleached-white face. His hair was tangled and his eyes were red. He walked slowly, supported by two corrections officers.

"He's sick, Auntie Em," Julie said in hushed tones.

Auntie Em grabbed Molly's hand. "This is worse than I thought." She started to rise. "We got to do something."

Julie put a firm hand on her arm and eased her back into her seat. "There's nothing you can do now, Auntie Em. You just have to get through this. Once the judge says he can go, I'll personally expedite the papers to get him out of here."

Molly saw the appreciative look in Auntie Em's eyes. "Thank you."

Tommy looked at them and then put his head in his hands.

❦

All the cases seemed to run together. Mary Stanton, who used to work in the factory with Auntie Em, entered a plea of not guilty. Auntie Em had been right—she was charged with assaulting her husband. Ed Stewart, who was the janitor at city hall, also entered a not-guilty plea. Matt Cline said he was guilty and the judge fined him $100. He grinned and winked at Molly as he walked out the door. He and Molly had gone to high school together.

Molly knew that clam diggers were often arrested for clamming in a closed area. They didn't believe the state when a flat was closed because of health reasons. They figured the state closed the flat to give the resource a chance to rest. So they'd sneak back, hoping the clam warden was busy in another part of town. Eventually, Molly heard the judge read Tommy's name.

Her brother stood up and was escorted to the table. Joe Matthews, Tommy's attorney, seemed to appear from nowhere. Tommy sat down on the chair, but Joe reached down and helped him stand.

The judge read the case number, CRV210–03. "Thomas Bean, you have been charged with violation of bail conditions." He looked at her brother, then nodded to the district attorney.

"Your Honor, Mr. Bean was arrested on May third for possession of OxyContin. He was bailed the next day and the conditions of his bail were such that he was not allowed to use or possess any illegal substances and was ordered to stay away from Robbie Olson. When he was picked up a few days ago, he and Robbie Olson were together and he tested positive on a urine test. I don't think Mr. Bean appreciated the fact that if he violated the conditions of his bail, he would be sent back to jail to await arraignment. Which"—the assistant district attorney looked at the file in front of him—"is in three weeks, Your Honor."

"Mr. Matthews." The judge turned to Tommy's attorney.

"Thank you, Your Honor. The fact is this is my client's first offense, except"—he too looked at his notes—"he told me he was arrested a couple of years ago for speeding. Other than that his record is clean. We are not talking about a habitual offender here, Your Honor. We are talking about a member of this community who has, up until a week ago, been a productive member of society. I think putting him in jail until he is arraigned is excessive. He tells me he plans to stay with family until his court date. I think he should be let out on his own recognizance. He lives here. He will make that court date."

The judge looked back at the assistant district attorney. "Anything else?"

"Just this, Your Honor. If you are going to set bail, I would keep the bail at five hundred dollars."

"Done." The judge wrote on the file, set it aside and picked up another.

Joe Matthews leaned over and said something to Tommy. He then turned and looked for Molly. He beckoned them to follow him out of the courtroom. He closed the door behind them.

"Hi, Julie, Molly, Auntie Em, Allan." He paused. "They are going to take him back to the jail, process him and you can pick him up at the front door." He turned to go back to the courtroom. "By the way, make sure he makes that court date, or whoever put up the bail for-feits it."

"He'll be there," Auntie Em promised.

"Thanks, Julie," Molly said after the attorney went back into the courtroom.

"Hey, I wanted to help."

"Thank you," Auntie Em said begrudgingly. "It felt right that you should be there."

"Thank you, Auntie Em. Anything else I can do?"

"No," Molly said. "We'll be out front to pick him up."

"Good. See you soon." Molly watched as Julie stuck out her hand and shook Allan's. "I've missed our get-togethers," she told him qui-etly as she turned toward the door.

⨯⨯⨯

Auntie Em said very little after they got into Molly's truck. Allan had stayed with them while Tommy's paperwork was being processed. Then he gave them a hug and left with a promise that he would call them both later.

"You okay?"

"Tired." Auntie Em sighed.

"Hmm. I can understand why. You didn't get much sleep last night."

"He looked so awful."

"Yeah."

"During the night, I talked to myself. Told myself I needed to be prepared. But when he walked into that courtroom, I wasn't prepared."

"Me neither."

"We've never seen him like that. Not even when he was sick. Well, I'm going to take him home. I got up in the middle of the night and took a chicken out of the freezer. It's thawing right now. While he's sleeping, I'm going to make chicken soup." Auntie Em paused. "You want to invite Julie for supper?"

Molly turned to her in surprise. "No, why?"

"I saw how she was looking at you. She wants you back."

"So she said."

"What you going to do?"

"Nothing. I don't love her anymore."

Auntie Em sighed in resignation. "Good. I appreciate what she done for us today, but I don't like her."

Molly smiled. "I know."

"I like Carolyn."

"I know that too. Here he comes," Molly said, relieved that their conversation had been interrupted. Tommy walked slowly out of the jail. It looked like he was concentrating on moving his legs. His face was mottled and he looked exhausted.

Auntie Em slid across the seat next to Molly just as Tommy opened the door.

"I don't want to talk," he barked crossly.

Auntie Em slipped her arm through his. "You don't have to. You're going home, going to bed, and then tonight, you're going to have chicken soup."

The next morning, Molly got up early to go to her boat. Auntie Em and Tommy were still asleep. When they had gotten back to Auntie Em's house, Tommy showered and went right to bed. Auntie Em was exhausted and Molly insisted she lie down and nap. Molly walked down to the shore and sat on the rocks. She stretched out on a rock and fell asleep. At dinner, Tommy ate very little and then went back to bed. She helped Auntie Em clean up and they sat in the kitchen, drank tea and talked. Auntie Em went to bed early and Molly lay in her room and read. She could hear the soft snores of her brother through the wall. Molly was worried. Tommy was a drug addict and she didn't know how to solve the problem.

Julie had suggested that she talk to his attorney about getting him into counseling. She said it would look good when he went to court because it would help convince the judge that he was turning his life around.

But what if he doesn't want to turn his life around, Molly thought. Their father hadn't wanted to. She tossed her gear on board. Cat was standing on the table waiting for her.

"Good morning, Cat. I trust you slept better than any of us last night." She petted the cat on the head and picked her up and carried her into the cabin. She picked up the cat's dish and washed it out, opened a can of cat food and set it on the floor.

Cat was more interested in rubbing against her leg than in the food. Molly picked her up and cuddled her against her cheek.

"Lonely, little girl?" She stroked the cat's back and set her on the table.

"Hey, Molly." The voice came from on deck.

"Yo, Kevin. Come aboard," she said as he walked toward the pilothouse. "I can't thank you enough for helping me out."

"No problem, Molly. You helped my dad out that time. Glad we could return the favor," he said. Kevin's dad also was a lobster fisherman and Molly and some of the other lobstermen helped pull his traps after he'd broken his leg. Molly had helped organize the group. "Dad said you might need me the rest of the week."

Molly nodded. "Maybe next week too. Auntie Em wants to stay home with my brother."

"Dad said I should stay as long as you needed help," the eighteen-year-old said.

"Let's cast off," Molly said.

Kevin had been raised around boats, and she watched as he cast off the lines and prepared the bait.

Molly moved Cat away from the depth finder screen and started the engine. It should be just another day on the water, she thought, except that Auntie Em was not on board and her brother was a drug addict. All in all, Molly thought cynically, it had been a fairly good week. Those dour thoughts continued as she headed toward the first string of traps.

"You plan to go to college?" she asked Kevin when they had a break in the hauling. He was eating the ham sandwich she had given him.

He shrugged. "Don't know."

"It would help you, maybe get you out of here."

"Aw, Molly, you went to college and you're still here, so what's the big deal about going to school?" Kevin's long legs were stretched out in front of him. He was staring at his black rubber boots.

Molly didn't know how to answer. "Well," she mused, "it helps you to make choices."

"Like?"

"If you want to stay here, go away, do something else."

"It don't help yuh with what kind of bait to choose. The stench is just the same if yuh got college or not," he said dubiously.

Molly smiled. "True," she said, amused. "But I think what it did for me, it made me think of this more as a business and it made me a better businesswoman."

"Dad's a good businessman. Said he learned from the—"

"College of hard knocks?" Molly finished.

Kevin knit his brow. "No, the college of the sea. Said it taught him everything."

"And who am I to argue with that." Molly stood up, her sandwich finished. "Want another sandwich?"

"Sure."

"How about two more?" she said, walking back to her cabin, glad she had packed extra food. She was feeding a teenager, not a senior citizen.

"Sure, I worked up an appetite," he said.

The rest of the day the two pulled lobsters from the traps and banded them. Kevin's muscles were a bonus because when Auntie Em was on board Molly did all the heavy lifting. She didn't even have to ask Kevin; he automatically grabbed for the trap and pulled it on board. Molly smiled. His father had trained him well.

Molly saw the *Carolyn S.* doing a slow dance on the waves. The sleek craft was tethered in the slip she had used before. Molly strained to see if Carolyn was inside. She drew back on the throttle and it felt like the boat was in slow motion as they went past Carolyn's boat.

Carolyn stepped out of the pilothouse and waved to Molly. Molly cut the engine. Her heart fluttered. *This is stupid*, she thought. "Kevin, toss her a line so we don't float away."

"Sure," Kevin said as he tossed the bowline to Carolyn.

"I was hoping I'd run into you tonight," Carolyn said, her face glowing.

"I'm glad." Molly felt her nerves humming like a power line. *This is silly*, she thought. *The woman smiles and I crumple.* "Ah, Carolyn, this is Kevin."

"Pleased to meet you." Carolyn's smile was radiant.

"Same here," Kevin mumbled.

"Where's Auntie Em?"

Molly broke eye contact and looked away. "She was busy today." Molly noticed Kevin look from her to Carolyn, but he said nothing.

"Will be for the next few days," she added quickly.

"I was wondering . . ." Carolyn leaned against the railing. "I'd love to learn more about lobster fishing, thought maybe I could go out with you tomorrow. You and Kevin, of course," she added quickly.

"Sure." Molly felt flustered.

Kevin shrugged. "Okay by me."

"Great, what time?"

"We usually cast off around five."

"I'll be there." Carolyn smiled. "I'm spending the evening with Allan and Charlie, then I'll be back on my boat. How about if I pack lunch? I know you're out all day."

"Don't bother. I usually pack sandwiches," Molly said. "Whatever we need."

"I'll see you in the morning." She smiled mischievously at Molly. "Nice to meet you, Kevin." She tossed the bowline to him.

Molly stepped back into the pilothouse and started the engine. She could feel Carolyn's eyes on her as she moved her boat past Carolyn's toward her own slip.

"Wow," Kevin intoned enthusiastically. "She's not from around here."

"Bar Harbor," Molly answered absently.

"I hope she wears something other than those white shorts and white top when she comes on board tomorrow. She's going to get mighty messy."

"So do I." Molly didn't want to talk about Carolyn.

110

Chapter Nine

Molly sat on the porch swing with Auntie Em. They had finished supper and her brother had grumbled something about going to bed.

She decided that his sullen mood was not going to interfere with her appreciation of the night. The sun had hidden itself on its journey to the other half of the world, but it had left behind blaze-red streaks that traveled through and across the clouds. The sky was a unity of reds and pinks and there was a cathedral-like stillness to this spring night. The evening sea breeze had started and Molly could smell the sea salt. In spite of her anger at her brother, a disembodied calm floated over her. She didn't want to talk but knew that Auntie Em had carried the burden of the day and now needed to unroll her thoughts.

"How was today?" Molly scrutinized Auntie Em's face. It had been so long since she had really absorbed a face she took for granted every day, the ragged lines that began at Auntie Em's eyes and traveled down her cheek, the skin that gravity had stubbornly pulled down to hang loosely around her neck. The wrinkles seemed to fold into each other like a pleated drape. The iron-gray hair was pulled tightly into a bun, daring even one strand to escape and fly loose. The olive-colored eyes made public her exhaustion. For the first time Molly felt a frenzy of fear grip her as she thought about living each day without Auntie Em. *Stop it*, she sputtered furiously at herself. *Stop painting ghosts on the wall.*

"He mostly slept. When he got up he'd come downstairs for a while, sit in the kitchen chair and just stare out the window. I tried to feed him. He mostly snapped and snarled. I don't know this person." Auntie Em's voice was soft, almost inaudible.

"No," Molly said heavily. "We don't have to do this."

Auntie Em turned on the swing to look at Molly. "I don't understand."

"I was thinking about it tonight, at the table. You should not have to do this." Molly cleared her throat. "I know what Julie said, that the worst was over. That he mostly came down while in jail. But I see the pain he is causing you and I don't think we have to do this—"

"But we do," Auntie Em interrupted. "Molly, he's your brother. I don't understand this drug he was taking, so I went up to the college today and Allan gave me some stuff to read about it."

"You did?" Molly was momentarily startled. "Of course you'd go in search of information."

Auntie reached out and took Molly's hand in hers. "I read mostly all of what Allan gave me," she continued. "It said this stuff's like heroin, only worse. I didn't know that. I just thought it was something like marijuana. I knew about that garbage. I read about it when you was into it."

"Really?" Molly couldn't disguise the surprise in her voice. "You read about grass too?" Molly shook her head, surprised that she would be surprised. Although Auntie Em hadn't graduated from high school, she wasn't afraid to seek out information about things that puzzled her.

"Course. I was worried. We didn't have that rubbish when I was growing up, so I needed to know more. I read about it. How else would I be ready to help you when you needed it?"

"You're exceptional." Molly cuddled closer to her and put her arm around her shoulders.

"Not really . . ." Auntie Em said as her voice trailed off.

Molly suppressed a smile. Auntie Em might not be afraid to seek out information, but she never felt comfortable with a compliment.

"I just needed to know more about it. What I can't figure out is how they know which drugs are going to give them that high they talk about? That part I don't understand."

"I don't know that they know so much as they just experiment with every kind of drug they can find. I doubt they're reading medical books about the kinds of prescription drugs that will give them the ultimate high."

"I expect you're right. I also read that some doctors are real quick to hand out pain medication, and around here most everyone has a Jefferson County bad back or whiplash. So I guess some of the doctors started giving that out. Stick on an insurance collar and expect to collect a buck."

Again Molly suppressed a smile. "Insurance collars."

"You know," she said matter-of-factly, "they tell the doctor they got a pain in their neck, they get these pain pills and those plastic collars that make them look like they got too much starch in their shirt and the insurance company pays them off . . ."

"And their necks heal soon after they get their money," Molly concluded.

"I know." Auntie Em rubbed her hand over Molly's and continued her monologue as if she had crossed over some sort of Rubicon. "There is this euphoria they get when they take the drug. Then they come down. One pamphlet said it was like having the flu only ten times worse. The bad kind messes you up." Auntie Em waved her hand as if tossing words in the air. "Diarrhea, insomnia, muscle pain, vomiting, nausea, bad stomach cramps . . ." She paused and said tentatively, "I don't think Tommy's that bad."

"How do we know?" Molly remained unconvinced.

"We don't," she said huskily. "We got to hope it isn't. But we need to get help."

"What does the information suggest?"

"A drug treatment center. Course we don't have that here. Allan said the ones in Maine are full with a long waiting list. He knows because they're dealing with the problem at the college. He said we have a counseling group that has helped addicts. I want to get him in that. Then there's that drug court. I want to get him into that. It will keep him out of jail, if he graduates," she said cautiously. "I plan to talk to Billy about that. See if he can help."

"And if he doesn't want to join the counseling or go into drug court?"

"He won't have a choice."

Molly sighed in resignation. "Auntie Em, Tommy isn't going to do what you want. He's not a child." Molly paused. "Well, maybe a sick adult child, but he's not going to do what you want."

"I think he will."

"Why do you say that?" Molly asked dubiously.

"He's not lost yet," Auntie Em said quietly. "I think he's ready to heal."

"I hope you're right." A soft shudder moved up her spine and she shivered.

"You're cold." Auntie Em stood up.

"No, I—"

"You got to go to bed. You have to get up early. Come on, we can talk about this later. It ain't going away, for a while."

"No, it isn't, and I'm tired." Molly stretched and stood up. She helped Auntie Em out of the swing and hugged her. "I love you, Auntie Em."

"You and Tommy's all I got," she whispered, her voice on the brink of tears.

"I know and I'll do everything I can . . ." Molly could feel the tapestry of sadness surrounding them.

"Listen to us," Auntie Em said reprovingly. "Like we're going to cry or something. Won't help. Now why don't you sleep here in your own bed?"

"I'd love to Auntie Em, but I have to get up so early. I don't want to disturb you."

"Humbug, you're not going to wake me up."

"Honest, Auntie Em, I feel more comfortable sleeping on the boat and Cat hates it when I'm away." Plus, Molly thought, she was secretly hoping to see a light on in Carolyn's boat. She might stop and talk. For the first time in days she was looking forward to pulling traps in the morning, and she knew it had more to do with Carolyn than the work.

"I hear that sound."

"What sound?"

"That Bean determination." Auntie Em shook her head. "No point in arguing. There's a sound you get in your voice that goes along with that stubborn streak of yours."

"Stubborn streak?" Molly's voice went up. "Stubborn streak. I don't think so."

"You have it, Molly Bean. Most times it's good. Kept you going in a man's profession. Other women would have quit. Worked against you with Julie, you knew that wouldn't work, but you was stubborn. Made up your mind you was going to make it work."

"Maybe." Molly's tone was cynical.

"I know so." Auntie Em hugged her. "You go to your boat. You'll sleep better. How's Kevin doing?"

"Good." Molly started to say something, then stopped.

"He's not me."

Molly shrugged. "I miss you being there. We've worked together off and on now for a lot of years. You know my moods. With Kevin he either doesn't talk or if he does he thinks like an eighteen-year-old. I just miss you."

"I'll be back there soon. I just have to help Tommy get through this, but I know one thing, Molly. You don't have to work as hard with a young back like Kevin has. With me, you have to maneuver the boat then run over and pull the trap from the water. That's extra work for you. Maybe you should think about hiring a young back."

"Never. As long as you want to be my sternman, the job is yours . . ." Molly said as her voice trailed off. "Besides, I miss you, that's all."

"Good. You'll appreciate me more once I'm back," Auntie Em teased.

"I appreciate you, Auntie Em." Molly turned and hugged her again. "I'll see you tomorrow night."

Molly carried supplies to the boat. She had been up since four o'clock. When she had gotten back to the boat she was disappointed to find that Carolyn's boat was dark. She had fed Cat, prepared some of the food for the next day and gone to bed. Now she was quickly getting everything ready for the morning sail. What usually was routine became frenetic as she double-checked to see that her bed was made, the pilothouse cleaner than usual.

"Good morning." Carolyn smiled radiantly. "Permission to come aboard."

Molly bowed gallantly and made a sweeping gesture. "Come aboard."

"Do I get a pair of those?" Carolyn pointed at the orange slicks Molly was wearing.

"Only if you plan to work."

"Dig them out, lady. I'm here to work." Carolyn offered her a bewitching, dazzling smile.

"I have extra pairs in here." Molly turned away. She felt herself teetering on the edge. She wanted to reach over, pull Carolyn against her and kiss her. Instead she walked through the pilothouse and down the steps to the cabin. Carolyn followed closely behind, her perfume hanging around them like a commodious cloak. Molly reached into a drawer and pulled out a pair of slicks. "They maybe a little big."

Carolyn shrugged. "I'm sure they're fine. Do I put them on over my jeans?"

"Yeah, it'll be cool out on the water so the layers will help."

Carolyn leaned against Molly's bed and stepped into the slicks. She stood up and pulled them up to her hips. She reached down and pulled the suspenders over her shoulders. The pants hung low on her tiny hips. She laughed. "I think I need to adjust these," she said as she started to fuss with the suspenders.

Molly watched her. Never had orange slicks looked so sexy, she thought. "How was your visit with Allan and Charlie?" she said to distract herself from looking at Carolyn's hips and at the way her hands moved the small metal clasp on the suspender.

"Good. We had dinner. I got back here about nine o'clock," she said easily. "I had a date with some lobsters, so I went to bed early." She paused. "Damn, this one's stuck. Can you help me?"

"Oh . . . sure," Molly stammered like a ninny.

Carolyn stepped next to her and held the suspender away from her breast so Molly could fix the metal clasp.

Molly held the clasp with one hand and unsnapped it with the other. "There." She stepped back. She was not going to slide the clasp up toward Carolyn's breast. Molly could feel sweat gathering between her fingers. There was something absolutely beguiling about this woman, she thought.

"Thank you." Carolyn moved the clasp up, compared it with the other one and snapped it. She hooked her thumbs in the suspenders and pulled them away from her breasts. "How do I look?"

"Like a flatlander trying to be a lobsterman," Molly said impishly.

"Hmm. A flatlander. Well, I have just the thing to fix that." Carolyn reached in her jacket and pulled out a baseball hat and put it on. "Now?"

"Like a flatlander with a baseball cap," Molly said with mock seriousness.

117

Carolyn cocked her eyebrow. "I think . . ."

"Hey, Molly. You down there?" Kevin called.

"Be right up." Molly jumped.

Kevin stuck his head in the cabin door. "I thought I heard voices down here. Hey, Carolyn. You look great, just like a lobsterman."

Carolyn nodded in triumph as she looked at Molly. She headed toward the steps to the pilothouse. "Well, thank you, Kevin."

Molly watched. *This is stupid,* she thought. *I jumped like I was caught with my hand in the proverbial cookie jar. Take control, Molly Bean,* she scolded herself as she followed Carolyn up the steps.

"Ready to cast off?" she growled at Kevin.

"Sure thing." Kevin jumped onto the marina deck and threw first one and then the other line to Carolyn. He hopped back onto the boat. The two silently coiled the ropes neatly on the deck.

Molly started the engine and let it idle. She could see Kevin talking with Carolyn. He pointed at the pot hauler. Molly knew he was telling Carolyn to stay away from the rope that soon would be lying on the deck after the lobster trap had been pulled on board. He pointed at her boot and pointed to the water. Molly figured he was sharing the tale of the sternman who had gotten his boot caught in the rope and pulled overboard. It had happened not that long ago and the story was still potent and fresh. Molly watched as Carolyn smiled and nodded in agreement.

Molly backed the boat between the finger-piers and increased the throttle speed. She kept one eye on maneuvering the boat through the channel and the other on Carolyn.

Kevin pointed at the bait tub. Now this ought to be a sight, Molly thought. Carolyn was not going to stick stinky bait into a bag. Kevin handed Carolyn a rubber glove. Molly watched as she slipped it on. The glove was three times the size of her hand, but she gamely pulled it as high on her arm as she could.

Kevin then reached into the bait tub, grabbed a handful of fish parts and stuffed them into the bait bag. He pulled the strings on the top, like closing a purse, and set it aside. He handed a bait bag to Carolyn. Carolyn turned and looked at Molly and amusement did a jitterbug in her eyes. She dipped her gloved hand into the bait barrel and pulled out the rotting fish heads. Some of the fish heads fell at her feet as she pushed the rotten mess into the bag. She laughed as she tried to pull the strings on the top of the bag, her gloved hand making the task impossible. When Kevin reached for the bait bag to help pull the stings, she laughed and pushed his hand away. She pulled off the rubber glove and threw it on deck. She tied a knot in the bag and set it next to Kevin's. She then reached for another bag and dug her bare hand into the bait.

Molly could feel her blood pressure rise. That was the sexiest thing she'd ever seen a woman do. *You're sick, Molly Bean,* she scolded herself. *Sick.* She turned her back to Carolyn, pointed the bow of the boat toward the open sea and opened the throttle on the engine. The boat sped toward Molly's trap farm.

"How many traps do you have?" Carolyn asked over the low growl of the engine. They had just finished pulling all the traps on the north end of Roger's Island. Carolyn was standing next to Molly in the pilothouse. They were headed to another string of Molly's traps on the other side of the island.

"Between six and eight hundred."

Carolyn laughed, her dark eyes on Molly. "Please tell me we are not going to pull all of those today." She paused to rub her neck. They had been pulling traps all morning and Carolyn had gamely worked with Kevin, refilling bait bags and sizing and banding the lobsters.

"No." Molly smiled. "We do a little more than two hundred a day. As soon as we get around here we're going to eat and then pull as many traps as daylight allows and then head back." Molly looked at the crates full of lobster. "It's been a good morning."

"And no shorts." There was a teasing look in Carolyn's eyes.

"No shorts." She paused, embarrassed. "I don't usually break the law like that, it was just . . ."

"One of those moments," Carolyn said, her voice frolicsome. "Like speeding or jaywalking or . . ."

"Enough." Molly laughed. She eased back on the throttle. "Tie on to the buoy," she called to Kevin. "We'll stop and eat here and then finish up pulling." She asked Carolyn, "Would you like to wash up?"

Carolyn looked at her hands. "I would."

"You go and use the head first." Molly cut the engine.

Kevin stepped into the pilothouse. "Lines secure. I'll get another bucket to sit on."

"We're going to eat in the cabin." Molly went inside and opened the refrigerator. Kevin followed. Cat jumped down off the table and onto the refrigerator, then rubbed up against Molly's arm. She pushed the cat away.

"What's in there?" Kevin asked.

"Lunch."

"Can I help?" Carolyn asked, emerging from the head and rubbing her hands together.

"What would you like to drink?" Molly asked. "I've got bottled water, soda, coffee, tea."

"Bottled water, please."

Molly opened the refrigerator and handed Carolyn bottled water.

"Wow, look at all that food," Kevin enthused as he reached for a can of Coke. "Glad you're on board, Carolyn, otherwise we'd be eating ham sandwiches again out on deck with fish heads and seaweed at our feet."

Molly could feel the heat creeping up from her shoulders to her neck. *God*, she thought, *it'll be all over my face.* She looked away from Carolyn. "Don't you want to wash up?" she barked at Kevin.

He stepped out on deck, reached over the side of the boat and sloshed his hands back and forth in the water. Back in the cabin, he reached for a napkin and wiped his hands. "Dad says that's the cleanest water on earth." He nodded toward the ocean. "Says all the flushing it gets every day just keeps it right."

"Can't argue with your dad." Carolyn smiled at Molly.

"Why don't you two sit," Molly said as she reached into the refrigerator and set containers on the table.

Kevin started to open the containers. "Wow, potato salad. What's in here?" he asked opening another container. "Double wow, Italian subs." He continued to open more containers as Molly placed them on the table.

"This is very nice." There was a flirtatious look in Carolyn's eyes. Molly swallowed and suddenly her throat felt like it had a whole banana stuck inside it. She mutely handed Carolyn a plate and silverware. Cat jumped onto Carolyn's lap. Carolyn laughed.

Molly reached over and pushed her down. "Sorry."

"It's okay." Carolyn smiled. "She just wants to cuddle."

Kevin piled potato salad on his plate and reached for a sub. "This is great," he said. "You coming with us on Monday?" he asked Carolyn, his mouth full.

"No, I have to head back to Bar Harbor." Carolyn spooned potato salad on her plate and reached for a submarine sandwich. "This is nice," she said softly. "Thank you."

"You're welcome." *This is crazy*, she thought. *The woman smiles and my heart does a two-step. I'm thirty-five years old and I am going to have a heart attack. My obituary is going to read, "Died unexpectedly. Her heart gave out under some of the most powerful brown eyes ever."*

"You work there?" Kevin's question interrupted Molly's sappy thoughts.

"Uhm," Carolyn murmured.

"What ya do?"

"I'm an attorney."

"Like, cool. You here to help Tommy?"

Carolyn gave Molly a quizzical look. "Tommy?"

"No," Molly answered quickly. "She's visiting with Charlie. They went to school together." Molly ignored the question in Carolyn's eye. "You want another sandwich?" she asked Kevin. She did not want to talk about her brother.

"Sure."

"So, do you go to school?" Carolyn asked Kevin. Molly sensed that Carolyn had understood her discomfort.

"Graduated last year from high school," Kevin said between mouthfuls. "I'm going to save my money and then buy my own boat so I can be a lobster fisherman like Dad and Molly. I mostly work as a sternman for my dad. I'm just helping Molly out now that Auntie Em's busy."

"I tried to talk Kevin into going to school, if not the university here, then the community college in Calais," Molly said, not wanting the topic to turn back to her brother.

"It wouldn't hurt," Carolyn said to Kevin.

"I know, but I didn't much like school when I was there. I figure my dad's been real successful doing what he does. My grandpa did it. Seems only right that I do it."

"It's hard to argue with that logic." Carolyn smiled. Carolyn then asked Kevin about his family, his other brothers and about the lobster business.

Kevin pushed his chair back from the table. "That was good. I'm just going to use the head."

"I'll clean up and we'll finish hauling," Molly said as she stood up. "Did you get enough to eat?"

Carolyn laughed. "Gosh, yes, that was wonderful. Can I help with cleanup?"

"No, I'm going to toss everything in the refrigerator and deal with it later." She reached for the garbage pail and threw the paper plates inside. She put the dirty silverware in a plastic bag; she would wash them later. Carolyn put the covers back on the food dishes and handed them to Molly, who tucked them back inside the refrigerator. Molly wiped the top of the table with a napkin.

"I'm looking forward to tomorrow," Carolyn said as she looked out the porthole at the island. "Can we do some exploring on the island?"

"Absolutely." Molly followed her gaze. "It's been years since I've been there." She paused. "No, more like forever. I don't think I've picnicked there since I was a kid and Auntie Em and Uncle Ben brought us on Sundays. Used to be families would all come here and picnic, not so much anymore."

"People get busy with their lives, I guess," Carolyn said. "Now people have barbecue grills and they don't seem to go places to picnic. It's the same in Bar Harbor. We used to picnic on the islands around there when I was younger, but I don't know, it just seems like there's never time now that I'm an adult." Carolyn stopped and stared at Molly. "Life shouldn't be like that. We should take time to picnic on islands and walk on the beach," she said softly. "I'd love to take a walk on the beach with you."

Molly felt a soft shudder move up her spine like someone had floated a feather over skin. "I—"

"Ready," Kevin interrupted as he came out of the head. "We going to pull this bunch here and then head back to the marina?"

"Yes." The question jarred her. *This is silly*, she thought. *The woman simply asked to go for a walk on the beach, not join her in bed.*

"Let's do it." Carolyn smiled provocatively at Molly at the same moment she patted Kevin on the back. "Let's go pull some more traps, mate."

Carolyn followed Kevin on deck. Molly followed them up into the pilothouse and started the engine. She eased the boat next to the first trap and watched as Kevin used the gaff to snag the line. He and Carolyn were laughing and talking.

∽⌇∾

At five, Molly had dropped Carolyn off at her boat so she could get ready to go to Allan and Charlie's. She and Kevin had gone on to the co-op. After they returned to the marina, Kevin helped her scrub down the boat and then he left. Molly showered and put on clean clothes.

Now driving to Auntie Em's, she saw the police cruiser behind her. Its blue lights flashed and Molly pulled over. Julie hopped out of the cruiser.

Molly turned off the engine and opened the door. She stepped out of the truck. "Anything wrong, Julie?"

"No, I just saw your car come out of the marina, thought I'd stop to say hi."

Molly sighed impatiently. "That's it? You pulled me over to say hi."

Julie grinned. "I figure it's about the only way I'll get to see you. I can't go over to Auntie Em's—she'd run me off—and it seems I can never find you at your boat. I was wondering if you'd like to have dinner tomorrow." Julie leaned casually against the door of Molly's truck.

"Busy."

"Really busy, or just get-rid-of-the-old-girlfriend busy?"

"Both."

"New girlfriend?"

Molly stared at Julie and did not answer.

"I understand a new woman's been around town. Come in on her boat from Bar Harbor, a real good-looking woman, from what I hear."

"Well, you can hear almost anything in Gin Cove, Julie. So I wouldn't invest much energy in that one. Look, I'm late getting to Auntie Em's. I don't want her to have to hold supper."

"How's your brother?" Julie did not move.

"Better."

"I'd like to help you, Molly. You don't have to go through this alone, I mean with your brother."

"I'm not." Molly eyed her suspiciously. "I've got Auntie Em."

"I just mean—"

"Look, Julie, it doesn't matter what you mean or what you want to do. I don't know if you want to help me with my brother or not. I just don't care. That's what you need to understand. You live here, I live here, so we are going to have to see each other, but except for a civil nod to each other I am not interested in anything else."

"Come on, Molly, I deserve a second chance." Molly could hear the frustration in her voice. "We deserve a second chance."

"No, we don't." Molly made a curt, dismissive gesture. "That's just background noise in my life, nothing more, Julie. Now, if you'll just get your backside off my door, I have to go see Auntie Em."

Julie stepped away from the truck. "You're angry."

Molly laughed. "No." She took a deep breath and rubbed a hand over her tired brow. "That's where you're wrong, Julie. I'm not angry. To be angry would mean I care, and I just don't care." Molly opened the door to her truck and got in. She slammed the door and drove away. In her rearview mirror she could see Julie watching her.

As soon as she pulled into the driveway, Molly saw her brother sitting on the swing. She went up and sat down next to him. He looked less tired. His red hair was combed and she could smell his aftershave. She hesitated, unsure if what she said would draw a curt response, so she waited.

"Auntie Em suggested I come out here and soak up some fresh air," he said moodily. "Said it would do me some good."

"And is it doing you some good?"

Tommy shrugged. "It's going to take more than fresh air."

"It is," Molly said cautiously, uncertain how far this discussion was going to go.

"I also think she hopes this will give us some bonding time. She knew you'd be home soon." Tommy looked obliquely at his sister.

"She's trying—"

"You can say that again," Tommy interrupted.

"I didn't mean trying as in trying . . ." Molly looked at her brother quizzically. "You're yanking my chain."

"A little." His smile reminded her of when he was a kid.

"You have Lulu." It was more a statement than a question.

"Lulu?" Molly was confused.

"My cat."

Molly shook her head. "I didn't know her name. I just called her Cat."

"Does she answer?"

"When she's in the mood." Molly was surprised at the surge of sadness that had come over her. She was waiting for her brother to ask her to give the cat back.

After a moment her brother asked, "So how's the lobstering business?"

"It's been good. Last year the stocks were down. I actually worked more traps just to make a profit. This year the stocks have been terrific."

"I don't miss it," Tommy said quietly. "I hated it when I fished with Pa, and I hated it with you."

Molly hesitated. "Hated it because it was me, or because of the business?"

"The business. I never signed up with anyone else." He rubbed his cheek. "It wasn't you. Hell, I had no desire to own my own boat."

"I didn't know." Molly shook her head. "Maybe I could have helped you do something else . . ."

"Don't churn the bait on this one, Molly," Tommy snapped. "I hated the business. I hated the smells. I'd shower and I could smell that stench of dead fish on me. I'd wash my hands and I could still smell it."

"I'm sorry, Tommy. I didn't know." Molly shifted on the swing and looked at him. She was startled at what she saw. Her brother was ten years younger than her, yet his face looked used up. The drug-induced cloud that had covered his eyes the first few days was gone, but his eyes look shattered, the brilliance gone. "I didn't realize you were so miserable."

"Trapped, just like the lobsters." His laugh was harsh. "Now I'm boiled just like them. Maybe I have more in common with them than I thought."

Molly laced her fingers together and rested her chin on them. "How long has this been going on?"

"Long, Molly. Too long." He turned and looked at her. "I've done it all."

"Honest?"

"I won't be any more honest than I am right now. Coke, heroin. Ecstasy. Oxy. Gibbers."

"Gibbers?"

"Pot."

"I didn't have a clue," Molly murmured.

"No, I don't expect you did."

"Last year, when you were on the boat, you were high?" Molly asked wearily.

"Sometimes. It's worse lately. I've been getting higher more often."

"I know there were times when you had some serious mood swings. I just thought you were mad at me about something." Molly shook her head. "I should have asked you what was going on."

"I wouldn't have told you."

"Does Auntie Em know?"

"No, and I'm not going to tell her and I know you won't." Molly noted the testiness in his tone.

"No."

"She's worried about you, though."

"Me?"

"Worried you won't have anyone in your life if something happens to her. Says you've met a new woman."

"I don't know. She's from Bar Harbor, a friend of Charlie's. We're all going on a picnic tomorrow." Molly paused. "Say, why don't you come along?"

"I don't have the energy for a picnic. I barely had the energy to come out here and sit on the porch. That's the downer part." He laughed cynically. "I like the upper part better."

Molly rubbed her hand against her leg. "Tommy, I—"

"At least one of the Bean kids has good taste in women," he interrupted. "You always did. Remember Jenny Lou Bagley?"

"Vaguely."

"I had it real bad for her." Tommy looked at Molly, his eyes heavy with sadness. "She had it real bad for you."

"Me? She was your age." Molly suddenly remembered. "She was ten years younger than me. I thought she was just a kid who liked to hang out with you."

"She liked to hang out with me because she wanted to be near you. I heard she's living in Portland with a woman."

"Tommy, I never knew."

"No, you were always busy running around showing off, the best at sailing, the best at softball, the best at . . ." Molly could hear the bitterness in his words.

Molly looked down at her hands. "Anything else?" She spoke so softly she thought maybe the words had not come out.

"Your being a lesbian didn't help. Remember that time you found me crying behind the school 'cause what those kids did to my face?"

"Yes." Molly could feel her stomach churning. "Because I was a lesbian?"

"Bingo." Tommy's laugh was harsh. "As a kid I got beat up by you because you didn't want me hanging around and I got beat up by the guys because you were around."

Molly felt the tears. "I didn't know. Did you tell Auntie Em?"

Tommy shrugged. "No. What could she have done? Pa was mostly drunk. When he was sober he was out lobstering. Funny, I tried to like you, but I mostly didn't."

"I'm so sorry." Molly put her hand on her brother's arm. He pulled away. "I didn't know." She felt as though she had a foot against her chest and her lungs were collapsing. She found it hard to breathe. "Please let me help now." The words sounded distant even to her own ears, as if they had not come out of her mouth.

"You know, I'm mostly over the whole little brother resentment thing. Hell, I don't even care anymore who you sleep with. Seems like even the town don't care anymore. I just don't want your help. I am in a mess, a screwed-up-my-life mess. You see, Molly, you just don't get it. It's too late." Molly heard the sorrow in his voice.

"Tommy, let's talk about beating this one, together."

"What? Being pals? Brother and sister? Or the drugs?" Tommy said darkly. "I've said all that I'm going to say. This one's not going to go away, Molly."

"It could."

"It can't." Tommy crossed his arms over his chest. He rested his chin on his chest. "A couple of times I quit cold turkey. Each time, it's been harder. This last time, the worst."

"Tommy, don't give up on this."

"I did that a long time ago." He stood up. "I'm not smart enough to know why I like this stuff so much. I just know the world don't dare touch me when I'm high."

"Tommy, that's just drug dependency. We can change that."

"Molly, this therapy session is over." There was a low growling fury in her brother's voice.

She stood up and touched his arm. "No pressure from me, Tommy, know that."

Tommy turned to her and put his hands on her arm. "And know this, Molly. I don't want to be helped. Not by you."

With that he quietly opened the screen door and walked inside.

"Everything okay?" she heard Auntie Em ask.

"Good, Auntie Em," Tommy answered. "Look, I'm just going to go up to my room for a while, rest some before supper."

"You do that."

Molly sat back down in the swing. Her heart felt like it was going to blow through her chest it was pumping so hard.

"You okay?" Auntie Em asked through the screen door.

Molly wiped her face on her sleeve. She shook her head no. She heard the squeak and the movement of the swing as Auntie Em quietly sat next to her.

"Come here." Auntie Em pulled Molly into her arms. Molly put her head against her aunt's shoulder and sobbed. "There's lots of pain tonight."

"I didn't know he hated me so," Molly said through her sobs.

"What did he say?"

"Just stuff about my being a lesbian."

"Oh." Auntie Em paused. "I don't think he hates you." She stroked Molly's hair. "I think he's just trying to put all of his anger about his problem and everything on someone else."

"I don't think so, Auntie Em." She then told her about what Tommy had said. "I never thought . . ."

"I'm not making excuses for your brother, but he has had a harder time than you. You were older when your mom died. That didn't make it easy, but it seemed like Tommy just turned inside out. After that he just stayed by himself."

"If I'd known . . ." She shrugged.

"You'd done what? Lived a lie. Not be who you are?"

"I don't know." Molly sat up on the swing. Her face burned from the tears.

"I just never thought he hated me so. I knew that our age difference had a lot to do with our not being close. Hell, Auntie Em, I was in college when he was going through his teenage years."

"And what would you have done?"

"Helped you," Molly said. "Helped Tommy. Been here for both of you."

"It wouldn't of mattered. He never said what he was so unhappy about." Auntie Em took Molly's hand and rubbed it between hers. "Your brother was easier to raise than you. He'd come home from school, mostly go up into his room and just lie on his bed and stare. He was just this solitary little boy. I talked to him, even took him to the doctor a couple of times. Doc said he'd grow out of it. Just said

130

he had some kind of adolescent sullenness. I guess I'm more responsible. I should have figured it out."

"This blame doesn't rest at your feet." Molly pulled Auntie Em tightly against her and held her. She felt Auntie Em's warm tears against her neck. "I just don't know what to do next." Molly gulped.

Auntie Em pulled a handkerchief from her pocket and wiped her eyes. "We keep trying to help him. We're family."

"Even if he don't want help."

"Even if."

Chapter Ten

Carolyn carried the tray with the coffee onto the patio. She put the tray on the table and sat in one of the chaise lounges. She picked up one of the cups; the other two were for Charlie and Allan. They had sent her up to the widow's walk while they prepared their surprise dessert.

She thought about the day she had spent on the boat with Molly and about the lunch Molly had prepared. She had told Charlie and Allan about it and they had chortled. Allan said that Molly never cooked and that Carolyn should consider the small feast a flirtation lunch.

Carolyn wasn't so sure. She had flirted, but Molly seemed distant.

"Here we go, love," Charlie said as he carried the flaming dessert onto the patio. Allan was grinning behind him.

"What is it?" Carolyn exclaimed.

"Cherries jubilee. One of our favorites." He set it down and took one of the bowls Allan was carrying. He spooned the ice cream and cherries into the bowl. The small blue flame danced in the evening sea breeze. "Blow," he told Carolyn. She blew the flame out and watched as a small line of smoke floated into the air.

Allan also blew his out.

"Don't you just love this dessert?" Charlie said as he blew his out. "It has both showmanship and color."

"It's delicious," Carolyn said as she blew on the dessert to cool it. She paused, her spoon in the air. "Allan, can I ask you a question?"

"Of course."

"Who's Tommy?"

Allan glanced at Charlie. "Did Molly mention him today?"

"No, Kevin did. When I told him I was an attorney, Kevin asked me if I was here to help Tommy. Molly changed the subject."

"He's her brother." Allan looked to Charlie for help.

"Tommy has had some problems lately," Charlie said carefully. "Legal problems."

"As in . . . ?"

"Drugs," Charlie said thoughtfully. "Bad drugs."

"Was he arrested?"

"A couple of weeks ago. He's out on bail. Staying with Auntie Em," Allan added.

"That explains a lot, I hope."

"What do you mean?" Charlie asked.

"Well, I've been flirting with this woman and she has been about as responsive as the lobsters she catches. In fact, they're more responsive. At least they wave their claws in the air when confronted."

Allan smiled. "You have to know Molly."

"Well, you can't say I haven't tried. I went over to see her the night before I left. I spent today on her boat. I am going to see her tomorrow. What do I have to do, send her flowers and a singing telegram telling her I like her?"

Allan laughed. "Molly is wonderful but very reluctant to put her feelings on the line."

"I agree." Charlie picked up the thread. "She's reticent when it comes to expressing her emotions. She's known Allan almost her entire life, yet I've never once heard her tell him she loves him. Yet she does." He poured more coffee for himself. He held the pot out to Carolyn, but she shook her head no.

"That's true. I will give her a hug and tell her I love and adore her, and she blushes," Allan added.

"Plus there's another wee bit of a problem," Charlie said quietly. "There's the Julie factor."

"Another woman? I thought you said she wasn't with anyone."

"That's true." Allan quickly picked up the story. "Julie dumped Molly, left the area and moved in with a nurse from here who just happened to move to the same area, get my drift? Months later, Julie's back."

"Here?"

"Here," Charlie said softly.

"And Molly is . . ."

"Not happy," Allan said expressionlessly. "Julie has been around—"

"A pest," Charlie interjected.

"I love the way you two finish each other's sentences."

Charlie smiled. "We do, don't we. We've been together too long."

"Just long enough," Allan countered. He reached over and squeezed Charlie's hand.

"So, I have a former girlfriend and a family crisis to deal with. Anything else you want to tell me?"

"Yeah," Allan said gently. "Don't give up. Molly is special, and although her life is topsy-turvy right now, she's worth all the effort."

"It doesn't sound like her life is going to settle down anytime soon." Carolyn sat forward on the chaise and set her cup on the table. "This is way too complicated."

"When is life not complicated?" Allan countered.

"Not in a relationship. Not in the beginning." Carolyn stood up.

Allan also stood up and put his hand on Carolyn's arm. "When we invited you here, we did it so you and Charlie could reconnect. That was what was most important. Molly was an afterthought. Someone we thought you would like to meet. Julie wasn't in the picture and her brother certainly was not a problem. This all has unraveled in the past few weeks. Look, I'm sorry."

"Allan, I'm not blaming you or Charlie." Carolyn returned to the barb that was pricking her. "But even with all of these problems, she has shown no interest in me. Has she ever hinted that she might be interested in me?"

Charlie looked at Allan. "You're the one who talks with her the most."

"No." Allan shrugged. "She hasn't said a lot about you, but then she's had a lot to deal with lately. Mostly we talk about her brother."

"I wonder if the picnic is such a great idea tomorrow. Maybe I should just go back to Bar Harbor instead." Carolyn rubbed her temples.

"Please don't do that," Allan begged. "Let's give it one more chance. This will be the first time since this all happened with her brother that Molly's going to be doing something other than working and worrying . . ."

"And," Charlie added—"she did fix that great lunch today, something Molly never does. Maybe she was trying to impress you."

"Maybe, and maybe she just felt like cooking."

"Not my Molly," Allan said with a grin.

"All right." Carolyn slipped backward into her morass. "One more try, but short of throwing her down on the rocks and making mad passionate love with her, I don't know if this woman even has a clue that I'm on this earth."

"Whoa." There was a teasing look in Charlie's eyes. "If you're going to do that please warn us so we can scoot to the other side of the island."

"Don't worry. I'm not that bold." Carolyn laughed.

"Well, my dear." Allan pretended to look shocked. "Remember we're an old married couple and very unused to that kind of passion."

Charlie slapped Allan on the arm. "I beg your pardon, mister. Boy, are you in for it tonight."

Chapter Eleven

It was Sunday and Molly was relieved she didn't have to pull traps. She was eager to see Carolyn. She was on the deck of her boat when Allan and Charlie drove into the marina. She was disappointed when she didn't see Carolyn get out of Allan's truck. She thought about her conversation with her brother only days before and wondered at how much more disappointment she could take. She quashed the emotional response that was whirling inside of her. What if Carolyn had decided not to come?

"Hi, kitten," Allan said as he walked across the marina. He was carrying two large coolers.

"Hey, Molly." Charlie was walking behind him carrying a picnic basket.

"Hi, guys."

She didn't want to ask, but the question seemed to explode from her mouth. "Where's Carolyn?"

Allan gave her a quirky look. "Don't worry, we're joining her. Charlie brought her out early this morning; we're going on her boat. She wanted to make sure everything was all right before we all descended." He handed Molly one of the coolers.

"Saw you on deck and thought we'd all walk over together."

Molly followed them across the pier.

"How's your brother?" Allan asked.

"I don't know." Molly lapsed into thought as she recalled their conversation the night before. It was clear he did not want help, and his anger at her was a prick that had not gone away much as she tried to rationalize his anger. At first she was angry at him and had decided that he did not deserve her help. Then she had thought about the drugs and how much they had changed him, and she tried to reassure herself that it was the drugs talking, not her brother. Then she went back to anger. Throughout the night, she had tried to shrug off the sadness that had been her constant companion, but failed. After they talked, Tommy went to his room and when Auntie Em called him for supper, he said he wasn't feeling well. She and Auntie Em had eaten and Molly returned to the boat. "I guess about the same."

Carolyn was standing on deck when they approached her boat. "Welcome," she said. Molly noticed the glow on her face. "I thought I would be the captain today, since you're always at the helm of your boat." She smiled at Molly.

Damn, Molly thought, *there goes my ability to swallow again.* "Always happy when there's another skipper," Molly mumbled as she shifted from foot to foot.

"Allan, Charlie, welcome aboard," Carolyn said, reaching for the cooler Molly was holding. Their hands touched and Molly felt as if she had been liquefied. The deck had built-in padded captain's chairs, not the turned-over buckets Molly offered her guests.

Molly stepped on the boat. Charlie was right behind her so when she stepped out of the way to let him on board, she bumped into Carolyn. Carolyn smiled mischievously. Charlie turned to reach for the cooler Allan was carrying. Allan tossed them the ropes and then stepped on board.

"Join me up front," Carolyn said to all three.

"You two go ahead," Charlie intoned. He looked at Allan. "We're going to soak up some sun. We have those inside jobs where we wilt during the week and flower on weekends."

Carolyn and Molly laughed.

"I want to thank you for yesterday. I had a good time," Carolyn said as she started the engine. She eased her boat out of the slip and into the main channel.

"Me too." Molly looked around the pilothouse. "Very nice." She admired the long sleek lines of the thirty-three-foot sport boat. Molly could feel the power of the 350-horsepower diesel engine as Carolyn advanced the throttle. The fiberglass hull seemed to skim on top of the water instead of plow through the waves like Molly's boat. Bronze gauges embedded in teak wood adorned the bulkhead. Molly could only guess what the sleeping compartment looked like. She thought of her boat as Motel 6 compared to Carolyn's Park Plaza.

"It suits me." Carolyn's smile was provocative.

Molly watched as Carolyn turned her eyes to the open water. *That it does,* Molly said in silent agreement. It was sleek and smooth and very sexy, like its owner. She looked out the door of the pilothouse and saw Allan and Charlie sitting on the captain's chairs. They were holding hands and laughing and talking. Molly felt a torrent of melancholy envelop her. She had forgotten how much she had missed the singular emotional closeness you felt with someone you were intimate with.

"I'm looking forward to this picnic." Carolyn smiled. "It looks like Allan and Charlie brought enough food to feed us for days."

Molly grinned in agreement. "They both love to cook, and you never know what surprises they're concocting. Every meal is a joy."

"I agree. I've eaten myself into a catatonic state." Carolyn laughed. "Last night they served cherries jubilee, fire and all."

"That's Charlie's specialty. I've had it and I'll tell you, you don't eat just one helping."

"Agreed," Carolyn said as she turned the wheel of the boat and eased back on the throttle.

"I know I said I would take us out to Roger's Island, but I was wondering, would you like to skipper the rest of the way?" Carolyn moved away from the wheel.

"I would," Molly said, stepping in where Carolyn had been. "I'd like to see how she feels." As Molly eased forward on the throttle, the engine came alive and the boat seemed to skim on top of the waves.

Carolyn stood next to her, their arms touching. "Do I get to drive your boat sometime?"

"Of course." Molly could feel herself teetering on the edge. She gripped the wheel even harder. *Let go, Bean, and you are going to crush this woman against you and kiss her.* "I think you're going to find that it slogs along compared with your boat's sprint."

"Slog is nice." Carolyn smiled.

Molly swallowed, uncomfortable with the too-flirtatious tone they were using. She was relieved to see Roger's Island in the distance. "Any preference as to where we land?"

"You're the skipper now. Is one spot better than another?"

"Actually no. It's one of the few islands that is reachable from any side. It's boat-friendly." Molly felt better now that she was talking about the island. "In fact, if you're ever traveling up from Bar Harbor and the weather changes and you need a secure place to ride out the storm, this is the island to do it. On the other side there's a sandbar. If I was in trouble, I'd run my boat up on that and wait for the tide to come in and float me back out."

Carolyn looked at the island. "Thanks. I'm usually pretty careful—I don't head out unless I know the weather."

"No doubt. Most seamen are, but this ocean switches moods in the time it takes for you to snap your fingers, and you can find yourself in a mess." Molly eased back on the throttle as she guided the boat near the beach. "How about dropping some anchors out there?" she called to Allan and Charlie.

"We're on it," Allan called back.

Charlie stuck his head in the pilothouse. "You want to eat on board or wade ashore?"

"This lady promised me a tour of the island." Carolyn smiled mischievously. "I'm game to wade. How about you?" she asked Molly.

"This ocean has gotten me wet before—it wouldn't be the first time."

"Let's do it." Charlie stepped back on deck and picked up a cooler. "We're wading, love," he said to Allan.

"Fine by me." Allan grabbed the second cooler and swung his legs overboard. "Oh, this ocean is cold."

Molly picked up the picnic basket and swung her legs overboard. She held her other hand out to Carolyn to help her. Carolyn's hand felt warm compared with the cold water that now hugged her legs.

"Wow, this is cold," Carolyn said. She waded next to Molly.

"It's never warm, not even in the middle of August. That's why we carry survival suits."

"But you don't wear yours."

Molly laughed, embarrassed. "They're so bulky. Hard to work in. I figure most boats don't sink immediately so you have time to get them on."

They were standing on the edge of the shore. Carolyn looked seriously at Molly. "I've been around water my whole life, just like you, and you know that's not true. Waves have swamped boats, things have happened and boats have sunk immediately. So taking time to put on a survival suit is great in theory, not necessarily reality."

Molly scratched her ear. "Probably."

"Hey, you two, we going to talk or eat?" Charlie called.

Molly was glad for the interruption. She didn't want to talk about survival suits.

141

"This conversation isn't over." Carolyn smiled sweetly.

Carolyn and Molly followed Allan and Charlie up onto the sandy beach. They already had selected an area in the grass, just above the beach. Charlie knelt next to one of the coolers. "This is pure ambrosia. Allan and I have been planning this menu for weeks. Are you ready, ladies?" He cocked an eyebrow at Carolyn and Molly.

"Go for it," Molly said laughingly.

"We begin with crab cocktail," he said, pulling out a container. "Of course, the crabs are from right here in our ocean."

Molly smiled at Carolyn. "I feel like I'm at one of those pricey restaurants in New York."

"Or Bar Harbor." Carolyn's smile was lively.

Allan handed them lettuce-lined cocktail cups and tiny forks. "This is *chez* Allan *et* Charlie," he said, adding an accent on the last syllables of their names.

"Oh, this is wonderful," Carolyn said as she tasted the crab cocktail. "Are we lucky?" she said to Molly. "I don't think lesbians cook this good."

"I know this lesbian doesn't." Molly laughed.

"There's more," Charlie said as he reached into the picnic basket. "This is my own herb bread." He broke off pieces and handed them to Carolyn and Molly. "And, we have wine. Just to tickle the flavor of the crab."

"Allan," Molly said between mouthfuls, "Charlie is beginning to worry me. 'Tickle the flavor of the crab'?"

"Humor him." Allan smiled affectionately at Charlie. "He is having a ball."

"Do you know," Carolyn said as she finished her crab cocktail, "when we were in college, everyone else would go to the dorm cafeteria. Not us. Charlie had an electric fry-pan hidden in his room and we used to pig out on some of the best food. Illegal as all get out. He never got caught and we burned candles to cover the smell. Our junior year, four of us moved into a house and shared the cooking—we all were home the night Charlie cooked."

"That was fun." Charlie smiled nostalgically at his friend. "We had a lot of fun back then."

"Yes, we did."

"Okay, you two," Allan cut in as he reached inside the picnic basket. "You two can reminisce later."

"Now for my part of the meal. Haddock-shrimp bake and," he said as he touched the bottom, "it's still warm." He handed new plates to Carolyn and Molly and served them each a large portion.

"Oh, God, I just died and went to heaven," Molly said. "Allan, this is wonderful."

"Just 'wonderful'? What? words fail you?" Allan was ribbing her.

"Let's see . . ." She pretended to ponder the question. "Wonderful, phenomenal, extraordinary. Let's try another, something I hear Kevin use all of the time. Awesome," Molly said with emphasis.

"I agree," Carolyn said. "Please tell me there's no more."

"Well, just these." Allan uncovered another dish. "Creamed vegetables au gratin."

While they ate, they talked about living in Gin Cove and about the murder. Allan said the police offered little insight as to what was going on. Carolyn told them about her life in Bar Harbor. They laughed and shared stories about their jobs.

"I can't eat another thing." Carolyn leaned back on her hands after finishing the haddock.

"Me neither. That was outstanding, guys, thank you."

"We're not done," Allan said, reaching inside the cooler again. "We have dessert."

Molly held up her hand. "Would you let us rest," she protested, then curiosity dominated and she asked, "But what is it?"

Allan laughed. "Double chocolate soufflé."

"I love this." Molly looked at Carolyn. "They made this for me before. It is—" She stopped. "Words fail me this time."

"Well, if it's like some of the other desserts they've fixed when I've been here, I know it's to die for."

"Do you want to eat it now or save it for later?" Allan asked.

"Later," Carolyn and Molly said together. Molly added, "We're full from everything else. How about I help you clean up."

"How about you two take a walk. Carolyn said you promised her a tour of the island. Charlie and I will clean up." Allan winked at his friend.

"Would you like to go for a walk?" Molly asked. "The island is not that big."

"Let's do it. It beats doing dishes," Carolyn said, clearly amused.

Molly led her along the beach to the southern end of the island, where they climbed some hills.

"An island like this would have houses on it in Bar Harbor," Carolyn said, looking out over the ocean.

"Well, this one would also, except the woman who owned it left it to the town as a bird sanctuary. They can't build on it, they can't sell it, so all it does is sit here. Home to a variety of seabirds and, on occasion, a safe haven for boaters."

" And lobstermen and women?"

"Yes, on occasion," Molly said quietly. "Carolyn, please understand, I know you're very seaworthy . . ."

"Like an old boat," Carolyn teased.

"No, not like an old boat," Molly protested. "It's a long trip by boat up here and I just want you to be careful. The ocean can be well-behaved, but it can be bad, wicked bad."

"So serious." Carolyn turned and must have seen the concern in Molly's eyes. "I will listen," she said solemnly. "I won't take chances. But what about you?"

"I've been on the water even before I could walk. My father and mother used to picnic on this very island. I love the ocean and respect it."

"Molly, I'll be careful." Carolyn looked at her. "I promise."

An intimacy lingered between them. Molly could almost touch it with her fingers. Then she thought about her brother and the challenges that her family faced and she mentally stepped back. "We'd better finish up this tour," she said quietly. "I know they expect us back."

"Of course." Carolyn paused. "Molly, I—"

Molly held up her hand. "Carolyn, I have these family problems to deal with right now and I don't know where they're taking me and . . ."

"Your brother?"

Molly frowned. "Allan and Charlie? Did they talk about that?"

"No." Carolyn clearly didn't know what to say. There was an awkward pause. "I asked them, after what Kevin said on the boat yesterday. They told me very little, just . . ." Carolyn put her hand on Molly's arm. "If I can help, I will."

"Really? As an attorney?"

"Really." Carolyn smiled. "As an attorney."

"Let's sit here." Molly pointed at some rocks. She then told Carolyn about her brother, the arrest and their conversation the night before. She was too embarrassed to talk about her brother's feelings about her lesbianism. "Basically, what he is telling me is that he doesn't want help," she finished up.

"That's hard. He has an attorney?"

"I hired one. A local fella. I'm not real confident he's going to do much."

"Why?"

"The police chief told me in one of the many conversations I had with him that the guy is good, but he's going to convince my brother to enter a guilty plea. He'll negotiate a reduced sentence and everyone will go on their merry way."

"Don't look at that as a negative," Carolyn said. "That happens a lot. From what you've told me, your brother had drugs on him. It's pretty hard to go into court and argue that the drugs were not his."

"I guess. I just expect more. I don't expect a defense that will razzle-dazzle the judge, but I would like to think that he'd put up a defense."

"Molly, don't be too hard on him. What's your brother saying?"

145

"I think he plans to take the plea."

"Any prior convictions for drugs?"

"A speeding ticket a couple of years ago, that's about it."

"He should take the plea. It will probably mean avoiding jail time."

"Auntie Em wants him to go to drug court."

"What does your brother want?"

"Not drug court."

"Drug court is hard. You have to be a willing participant. It means a probation officer, counselor, police officer, health care provider and judge are all looking over your shoulder and insisting you remain clean. In return you get a reduced sentence or no sentence. It's a hard sell to your brother because this is his first offense, so he more than likely won't see any jail time. The jails are full, overflowing with people who have committed more heinous crimes than being asleep with a couple of prescription pills on them."

"Boy, I really don't think I like this form of justice. I have a brother who's admitted to me he's a drug addict. Doesn't want to get off the crap. And a justice system that says because he has no prior record he's going to get a slap on the wrist, put on probation and let go to suck more drugs into his system." Molly stood up. She anxiously rubbed both hands through her hair. "That system stinks, Carolyn."

"You're brother is twenty-five years old. He's an adult. You can't force him to do something he doesn't want to do."

"Then put him in jail." Molly couldn't camouflage the frustration in her voice. "Force him to confront his problem."

"Molly." Carolyn paused. "I'm not saying that the system works, I'm just saying the system can't fix your brother's problem."

Molly started to pace back and forth. "So if you were his attorney?"

"I would tell him to take the deal."

"Even though you know it might kill him."

"Not necessarily. He can get help on the outside," Carolyn said quietly.

"Let's go back." Molly knew she had to keep a tight rein on her emotions.

"Molly, I'm sorry." Carolyn touched Molly's arm. Molly pulled it away. "I'm not going to lie to you."

Molly blew out the air she was holding inside. "Carolyn, I'm not angry at you. I'm angry at the world right now. Let's go back," she said more calmly.

Carolyn nodded.

Molly had hugged Charlie and Allan after they had returned to the marina. They clearly had sensed the distance that had developed between her and Carolyn after their walk and, in an obvious attempt had tried to mollify the situation, invited Molly back to their house for a cup of coffee, but she declined. She and Carolyn had been polite to each other, but Molly hadn't wanted to engage in conversation. Now back on her boat, Cat fed, she was angry at herself for getting angry at Carolyn. *Shoot the messenger, Bean,* she said to herself, that's what she'd done. All those weeks of frustration and anger had ruptured and the person who ended up taking the hit was Carolyn. Allan and Charlie had stayed on board with Carolyn. She could imagine the earful they were getting. Molly curled up on her bunk. She picked up the book she had been reading and stared at the pages. She tossed the book on the floor.

Molly got up on the first knock. She put on her robe and turned on the lights in the cabin. Allan was leaning against the door.

"I thought you'd gone home," Molly said grumpily.

"And why would I do that?"

"Because it's late and you have to go to work tomorrow."

""Tomorrow's a holiday, I don't have to go to work. However, I have a friend who is tearing up people and I go home?" Allan followed her into her cabin. "I don't think so."

"I was a jerk. Is that what you wanted to hear?"

147

"That and more. The woman offers her help and you take your anger out on her."

"She been complaining to you about me?"

"No," Allan said softly. "She didn't say a word. Charlie and I figured it out. Charlie went home and I came to see you."

"Look, I apologized to her. I can't do any more."

"Molly, I love you dearly, but while I am being patient with you, you are being petulant."

Molly sat down on the chair in her cabin. "Allan, I'm sorry. I don't know what happened. I just lost it." Molly jumped up and began to pace back and forth in the small cabin. "I can't take this anger out on my brother or Auntie Em and I just lost it. And I'm so sorry."

"Tell her."

"I did."

"Tell her again."

"I can't," Molly said, irritated.

"Why?"

"I'm embarrassed."

"So swallow that redheaded pride and go see her, tonight. Tell her you're sorry, again."

"Allan, I can't."

"Why?"

"Because I'm . . ." Molly put her face in her hands. "I'm going to cry." She sobbed.

Allan took Molly in his arms. "Come here, kitten. Now I'm the one who's sorry."

"For what?" Molly's words were muffled against his chest.

"For making you cry."

Molly stepped back and wiped the tears on her sleeve. "You—" She hiccuped. "Didn't make me cry. It's been there ever since the night Tommy was arrested. The tears, Allan, are like the anger, they are just there." She then told him about what Tommy had said about her being a lesbian and how she at first tried to shrug it off, but how the anger kept coming back.

"Come here," Allan said, holding out his arms. "I'm so sorry. He's just trying to transfer his anger to someone else."

"I know, Allan." Molly leaned her head against her friend's chest and cried. "But it still hurts."

"I know, sweetie." Allan rubbed her back. "But you can't take it out on Carolyn."

"You know what really makes me angry?" Molly said between sobs. "I really like her. I really, really like her."

"I know, hon."

"And now I've blown it."

"I don't think so."

Molly wiped her nose on her sleeve.

Allan laughed. "Let me get you a Kleenex." He stepped into the head and returned with a box of Kleenex. "Here." He handed them to her. She blew her nose and wiped her eyes.

"Did she say anything at all about me?"

"Nothing. Charlie tried to talk to her alone, but she said everything was fine. Charlie and I figured that something happened. You go off chummy as all hell and come back barely talking to each other. It didn't take a genius to figure out something had happened." Allan sat down on the chair. "Molly, I think you should talk to her tonight."

"Allan, I can't. I'm embarrassed. I don't take my problems out on other people. I don't know what happened. One moment we were talking and the next I was blaming her for the entire judicial system. God." Molly wiped her eyes again. Cat rubbed her muzzle against Molly's hand. "I was an ass."

"Well, love, I have to admit this wasn't your best moment." Allan paused. "But I think Carolyn understands. I think you need to talk to her before she leaves."

"Redheads look awful after they cry."

Allan put his head back and laughed. "No worse than anyone else who cries."

"Not true. Bloodshot eyes and red hair just don't blend. I don't want her to see me like this." Molly sat down next to Allan. "I promise you I'll talk with her in the morning. I am up earlier than anyone, and I'll wait on the dock if I have to and tell her I'm sorry. I'll grovel and tell her I'm sorry."

"Don't grovel, just be you." Allan stood up. "I gotta go. Are you all right?"

"Actually, yes. The tears helped. They gave me a gosh-awful headache, but they helped."

"Hey, what are friends for?" Allan said with a wry grin.

"Go ahead." Molly smiled in spite of her tears. "Make me feel better."

"I hope I can, kitten."

Molly reached out and touched his cheek. "Allan, thank you." Molly stopped. "Thanks for coming over tonight."

Allan leaned over and kissed her on the cheek. "You're my best girlfriend and when my best girlfriend hurts, I hurt. Know that, Molly."

"I do." Tears burned her eyes once more. "I'm going to cry again."

"No, you're not. You're going to go to bed and when you wake up, you're going to tell a very nice lady who likes you a lot that you're sorry. Agreed?"

Molly smiled. "Agreed."

Chapter Twelve

Molly dressed quickly. It was five-thirty Monday morning and she wanted to talk to Carolyn before she left for Bar Harbor. Her conversation with Allan was still a palpable memory of the night before. She stepped into the pilothouse. She opened her eyes wide; Sunday had been a perfect day of sun and warmth but not now. The morning sky was enraged. Black clouds spilled over and over on top of one another, leaving no dividing line between clouds and sky. The ebony expanse had enveloped Gin Cove. A bad storm was coming, Molly thought, a really bad storm.

Northeast winds acted like an undulating whip, creating an unrelenting fury to the water. The water whacked the side of her boat. Molly frowned. The noise hadn't awakened her, but then she remembered what Allen had said last night that this thing with her brother had twisted all aspects of her life. Last night she had fallen into bed exhausted from the crying and depleted from the weeks of worry. Now, she planted her feet as the boat rocked with the pounding waves.

She picked up her cell phone and called Kevin. A sleepy voice answered.

"Kevin?"

"Yeah, Molly?"

"Sleep in, my boy. We're heading for a first-class storm."

"Saw it when I got up. I went back to bed."

Molly smiled. She forgot Kevin had also been raised on the water. "Sorry to wake you."

"Sa-right, Molly. See ya tomorrow."

Molly took her jacket off the hook near the door and put it on. She dropped her cell phone in her inside pocket just as it rang. It was Charlie.

"Hey, Charlie, how are you this morning?"

"Actually, worried. I've been trying to call Carolyn on her cell phone. Is she still in the marina?"

"I was just going to talk to her." Molly opened the door and stepped on deck. "Why don't you hang on. Once I get down to her boat you can talk to her." Molly started toward the end of the pier. "How are things over there?"

"Bad. Everything looks black." Charlie was clearly worried.

"Not much better here." Molly stopped. "Charlie, did Carolyn tell you what time she planned to leave?"

"She just said early."

"The slip's empty." Molly looked out toward the water. "What's her number? Let me try and reach her from here." She listened as Charlie recited Carolyn's number. "I'll call you back."

Molly punched in Carolyn's number. *Come on*, she thought, *pick up*.

"The cell-phone customer you are trying to reach has either traveled outside the coverage area or is unavailable. Please try again." Molly huffed as she punched in the number again. She hung up as the message repeated itself.

She dialed Charlie and Allan's number. "I can't reach her," she said to Charlie, who had picked up on the first ring. "I'm going back to my boat and see if I can raise her on my CB."

"Call me when you reach her," Charlie said. "And tell her to turn her little butt around and get back here. She can stay here tonight. You too, Molly. This is going to be a bad one."

Molly ran toward her boat. "I'll reach her, Charlie, don't worry."

She opened the door to the pilothouse and pushed Cat away from the equipment. She picked up the microphone. "This is the *Finest Kind* calling the *Carolyn S*. Do you copy?" Molly willed herself to keep calm in her voice. She leaned the microphone against her cheek. "Come on, Carolyn, answer," she whispered to no one. "This is the *Finest Kind*. Carolyn, if you are out there, answer. You are headed into a bad storm, you need to turn around now."

"Molly." Her radio crackled.

"Clayton?"

"Yeah, I saw the *Carolyn S*. head out to sea more than an hour ago. Went right past the co-op. You think she's in trouble?"

"Don't know, Clayton."

"You better call the Coast Guard." Clayton's voice sounded scratchy as the radio crackled and popped.

"Let me try to reach her. I fail, I'll call the Coast Guard," Molly told him.

"Ya need help, let me know. We'll get a search party going."

"Will do." Molly switched channels and clicked her microphone on. "*Carolyn S*., do you read?" Molly closed her eyes as she waited. *Please answer.*

"*Finest Kind*, this is the *Carolyn S*."

"Where are you?" Molly shouted into the microphone. She rubbed a hand against her mouth. *Stay calm*, she ordered herself, *stay calm.*

The radio screeched and snapped. "Roger's—" The radio stopped.

"Stay there," Molly yelled into her radio. "Stay there, I'm on my way." Molly knew that Carolyn's boat had been built for speed and was not ready to take on a storm with this much rage. She turned the key and the diesel engine grumbled. She ran on deck, jumped on the pier and tossed both lines into her boat. She swung her legs on deck and ran back into the pilothouse. She slammed the door as rain began to cuff the outside of her boat. She turned on her windshield wipers. "Hang on, Cat, this is going to be the ride of your little nine lives," she said as she lifted the cat from the console and put her on the floor. Cat wound her small body around Molly's legs.

Molly backed the boat out of the slip. She thought about Carolyn, hoping she had listened to her when she told her to run her boat aground at Roger's Island or at least get on the leeward side of the storm and use the island as a buffer. She pushed the throttle forward and the usually powerful engine labored as it carved tiny little channels through the waves. Ordinarily it would take her about thirty minutes to get to Roger's Island, but the enraged winds kept pushing the boat off course. Her cell phone rang. She gripped the wheel with one hand and answered.

"Where the hell are you?" Molly could hear the panic in Charlie's voice.

"I think she's at Roger's Island. I'm going there," Molly yelled into the receiver. The cell phone snapped and hissed.

"We . . . want . . . help." There was a loud roar and Charlie's voice dissolved into nothingness.

"Stay there," Molly yelled. "I'll call you when I make contact with her." Molly tossed the telephone onto the console, unsure if Charlie had heard her.

Molly turned the switch on her windshield wipers to a higher speed; the black arms played a rhythmic beat of *slap-slap* as they swished back and forth. The rain, now pounding horizontally, continued its assault on the windshield.

"It's just you and me, girl," Molly said to the cat that now seemed to be leaning into her legs. Molly gripped the wheel with one hand and reached down and lifted Cat onto her shoulders. The trembling feline wrapped itself around her neck like a bushy neckpiece. Molly gritted her teeth as Cat dug her nails into her jacket.

"*Finest Kind.*" Molly's radio crackled. "This is U.S. Coast Guard Jonesport. I repeat, this is U.S. Coast Guard Jonesport. Are you in trouble?"

Molly picked up the microphone, her eyes on the swells. "Negative. My boat is fine. I'm headed to Roger's Island. There may be a boat in trouble there."

"Molly, turn around."

"Danny?" she said into the microphone. He had been on duty on other rescues Molly had helped with.

"Ten-four, *Finest Kind.* Recommend you turn back. We are dispatching our search-and-rescue boat."

"Welcome the help, Danny, but you're more than an hour away. I'm—" Molly stopped and looked at her watch. "About twenty minutes away. I'll keep going."

"Molly, this is Clayton. Have several boats standing by. Do you need help?"

"Will let you know," Molly said to the microphone. "Have them ready, if I don't make radio contact with her soon, send out the fleet." The two other times captains had gotten into trouble, Molly and the other Gin Cove captains had gone to help.

The winds snapped and a single streak of lighting slashed through the clouds and seemed to hop just above the water. A few times the twisting winds slapped her boat from the side. She felt her boat want to break stride and turn with the wind, but she held the wheel steady. The boat pushed down into the bottom of the wave and then climbed up and over. Each wave felt like scrambling over a high hill. It took both hands to keep the bow pointed into the wind.

Molly kept an eye on her compass. Outside the world had turned passive gray, and the clouds and water had fused, becoming one color. She knew that if she kept pushing in a north northwest direction she would run into the island.

Cat shifted on her shoulders. "Hang tight, girl. As long as this engine keeps going, we are going to make it." *I hope*, she said silently. Molly had been caught in storms like this before, but she had usually only been just a few miles from shore when they hit. She could read the sky and she, like every other lobsterman, would suspend pulling if bad clouds began to form.

It had been more than twenty minutes and still no island. She knew that the harsh winds made it seem like she was dragging a colossal anchor behind her boat. Molly kept an eye on the depth finder, the other on radar. They would tell her if she was getting near the shallower water and the island.

Molly ground her teeth together. If she found—no. Molly stopped. When she found her she was going to give her hell. First she would yell, then she would fold her into her arms and hold her. No, she argued with herself, she would do more yelling first. Molly saw the change in her radar; she was closing in on the island.

"It's not that far now, Cat," she said out loud. Cat raised her head and then laid it back down on Molly's shoulder. "I don't blame you," Molly said. "I would love to put my head down and close my eyes."

She eased back on the throttle; the radar told her the island was right in front of her. Molly prayed that all the years of setting traps in the area would instinctively keep her away from them now; the last thing she needed was for her boat to get tangled in a lobster line. She tried to look beyond the gray out her window, but she couldn't see the island. Molly reached for her microphone—maybe she could make radio contact. "Carolyn, this is Molly, are you there?" Molly's radio hissed back at her. "Carolyn, it's Molly. If you can hear me, answer."

"Molly." The voice sounded scratchy. "Where are you?"

"Roger's Island. Where are you?"

"Oh, thank God." Molly could hear the relief in her voice. "Here, Roger's Island. I tried to get to the sandbar, but I couldn't get around the island. The storm is worse on the other side. I've just been trying to use the island to keep the winds from pushing me over. My main engine is dead. I'm using my smaller outboard to give me enough rudder to keep from being pushed out to sea."

"Can you give me some idea where you are? I can't see you." Molly could hear the anxiety in her own voice. She didn't want to run over her now that she was here.

"Near where we put ashore yesterday. I was able to get here just before the brunt of the storm hit. I've been mostly circling around in the same area, but the waves are higher now and my boat isn't doing well. And there's something wrong with my radio."

"I know where you are," Molly shouted into the radio. "I'll find you." She watched her compass as she turned her boat to the right of the island. She switched her radio to the emergency channel. "This is the *Finest Kind* calling U.S. Coast Guard Jonesport. Danny, I've made contact with the *Carolyn S.* She's near Roger's Island, will let you know when I find her."

"Ten-four, we have rescue boat en route."

"Ten-four," Molly answered. She switched back to the channel she had been talking to Carolyn on. "Carolyn, my boat is larger. I need for you to watch for me."

"I am, Molly. I can't see a thing."

"Just keep watching. You may need to go on deck. If your windows are like mine, you can't see a damn thing out of them." Molly eased back even more on the throttle; she didn't want to find Carolyn by ramming into her. Molly saw the tiny blip on her screen. "Carolyn, I've got you on my radar screen. Can you see my boat?" Molly kept her eye on the tiny blip on her screen. *Come on, Carolyn,* she thought, *you've got to see me.*

"I see you." Carolyn's voice crackled across the radio. "You are headed right toward me."

"About how far?" Molly strained to see through her windshield.

"It's hard to say, not far." Carolyn's voice was tense.

Molly rubbed the side of her arm against her windshield. "I can see you." She eased back on the throttle even more.

"What are we going to do, Molly?"

Now that she was here, Molly was wondering the same thing. Although the island had served as a barrier, the waves still were pounding the side of her boat. If she tried to come alongside Carolyn's boat, the waves could push them into each other. "We're going to use the island as protection. I'm going to get as close as possible and I want you to toss me your bowline. I'm going to try and pull us around to the other side of the island. The winds should be less severe there. You try and hold as steady a course as possible and I will come alongside."

Molly rubbed her arm against her windshield again; the fog inside kept occluding her view of the boat.

"Carolyn, I'm about as close as I want to get. When I tell you, I want you to put your outboard motor in neutral and throw me your bowline," Molly said into the radio.

"Okay." She could hear the tremble in Carolyn's voice.

"It's going to be all right. There's a small inlet not far from here, I think I can get us in close enough to ride this storm out." Molly again rubbed her windshield. "All right, I'm closing in now. Put it in neutral." Molly swung her boat to the right and slowed. She slipped the gear of her boat into neutral. She put Cat on the table and opened the door. Rain smashed against her face. She could see Carolyn on the back of her boat, holding the line. Molly motioned for her to throw it. Carolyn let loose and the line landed near Molly's feet. She grabbed the rope and tied it to the stern rail. Molly wiped rain from her eyes. She motioned for Carolyn to get back inside.

She stepped back into the pilothouse and eased the throttle forward. She watched the bowline tighten and her boat begin to pull Carolyn's. *Well, at least it was working,* she thought. Now if she could just get the two boats to the inlet. Molly could feel the drag on her boat and the huge diesel engine seemed to complain even louder as it pushed against the waves. Molly turned the wheel to the left. She had grown up playing on this island and now memory would be her map. The inlet was on the south end of the island. Molly kept a close eye on the radar. She knew that she now was between the island and her first string of traps. Thank God the island wasn't that big. Molly could feel the winds lessen as she moved closer to the inlet. The hills she and Carolyn had climbed the day before would be the barrier she needed to get Carolyn safely aboard her boat. She let out a breath as they rounded the tip of the island and she could see the inlet. It was still blowing and there was a chop, but nothing like what they had just been through. She eased the throttle back as she got closer to the island.

She picked up the microphone. "Carolyn, I want you to kill the outboard, I'm going to try and get you close enough so you can come aboard my boat."

"Can you do that?"

"Yeah, I can." Molly stepped back on deck, untied the rope and fed it through the snatch block on the pot hauler, and the wheel whirred as it twisted the line around and onto the deck. When Carolyn's boat was only inches away, she turned the switch off. Carolyn came on deck. Molly grabbed her gaff and hooked it onto the railing on Carolyn's boat and pulled on the gaff with both hands. Carolyn's boat banged into the side of Molly's. *Shit*, she thought. She reached out to Carolyn and grabbed her hand. "Throw your legs over the railing. I got you," Molly yelled. Carolyn grabbed the railing of Molly's boat with her other hand and threw first one and then the other leg over. Molly let go of the gaff and it fell to the deck. She pulled Carolyn forward with both hands. "Get inside," she said.

Molly eased back on the pot hauler and let some of the rope slip through. Carolyn's boat was now floating behind hers. She stepped back into the pilothouse. Carolyn had not moved from the center of the room.

"Come on, you've got to get out of those wet clothes." Molly pushed her toward her cabin. "There are towels down there and a robe. Put it on," she ordered. Carolyn's face was as gray as the sea. Molly was afraid she might be in shock. "Go." Her voice sounded harsh even to her ears. Carolyn didn't say a word; she turned and went down into the cabin.

Molly pushed the throttle forward on her boat and moved even closer to the inlet. She had been right; the high hills would protect them. She switched her radio to the emergency channel.

"U.S. Coast Guard Jonesport, this is the *Finest Kind*. Danny, I've secured the boat, passenger is fine. Will ride out storm here. No need to continue rescue mission."

"Ten-four, Molly. You sure you're all right out there. Weather folks say this thing's going to last all day."

"We're fine. I'm going to anchor south of the island. Do me a favor, radio Clayton and tell him to stand down. Call Auntie Em and a friend of Carolyn's, Charlie Hatcher. Let them know we are safe." Molly gave Danny the telephone numbers.

"Will do. You get into any kind of trouble out there," Danny said, "you radio."

"Ten-four."

With the two boats secured and the anchors dropped on her boat, Molly stepped into the cabin. Carolyn was sitting on the edge of the bed. She looked up. "I was so scared out there," she said, clearly agitated. Carolyn had taken off her wet clothes and was wearing Molly's robe. Her face was as wet as her hair.

Molly held her arms open. "Come here," she said quietly.

Carolyn stepped into her arms and sobbed. "I'm sorry. I . . ."

Molly held her tightly against her. Carolyn's whole body shook as she cried.

"I'm sorry. I'm not usually such a wimp, but I was really scared, especially after my main engine died." Carolyn wiped her face on Molly's robe.

"You're safe." Molly closed her eyes; she did not want this moment to end. Her robe felt so alive now that Carolyn was wearing it.

160

"Thank you," Carolyn said. "I knew you'd be the one who'd come. I just knew." Carolyn's eyes were fierce and Molly could feel the sparks move up and down her body. Carolyn rested her forehead against Molly's shoulder. "My God, you're soaked." She stepped back and looked at Molly. "You've got to get out of those clothes. You're absolutely dripping." She pulled Molly's jacket from her shoulders. Molly sensed that Carolyn was more controlled now that she was focused on something other than herself.

"I'm fine." Molly laughed as she slipped the wet jacket off. Her shirt and T-shirt were stuck to her body. Her curly red hair felt glued to the side of her head. She knew there would be thousands of ringlets. She had been so preoccupied with Carolyn that she hadn't even noticed that her feet were squeaking in her deck shoes. Nor had she noticed Cat crawling around her legs.

Carolyn reached for the towel she had used and wiped Molly's hair and face. "Please change your clothes," she pleaded. "Besides nearly drowning you, I don't want you to die from pneumonia."

Molly stepped into the head. She stripped off her shirt and pants. Even her underpants were wet. She toweled herself off and reached for her robe. "Shit," she muttered, Carolyn had her robe on. "Ah, Carolyn, could you reach in the top drawer near my bed. I have a pair of sweats in there."

"Sure," Carolyn called through the door.

Molly stood behind the door and opened it a crack. She reached a hand out for the sweats and instead felt Carolyn's hand in hers.

"Why don't you come out here?" The voice was low, inviting.

Molly swallowed. She felt like she had just stepped into the vortex of a new storm. The door opened and Carolyn stepped inside. She had taken off the robe. Molly could feel her blood percolate as she stared at Carolyn's breasts, the curve of her hips. She pulled Carolyn to her. Carolyn's lips were open, a sensuous invitation to what lay underneath.

This is what I wanted to do, Molly thought as her mouth explored Carolyn's. *I've wanted to taste her.*

"Come on." She had seen the sultry look in Carolyn's eyes and wanted more. She backed Carolyn up to the bed and bent over and took first one and then the other nipple in her mouth. Carolyn tasted salty from the seawater that had bathed her. "I've wanted to do this for so long," Molly murmured against her breast.

"Me too." Carolyn's voice was soft, almost inaudible. She touched Molly's neck and her hand traced a line down to her breasts. "I wanted to know how far these freckles went and now I know." Carolyn's mouth feasted on her breasts as if they were a banquet.

Molly closed her eyes. All the weeks of being near her and afraid to touch her erupted in her mind. She raised Carolyn's face to hers and knew from the look in Carolyn's eyes that she understood.

Molly pushed her onto the bed and stretched out on top of her. She pulled Carolyn's hips into hers and kissed her as powerfully as the storm that hammered the outside of her boat. Molly pictured the storm and could feel the boat rock underneath her.

I've got to make her happy. Molly's thoughts became a mantra as she listened to the change in Carolyn's breathing. The quick intake of breath as Molly's tongue swept over first one and then the other breast. The way Carolyn's hands gripped her shoulders as Molly's hand trailed down Carolyn's abdomen, resting just above that spot where she knew Carolyn's passion would come to fruition. Molly touched her, a slight sweep of her finger and then her whole hand bathed in Carolyn's wetness.

She felt Carolyn's body tense as first one and then another orgasm vibrated through her body. Carolyn's nails dug into her back, but she did not stop. She leaned over her and again tasted her breasts and the salt that her flushed skin produced. She trailed her tongue down her stomach, finally savoring the spot her hand had touched only seconds before. She felt Carolyn's shudder begin at her toes and course up her body. *I never want to stop*, Molly thought, *I never want to stop tasting the woman I love.*

Chapter Thirteen

Molly rolled over and felt Carolyn's body spoon into hers. She kept her eyes closed. Maybe, she thought, if she didn't open her eyes, this moment would never end.

They had made love throughout the night. Sometime during the early morning hours, the storms inside and outside the boat had diminished. The boat was now gently rocking back and forth. Molly eased out of the bed and reached for her robe. She opened the cabin door and walked up into the pilothouse, which was now bathed in sunlight.

Molly stepped on deck. The morning sun felt warm on her face. She checked her boat and it appeared to be fine. She looked at Carolyn's boat. Her CB antenna was lying on the roof of the pilot-house, but other than that, the boat was dancing on the gentle waves. It had taken a punishment during the storm but had weathered the thrashing.

"Good morning." Carolyn came up behind her and hugged her.

"That feels very nice." Molly turned to her. Carolyn had on one of her T-shirts and nothing else. "I like your morning apparel."

Carolyn laid her head against Molly's shoulder. "This is all I could find."

"It looks a lot better on you than me. And it's going to look a lot better when I take it off of you." Molly could feel the passion between them. *Where the heck is this coming from?* she wondered. They had made love all night and yet she wanted Carolyn as if they were making love for the first time.

"You want me to take it off now?"

"I want to make love to you standing up," Molly said. She could feel the fire curling inside her. She wanted Carolyn and she wanted her now.

She slowly slipped the T-shirt up and kissed her stomach. Carolyn's skin felt warm on her tongue. She then eased the T-shirt over one of Carolyn's breasts and her tongue stroked the underside, finally coming to rest on her nipple. With her hand, she gently massaged Carolyn's other breast. She could feel Carolyn's body go rigid. And she trembled as she heard Carolyn inhale sharply.

If I want to please her, I have to listen to her body. I want to please her, Molly thought as she nibbled on Carolyn's breast.

"My knees are going to collapse." Carolyn sucked in her breath.

"I've got you," Molly said against her breast. She backed Carolyn against the wall of the pilothouse. "You're not going to fall."

Molly trailed her tongue down Carolyn's stomach. Her hand replaced where her mouth had been and she began a slow dance with her fingers over Carolyn's breasts. As she listened to Carolyn's breathing quicken, Molly kneeled on the deck. Her tongue slipped easily between Carolyn's folds. Carolyn gripped her shoulders. Molly's tongue tingled as she felt Carolyn's first and then second orgasm.

Carolyn gasped. "I can't stand up."

Molly stood up and pressed her body against Carolyn's. Her hand

164

slid easily into Carolyn's wetness and her fingers stroked where her tongue had been. She then slipped her fingers inside and when Carolyn gasped, Molly knew she was in love. *I've got to please her, I am listening to her body, and I've got to please her,* Molly thought as she felt Carolyn stiffen.

"I want to do that to you." Carolyn laid her head on Molly's shoulder. "As soon as I catch my breath, I want to do that to you." Carolyn's eyes were heavy-lidded. Molly could see she was still turned on.

"*Finest Kind*, this is Auntie Em. Where the hell are you?"

Molly stepped away from Carolyn. "Yikes," she said as she stumbled into the pilothouse. Shit, she thought as she stubbed her big toe on the kick plate of the door. She picked up the microphone and inhaled deeply. Auntie Em knew every unevenness in her voice. "Auntie Em, this is Molly. Over."

"What are you doing?" She could hear the frustration and anxiety in Auntie Em's voice.

Molly leaned the microphone against her forehead. She thought about what she had just been doing seconds before and felt a wave of desire deluge her body. "I've been checking to see if there's any damage to my boat or Carolyn's." Molly inhaled deeply. Carolyn's smell had become so palpably a part of her senses.

"I expected you back here by now. I don't know what the hell you been doing this morning, but if you hadn't answered I'd of sent the Coast Guard after you."

"We're fine, Auntie Em. Carolyn's boat has sustained some minor damage. Mine is fine. I was just going to haul anchor and head back." Molly was relieved Auntie Em had radioed first and had not called the Coast Guard. She remembered what she and Carolyn had been doing and she felt a blush creeping up her neck as she thought about the Coast Guard blasting their horn to let them know they were nearby. Carolyn's hand rested on Molly's back.

"All right, and tell Carolyn she can stay here, till her boat's fixed." Molly heard the maternal insistence in Auntie Em's voice.

Carolyn shook her head no.

"I think she plans to stay on board her own boat until it's fixed," Molly said.

"Well, she's welcome to stay here. Tell her I expect her for dinner tonight."

"Roger, Auntie Em."

"Now you get your butt home here. I was worried, to say the least."

"I hear you, Auntie Em. We'll be home this morning." Molly put the microphone down. She looked at Carolyn. "Sorry about that."

"Don't apologize. She loves you and worries about you, Molly. Don't ever apologize for that."

Molly smiled. "Thanks."

"Well," Carolyn said matter-of-factly. "I think we'd better head back."

"I'd much rather continue doing what we were doing." Molly slid her hand up Carolyn's back.

"Sorry, Ms. Bean." Carolyn laughed. "You said we'd be home soon and we're not going to upset Auntie Em. Besides, I turned down sleeping overnight there. I'd rather spend the night on the boat with you. Then I have to head home."

Molly frowned. "You can't leave until everything's fixed. That could take days."

"Days?" Carolyn frowned. "Molly, I don't have days. I have a practice to get back to."

"It could take days," Molly said gently.

Carolyn sighed. She rested her chin on her hand. "This does create a bit of a problem."

"I think it's a wonderful problem." Molly kissed her on the nose. "A fabulous problem," she whispered as she kissed Carolyn's lips.

Carolyn kissed her deeply. "Nonetheless a problem." Carolyn stepped back. "God, I didn't even think about people worrying about

166

me back home. It's already Tuesday, I was supposed to be there last night and back at work this morning. I've got to call my secretary and reschedule my appointments. I've got to—"

Molly sighed. Reality had already begun to ooze in. "Look, let's deal with this incrementally. You call everyone you need to in Bar Harbor." Molly handed her her cell phone. "And I will deal with people back in Gin Cove. Plus"—she leaned over and picked up Cat, who had been rubbing against her leg—"I will feed Cat and then I want to take just a few moments for us."

"I want more than just a few minutes," Carolyn said softly.

"Me too." Molly rubbed a hand against Carolyn's cheek. "Let's deal with all those practical matters that always seem to clutter our lives and then I want to hold you." Molly could feel a thunderclap of excitement course through her body. She wanted Carolyn again.

Carolyn smiled. "Agreed," she said as she dialed her first number.

Molly stood at the helm. Carolyn had her hand on the back of Molly's pants; her fingers were hooked just inside. They had gone back into the cabin and they had made love again, this time at a more leisurely pace. Auntie Em might demand that she return home, but Molly took time to luxuriate in Carolyn's body and Carolyn had slowly explored every inch of Molly's body. Even now, standing at the wheel of her boat, Molly's body was still vibrating.

"Will it really take days to fix my engine?"

"Probably not." Molly could hear the disappointment in her own voice.

"I've got to go back."

"I know."

"How long will it take?"

Molly picked up the microphone on her CB. "Gin Cove Marine, this is the *Finest Kind*."

"Go ahead." The radio crackled.

"Tim, a friend of mine's engine on her boat quit, that's the big problem. She also has a broken CB antenna. How long?"

"That the *Carolyn S.*?" Molly shook her head; there were no secrets in Gin Cove. "Ten-four."

"Don't know why the engine quit. So that could take anywhere from an hour to days. Depends on what's wrong. As to the antenna, I have them all in stock. I can fix that in a half-hour as long as no wires broke. I expect we could get started on it today."

"We're about twenty minutes from the marina. I'm towing the boat." Molly knew she was telling Tim something he already knew.

"Let us know when you're tied up, we'll send someone down to the dock to take a look. Could have it fixed by this afternoon, depends."

"Ten-four." Molly set the microphone down.

"I was hoping he would say he couldn't get it fixed until next week. Give me an excuse to stay."

"You need an excuse?" Molly could feel her body tense as she waited for Carolyn's answer.

"No." Carolyn turned Molly's face to her and kissed her lightly on the mouth.

"You keep doing that," Molly said huskily, "and I'm not going to guarantee that you're going to make port in twenty minutes."

Carolyn laughed. "I don't want to leave." Molly heard the solemnity in her voice.

"I don't want you to leave."

"We're going to have to deal with life's complications, aren't we?"

"Probably. I don't want to."

"What *do* you want, Molly?"

"To make love with you again and again."

"And after that?"

Molly stopped. She hadn't thought beyond the storm. Last night all she could think about was finding Carolyn. Then when she was safe, safe in her arms, she had stopped thinking. Now with port just minutes away she had her brother to think about; the storm had not blown his problems away. What could she offer Carolyn? Life with a lobsterman? Somehow, she didn't think Carolyn was ready for that. "I don't know."

Carolyn stepped back. "I guess neither one of us thought beyond last night," she said hesitantly. "I don't think we were thinking at all. I know I wasn't." There was a note of distress in Carolyn's voice and Molly felt powerless to do anything about it.

Carolyn picked up Cat, who was lying on the console, and hugged her.

"I—" Molly saw the boats heading toward hers. "Shit."

"What? Oh, no. The welcoming party. Does this happen a lot?"

"Only when Auntie Em is leading it."

"She worries about you." It was a statement.

"I guess."

Molly eased back on the throttle and slipped the gearshift into neutral. Her boat floated across the top of the water. Molly looked back and Carolyn's boat also had slowed. She stepped on deck. Carolyn was behind her.

"I decided to come out and see how you were doing," Auntie Em called from the back of Allan's boat. "I wanted to make sure you hadn't had any more problems."

Allan eased his boat alongside Molly's. "I'm fine, Auntie Em," Molly said.

"Hi, Carolyn. You all right, dear?"

"Just fine, Auntie Em. Molly did a good job of rescuing me," Carolyn said as Allan opened the door to the pilothouse and stepped on deck.

Auntie Em beamed. "She's the best sailor hereabouts. 'Cepting you, Allan."

Allan winked at Molly. "We were worried about you."

"Thanks." Molly felt suddenly self-conscious in front of her friend. Allan was smirking and Molly felt the red creeping up her neck to her face. *He knew*, she thought. His smirk was a prelude to the kidding she was going to endure later.

"Brought Auntie Em out, she threatened to murder me and feed me to the lobster's if I didn't," he said.

Molly quelled a smile she could feel dancing on the edge of her lips.

"We're going to escort you home. I talked with Tim," Auntie Em said. "He'll be waiting at the dock to fix Carolyn's boat. Everything else all right with your boat, dear?"

Carolyn shrugged. "I think so. At least it didn't sink."

"Land, yes." Auntie Em said. "Now, you two get home. I got beef stew cooking and peach cobbler."

"Sounds wonderful." Carolyn smiled.

"Looking forward to it, Auntie Em." Molly couldn't achieve Carolyn's level of enthusiasm.

Molly stepped back into the pilothouse.

Carolyn stood silently by her side as Molly slipped the gearshift ahead and pushed the throttle forward. "Love family," Molly said between clenched teeth.

"We do." Carolyn hooked her thumb on the back of Molly's pants. "We do. We'll be alone tonight."

Chapter Fourteen

Carolyn sat on the porch swing. Molly was in the kitchen with Auntie Em, helping prepare dinner. Carolyn had offered to help but Auntie Em had shooed her onto the porch. Carolyn smiled as she thought about it—the woman had actually shooed her.

Soon after she and Molly had arrived at Auntie Em's, the gentle dowager had insisted that she shower and nap. She then gave her a pair of Molly's jeans and a shirt. The jeans required a belt, because they were too big for her slim hips. Molly was slender, but she didn't come close to Carolyn's size ten. The large shirt hung on her shoulders and reminded Carolyn of a tent and she was the pole holding it up, she thought ruefully. She ran her hand over the shirt. She liked the idea that she was wearing something that Molly wore. The checkered shirt smelled like Tide and fabric softener, and the smells and the fabric made her feel warm and comforted. Carolyn frowned.

If she couldn't be in Molly's arms, she could be in her clothes. She shivered as she recalled their night on the boat.

Carolyn stared at her folded hands and thought about a new problem in her life. Somewhere between the storm and the rescue she had fallen in love with Molly Bean. After her breakup with that other woman, the one she lately had been referring to as her ex, she had slept with two women. Those nights had satisfied the fiery passion, but she had not imbued any emotion into it. This time was different. She and Molly had made love, and although the passion was sated for the moment, she wanted more. But more than that, she wanted to be with her. She did not want to go home to Bar Harbor.

Soon after they had arrived at the pier, Tim had boarded her boat and, along with two other men, stripped it to its bare essentials. When she had last seen her boat, the cover was off the engine and a man was nearly standing on his head tinkering. Since then, Tim had not called and Carolyn knew that that was not good news. After she turned her boat over to them, she had helped Molly secure her boat and then they took Molly's truck to Auntie Em's. On the dock Auntie Em had said something to Molly about her brother and Molly had been silent on the trip home.

Auntie Em had insisted, after Carolyn got up from her nap, that Carolyn spend the night, but she had resisted the invitation. Auntie Em had even hinted she could sleep in Molly's room, but Carolyn wanted to be alone with Molly. She did not want to spend the night in a house of memories, a house where a woman named Julie had been. But Molly had not even hinted that they would spend the night together.

Later, when Charlie called, she declined his offer to spend the night there, fearing she would insult Auntie Em. Then Auntie Em insisted Charlie and Allan join them for supper, so the time alone she had wanted with Molly disappeared. She rubbed her brow. How complicated life seemed to be.

Carolyn tucked one foot under her, her other foot gently pushing against the wooden porch rail. She closed her eyes and felt her body catch the rhythm of the swing. Maybe if she just focused on the swinging, she thought, the past twenty-four hours would disappear and she would be back in Bar Harbor, the successful lawyer who had all the answers, without any of the problems. The squeak of the screen door forced her eyelids open.

"Hi."

"Hi to you." Carolyn stopped the swing and patted the seat next to her, inviting Molly to sit down.

"Dinner is almost ready."

"Molly, what's wrong? You and Auntie Em have had your heads together ever since we returned home. I hope it's not because of me."

"No-o-o." Molly dragged the word out for emphasis. She then laced her fingers between Carolyn's. "It's silly, really. My brother went out today for the first time since he's been here, and I just feel uneasy, that's all."

"Drugs?"

Molly shrugged. "Undoubtedly. I've suspected he's been using right here. Mood swings, more than just worrying about his upcoming trial. I just didn't know what to say to him."

"I'm sorry."

Molly stared at the night stars. "I was looking for a fix to the problem, and he was just looking for a fix."

"It's possible he left for other reasons."

"You don't believe that."

"No." Carolyn stopped the swing with her foot and turned to Molly. "What can I do to help?"

"Spend the night with me, on the boat." Molly hurried on, "I know I've been absorbed by my brother's problems, but I don't want to be alone tonight and I don't want to stay here."

Carolyn touched a finger to her lips and then touched Molly's lips. "I don't want to be anywhere else tonight. I just want to hold you and make the world go away."

❧

Molly felt her heart skip a beat as she thought about Carolyn's sensuous invitation to what lay ahead. "Do you know what I want?" Molly swallowed. There was something absolutely beguiling about Carolyn. "I want to be stuck in another storm again, with you and I want—"

Molly stopped when she heard the toot of the horn.

"Hi, loves," Charlie yelled. He opened the door and rushed up onto the porch. He hugged Carolyn and then Molly. "We were so worried about you." He paused and looked mischievously at them. "Anything you want to tell us?"

"Stop teasing," Allan said from behind Charlie. He was carrying a large pan. "I made a few hors d'oeuvres to go with dinner." He handed the dish to Charlie. "I want to give you both a huge hug. You had us worried."

"I thought I heard some male voices out here," Auntie Em said, pushing open the screen door. "You all get in here right now. Dinner's ready. What that you carrying, Charlie?"

"Just a few hors d'oeuvres, to go with dinner." He leaned over and kissed Auntie Em on the cheek.

"And what about you?" Auntie Em demanded, her hands on her hips as she looked at Allan.

"I'm going to give you a big hug," Allan responded.

"'Bout time," Auntie Em said as Allan encircled her in his arms.

Inside the kitchen Auntie Em pointed at the chairs. "Everyone grab a seat. This here's mine," she said, pointing to the ladderback chair nearest her.

Charlie set the pan in the center of the table and lifted off the lid.

"Oh, my," Auntie Em said. "Did you say a few appetizers?"

"Well, maybe we went a little overboard." Charlie reddened, clearly embarrassed.

"This is wonderful," Molly offered agreeably. "What are we snacking on?"

"Well . . ." Allan gestured to the neatly lined sections. "Crab-bacon rolls, appetizer kabobs and pickled mushrooms. I understand from Charlie that Carolyn loves mushrooms. Quit wrinkling your nose," he said to Molly.

"You don't like mushrooms?" Carolyn asked.

"I, ah, don't put fungus in my body," Molly stammered.

"Ah," Carolyn said as she reached for the mushroom. "I've a lot to learn," she said with mock seriousness.

Molly blushed.

"When she was a child, didn't matter how hard I hid those mushrooms in chili, spaghetti. I'd cut them up in tiny little squares and when she was done eating, there they'd sit on her plate like she'd built a little mushroom fort." Auntie Em laughed. "She'd have them all picked out."

"Could we talk about something else, please?" Molly's voice cracked.

"Here," Auntie Em said as she set small plates in front of each of them and then sat down. "Put those snacky things on these."

Auntie Em spooned several hors d'oeuvres on her plate. Molly smiled to herself. No hors d'oeuvres for Auntie Em, they were appetizers or snacky foods.

"These are some good, Allan, Charlie," Auntie Em said as she reached for seconds. "Don't you all fill up on that small stuff. I have a whole pot of beef stew for you to eat."

"Don't worry, Auntie Em," Allan said. "It smells delicious and I'm ready for a bowl."

"Good enough," Auntie Em said, getting up.

"Sit," Allan said. "Let me serve you for a change."

"Don't be silly." Auntie Em went over to the stove. "I haven't had anyone wait on me in years and I'm not about to start now," she said as she handed him a bowl and a bowl to Charlie. As Auntie Em ladled the stew, she said over her shoulder, "Now that you're rested I think it's time for you to share the rescue with us."

"It wasn't much," Molly said, staring at her appetizers.

"You're being modest, Molly Bean. You saved my life and you know it."

"I'm not much in a mood to talk about that," Molly grumbled.

"Nonsense." Auntie Em handed bowls of stew to Carolyn and Molly. "What you did was darn brave. Everyone's been talking about it. Course they don't know you like I do. When you set your mind to stuff, you're like a goat found new green grass, can't stop you."

"Well, it wasn't much," Molly said again, staring at her stew.

Carolyn looked seriously at her friends and Auntie Em. "Actually, it was something. I was terrified. The wind kept howling and the waves just kept pounding the side of my boat. My main engine was gone and that small outboard gave me rudder but no push against those waves. When I saw that white boat of hers, it was an angel in a storm." Carolyn stopped. She reached for Molly's hand. "I didn't say thank you," she said quietly.

"I wouldn't have done anything else."

Carolyn saw the intensity in Molly's eyes. "It really was a something rescue." She turned to her friends and felt Molly squeeze her hand.

"Shucks, you wouldn't have even made good lobster bait, you're so skinny," Auntie Em said to Carolyn. "How about more stew?"

"Not for me." Carolyn laughed. Auntie Em had cut through the tension.

"I remember a time when a certain woman we all know and love had to be rescued," Allan teased.

"Don't go there." Molly laughed.

"And what's going to stop me?"

"Me." The light in Molly's eyes danced. "I'll shave that beard of yours the next time you're asleep."

"Foul," Charlie said, jumping into the moment. "I love the beard."

"You don't scare me, Molly Bean." Allan placed a hand against his

176

chest as if to emphasize the seriousness of his words. "Molly was what? Eleven, twelve?"

"Oh, I remember that," Auntie Em said with a laugh. "That was before she and her brother moved in here. Whole town was out looking for her."

Carolyn could see the red creeping up Molly's neck. Her freckles seemed to pop out on her face as the blush spread across her cheeks.

Allan leaned back in his chair and folded his hands across his stomach. "Molly had somehow scrounged up a small skiff. She found this large limb in the woods and nailed it to the seat. She got the sheet off of her bed, cut it at an angle and nailed it to the limb." Allan stopped and looked at Carolyn. "Now, recognize that this sail she had created couldn't swivel in the wind. She wrapped the sail around the pole and rowed out past the pier. Now," Allan said, his Viking eyes dancing in the night, "visualize this little skiff and this skinny little kid and toss into that mix a nor'easter. Anyway, once she's out past the pier, Molly stands up in the boat, which is rocking back and forth faster than a seat on a Ferris wheel, and she unwraps the sheet. She holds onto the bottom with both hands. Well, the wind grabbed hold of that sail and that skiff took off across that water like a chicken being chased by a weasel." Allan was laughing so hard that tears were rolling down his cheeks.

Allan's story had them all laughing, including Molly, who was clearly trying hard to look serious.

Auntie Em was rocking back and forth holding her chest. "Do I remember," she said. "The rest of the lobstermen were steaming toward port and this little bundle was flying right past them. My husband saw her first and he turns 'round and starts chasing after her. Soon more boats were going after her. They was all yelling, 'Drop the sail, drop the sail.'"

"What happened?" Carolyn said between breaths. Her sides ached from laughing.

"I wouldn't drop the sail." Molly grinned.

"Tell Carolyn why," Allan said, gasping for breath.

Molly looked sheepishly at Carolyn. "I was running away from home."

"Running away from home?"

"You bet," Auntie Em said. "She'd had a fight with her ma and she decided she was going to England. Tell Carolyn why England."

"We'd been studying about the palace guard and I was going to England to join the palace guard. I liked their red suits. Imagine this red hair in a red suit."

"What happened?" Carolyn asked, still laughing.

"They caught me. Uncle Ben got in front of me and two other boats got behind me and they just slowed me down. My boat kept bumping into Uncle Ben's. I remember him looking at me over the stern and yelling, 'Molly Bean, you drop that sail or you're going to be fish bait.' Scared the heck out of me."

"Looked like an armada," Allan said. "Course it was all over the CB and everyone was out at the pier watching. Here comes Molly being towed by Uncle Ben and the other lobster boats all around her. They were afraid she might bolt."

"Course your Uncle Ben couldn't stay mad at you too long."

"My ma and pa sure did. Ma made me sleep for weeks on the half of the sheet I'd left behind. Pa said he was sending me to juvenile detention. Course he never did, but I think he would have if it'd been an option."

"And of course the whole town talked about nothing else except about the Bean kid. She was a hero at school," Allan said as he looked at his watch. "Oh, look at the time. I gotta get up early tomorrow. Let me help you clean up," he said to Auntie Em.

"Nonsense, this was a one-pot meal. You take your snacky food home with you. I won't eat that. Have just a few bowls and the pot I cooked it in. You go on along," she said to Allan and Charlie. "And I know you two want to get to the marina see how Carolyn's boat is, so you go. I'll be fine. Like a little exercise after I've eaten a big meal." She pushed them toward the door.

Allan gave Auntie Em a hug and stepped out onto the porch with Molly.

"How's things going with the investigation?" Molly asked.

Allan shrugged. "Couldn't say."

"Can't say or won't say?"

"Actually can't say. All we hear is the murder is still under investigation. Course the rumors on campus are rampant. Everything from being killed by a cult to a male student lover who couldn't live without her." Allan shook his head. "These kids watch way too much television."

Molly watched through the screen as Charlie hugged Auntie Em and then he joined them on the porch. Auntie Em then hugged Carolyn. Molly smiled to herself. Auntie Em would never hug Julie, although Julie had tried. Auntie Em said something to Carolyn and Carolyn hugged her again.

Chapter Fifteen

Molly flicked the lights on in the cabin. She picked up Cat's food dish and set it on the counter. Cat, curled on Molly's bunk, blinked at the lights. Molly picked Cat up and stroked her head. The cat purred. "Come on, friend, you need to eat." She set Cat on the counter and reached for a can of Friskies. She opened the container and poured the can into Cat's bowl. "You deserve a treat today. You were just as brave as we were with the boat pitching and rolling."

After they left Auntie Em's, Molly had walked Carolyn to her boat so she could talk to the men who were still working on it. Carolyn said she needed to change into her own clothes before joining Molly on her boat.

Cat delicately took tiny bites from the bowl. No matter how hungry Cat might be, Molly thought, she never hurried. Molly wondered why her life couldn't be like that. Right now she felt as though she was darting through life and depleting it rather than taking tiny bites. And why did she keep running away from the woman who had reconfigured her feelings of love?

She jumped when she heard the knock. She paused before she went to the door. She wanted Carolyn with her but didn't want any of the turmoil that a relationship demanded. Not now, at least. Until she knew what demands her brother's problems would have on her, she wasn't ready to talk about love. When they were younger, her brother and his problems were just a small irritant, like the bite of a black fly. Now they seemed to encompass his life, hers and everyone else's.

She saw the anxious look on Carolyn's face as soon as she opened the door. "What's wrong?"

"My boat will be ready by morning." Carolyn stepped into Molly's arms. "I didn't want it to be. Now I have to go home." There was anguish in her voice. "I called my secretary at home. I told her I'd be there around noon, which means I have to leave early in the morning."

Molly felt the same crushing disappointment. Just seconds before she was telling herself she couldn't deal with a relationship and now all she could think about was Carolyn's being hours away from her. "I don't want you to go," Molly said so quietly she wondered if she'd even said the words.

Carolyn stepped back and looked into her eyes. "Really?"

"Really."

"Molly, I think—no, I know—I'm falling in love with you." Carolyn bit down on her lip. "I'm sorry, I didn't mean to talk about that now. I know you're dealing with your brother and his problems, but I can't seem to stop saying how I feel."

Molly felt herself teetering on the edge. She saw the look in Carolyn's eyes, a mixture of hope and desire. She reached up and touched Carolyn's cheek. "I think I'm falling in love with you and I am scared out of my pants. I don't know how to deal with this."

"What are we going to do?"

"This," Molly said as she kissed Carolyn. The passion she had felt building in her all evening exploded and it felt like a rocket blasting through her body. A violent shudder moved up her spine. She ran her hands down Carolyn's back and pulled her hips tightly against hers. A tapestry of tension seemed to drape over her like a heavy cloak. "I want this night to last forever," she said against Carolyn's lips.

"Me too," Carolyn murmured.

Carolyn's eyes were sultry, her lips open and inviting.

Tonight, Molly thought as she began to unbutton Carolyn's blouse, *is all I am going to think about.*

Molly turned on her side and ran her hand over Carolyn's thigh. Carolyn stirred in her sleep, her hand curled under her chin.

"I don't want to sleep." Carolyn's voice was sleepy and soft, almost inaudible.

"Me neither." *This is so illogical*, Molly thought. *I can't be falling in love with someone I've known only weeks.* She had known Julie for months before they made love and it was months after that that she said out loud that she loved her. Then it was months after that when she wondered if she was really in love.

"You're thinking about the future?" Carolyn asked, more awake now.

Molly stroked Carolyn's back. "Yes."

"And?" Carolyn turned on her back.

Molly traced a line from Carolyn's lips down her throat to her breast.

Carolyn took Molly's hand in hers. "Do you know what I found most attractive about you from the beginning?"

"No," Molly said gently.

"Your hands." Carolyn took Molly's hands in hers and kissed her fingertips. She stroked each of Molly's fingers then drew a circle in her palm. "Your fingers are like steel enclosed in a velvet glove. I watched you pulling those traps the first time and I knew that I wanted you to touch me."

"Like this?" Molly caressed Carolyn's nipple.

"Like that." Carolyn voice was soft, almost indistinct.

"I would love to do this for a lifetime."

Carolyn took Molly's face in her hands. "Molly, I'm not going to ask anything of you. No pressure, now or later. I know you're upset because of your brother. Know this, though. I love you. I know it now and I will know it next year."

"And I love you," Molly whispered, deeply moved. "Just give me some time to sort through this."

"We have time, Molly." Carolyn ran her hand down Molly's stomach and pulled her to her. "I love you, Molly Bean. That's all we need to think about tonight."

Molly kissed her deeply.

"Do you know why I didn't want to stay at your Auntie Em's house?"

"No." Molly kissed her on the nose.

"I didn't want to spend my second night with you in a bed that another woman had been in."

"Julie?"

"Julie." Carolyn's voice was almost imperceptible. "I was jealous."

"Julie's never spent a night there. Auntie Em hates her."

Carolyn propped her head on her hand and smiled. "That makes me love Auntie Em even more."

"Auntie Em disliked Julie from the day she met her. On occasion Julie had dinner at Auntie Em's, but that was it. She never was invited to stay. So when she invited you today, I counted that as an endorsement."

"Then I'm sorry we didn't stay."

"Not me." Molly leaned over and kissed her deeply. "I don't want any muffled sounds. I want to hear you as I make love to you. Just like before."

❧

The sun was just peeking at the edges of the ocean as Molly walked Carolyn to her boat. "I hate this. I don't want you to leave."

"Funny, up until this weekend, I never quite thought of Bar Harbor as being that far away."

"I consider it a lifetime." Molly stepped onto Carolyn's boat and reached up and helped her aboard.

Carolyn smiled. "No one has ever helped me onto my boat. I like it."

Molly hesitated. "Carolyn, I don't know where this is going, but know this, I have fallen in love with you, and even though I have this turmoil going in my life, I want to talk about the future. Maybe not now, but soon."

"I'll be back this weekend, then let's talk about the future, okay?" Carolyn kissed her. "I've got to go."

"I know." Molly pulled Carolyn tightly against her and rested her forehead against her shoulder. "Now, please, if it looks like the weather is going sour, turn around and come back here. No more high seas adventures, okay?"

"Oh, I don't know." Carolyn stepped back and looked at Molly quizzically. "I think the last time ended positively, if not productively."

"I can't argue with that," Molly said huskily.

"I love you." Carolyn kissed Molly. "I'll see you Saturday."

"I won't think about anything else."

Molly watched as Carolyn started the engine on her boat and then stepped back on deck. Molly tossed first the bow and then stern lines to Carolyn. "Be careful."

"I will," Carolyn said.

Molly watched as Carolyn backed her boat out of the slip. Carolyn turned and waved.

"Touching." Molly jumped. She turned to face Julie. Molly could see Julie had sensed the connection between her and Carolyn. "Are you two in love?"

"I'm not going to answer that."

"You don't have to. It was clear the way you touched her. How could you? You know how I feel."

"Julie, I told you it's over between us and I'm not going to talk about it or anything else." Molly frowned. "What are you doing here?"

"Your brother's been arrested." Molly could hear the low growl of rage in Julie's voice. Molly could sense Julie's jealousy and wondered at it. After all, it was Julie who had left her.

"Where? How?"

"It's not drugs this time, Molly. The Maine State Police arrested him."

"I don't understand."

"Simple, Molly. Your brother's been arrested for the murder of Professor Davenport."

Molly stepped back. Julie's words felt like a steel fist had hit her in the chest. "I—"

"He's at the jail." Julie shrugged. "Being questioned now. They found him drugged out of his mind. Looks like the Beans have finally met with their comeuppance." Julie turned and started to walk away. "You want to see him," she called over her shoulder, "you gotta go through the Maine State Police."

Molly watched as Julie walked off the dock. Auntie Em, she thought. She had to tell Auntie Em before the talking drums called her.

Chapter Sixteen

Auntie Em sat quietly on the passenger side of Molly's truck and stared at the road. The two had said very little to each other since Molly had arrived at Auntie Em's house to tell her about Tommy. Auntie Em had insisted on going with Molly to the police station.

Now, driving to the station, Molly knew that Auntie Em's thoughts were like hers—a frustrated muddle.

"I don't believe it," Auntie Em muttered.

"You know what, Auntie Em? I don't know what to believe anymore."

"What did Julie say? Tell me again."

Molly shrugged as she recalled Julie's words. "Just that Tommy had been arrested for that professor's murder. I really didn't talk to her. She was surly, angry."

"Why?"

"I think because of Carolyn. She saw us on the pier." Molly

paused. "It was anger built on instant jealousy. Funny, when she left me for that other woman, she didn't even stop to think about how I felt. Didn't care about my jealousy. Now, we're not even together and I get this. It was bizarre."

"I never liked that woman. Serves her right. I'm glad she saw you." Auntie Em stared ahead.

"I guess." Molly turned onto Main Street, then followed the road past the closed shops. The lights were on at the Dunkin Donut shop and there were cars parked in front. Molly drove toward the police station. She could see the American and Maine flags in the distance. Julie's jealousy had startled her. She didn't trust what Julie might do next. She wanted to distance herself from her ex and concentrate on this latest problem with her brother. She thought about Tommy, the morning sun now just slightly above the horizon. He was watching it from inside the jail.

She had called her sternman from Auntie Em's house and told him she was not going to pull traps today. She hadn't told Kevin why. She knew that within hours he, like everyone else, would know. Molly found a parking spot in front of the police station.

"I thought you said the state police was handling this," Auntie Em said, looking at the building.

"They are, but they're here." After Julie had walked off, Molly wasn't certain where she and Auntie Em should go so she called Billy, and he told her that the state police were questioning Tommy. He asked them to see him before they asked to see the state police.

Molly held the door to the police station open for Auntie Em. She looked past Auntie Em to the police desk and was relieved when she didn't see Julie in the office. Molly wasn't prepared to deal with another verbal storm. No doubt her seventy-year-old aunt would cold-cock Julie if she said the wrong thing.

"Hi, Fibber," Molly said to the young officer behind the deck. Fibber Havlong was her brother's age. Molly didn't remember how he had gotten the nickname, but everyone called him that. Nicknames were as much a part of Gin Cove as the ocean. After she had grown up, she was relieved that she hadn't been stuck with a nickname. The usual Red and Carrot-top stopped when she graduated from high school.

"Molly, Auntie Em, hi. Billy said to let him know when you arrived," he said, turning to the chief's office. "Wait here."

Molly saw Billy through the door. He motioned them to come in.

Fibber held the door for them. "It'll be okay," he said quietly as they passed him.

Auntie Em reached out and squeezed his hand.

"Sit down." Billy motioned to the two chairs in front of his desk. "You okay, Auntie Em? Like a cup of coffee?"

Molly turned to look at her. Her face was rigid, her eyes drained. "You okay?" Molly reached for Auntie Em's hand.

"Just okay." Auntie Em squeezed Molly's hand. "A cup of coffee would be nice."

"Molly?"

"No, thanks."

"Cream, sugar?" Billy asked Auntie Em.

"A little cream."

Billy punched a button on his telephone. "Fibber, get Auntie Em a cup of coffee with a little cream, would you please?"

"Sure thing, chief. You like a cup?"

"No, I've swamped my kidneys as is."

"How bad is it?" Molly asked after the chief released the intercom button.

"Tommy was picked up by one of my officers. We got a tip. He was staying at a house in Jonesboro." Billy paused as Fibber knocked softly and entered.

"Here you go, Auntie Em." Fibber handed her the cup.

"Thank you."

Billy waited until Fibber had closed the door. "We could have called in the state police but they'd probably gone with an entire force. I sent two officers down there. Tommy said he'd come back with them. No fuss. Nothing."

"Julie said he's been charged with murder."

Molly noticed the frown first. "No-o-o." Billy stopped. "We were told to pick him up as a material witness."

"What's that mean?" Auntie Em asked.

"The state police believe he may know something about the crime." Billy looked at Molly. "Who told you that?"

Molly squashed the emotional response that was whirling inside of her. "Julie did."

"She's crazier than a bear shot in the ass," Auntie Em snapped. "Get rid of her."

Molly didn't know what to say to cover the awkwardness of the situation.

Billy cleared his throat. "Yes, well." He shuffled some papers around on his desk. "I'll check into that. Right now you need to know that Tommy has not been charged with a crime. Right now he's being questioned about what he knows."

"About the people who did it?" Molly asked.

"Probably, and about the crime—"

"I wished you were handling it," Auntie Em interrupted.

"Can't. State law requires that the Maine State Police handle all murder investigations. I think the state believes it keeps it neater."

"Well, they don't know nothing," Auntie Em fumed.

Billy held up his hand. "They're good, Auntie Em. Just give them a chance. What they know is not much, and they're hoping your Tommy can answer some questions."

"If he doesn't?" Molly asked.

"They'll hold him."

"Can we see him?"

"I don't know. Like I said, the state police are handling this. You need to talk to a Lieutenant. Bob Gardiner."

"You like him?" Auntie Em asked. "He any good? Or he into just railroading Tommy?"

Billy hesitated. "He's good, a little different from what we expect around here, but good."

"Different how?" Molly asked, concerned about Billy's tone.

Billy stood up. "Look, why don't I arrange for you two to talk to him. You can use my office." He walked to the door. "Give me a second. Auntie Em, you want more coffee, just ask Fibber."

Molly could feel herself slip backward into the morass she had been feeling soon after Julie had told her. The silence was stifling. Molly watched as Auntie Em toyed with her cup of coffee. She had drunk very little. "Coffee all right?"

"Just like on TV. They talk about police coffee, tastes like it's been cooking all day. It's true." Auntie Em set the cup on Billy's desk. "What do you make of all this?"

"I don't know."

"Julie lied to you. She lied because she was jealous," Auntie Em said.

"Seems so."

Auntie Em made a dismissive motion. "She better never say anything to me. I'll pound her."

"No." Molly sighed, exhaustion covering her like a woolen blanket. "We're just going to ignore her. We've got enough trouble."

"What she said to you was unforgivable," Auntie Em persisted. "It might be jealousy, but that's one woman hasn't got a right to even know that emotion."

"I'll deal with that later. Right now—" Molly stopped as the door opened. The man was more than six feet tall. His brown hair was thinning and he had moved his part down the side of his head to push more hair over the top of his white pate. He had on a checked polyester shirt and tan pants, the pants made more obvious by the fact that his large belly was pushing hard against his zipper.

"Ladies, I'm Lieutenant Gardiner." He shook hands with each of them. "I understand you have some questions?"

"You bet." Auntie Em stood up, her hands on her hips. "What you doing with Tommy?" Molly could sense the tight rein Auntie Em was holding on her temper.

"Nothing, actually." He sat down in Billy's chair. "He's being held as a material witness."

"Is he cooperating?" Molly asked quickly before Auntie Em could talk.

"No." The police officer studied his fingernails. "Right now he isn't saying much."

"Can we take him home?" Auntie Em asked.

"No." He looked at Auntie Em for the first time. "We have a court order. We can hold him as long as we like."

"He sick?" Auntie Em had sat back down in her chair.

"If you mean is he coming down off of a high," he said, again studying his nails, "yeah, you could say that."

"He getting help?" Auntie Em huffed.

"We're monitoring him. He isn't as bad as some."

"You want to look at me when I talk to you?" There was a steely chill in Auntie Em's voice. The lieutenant looked up and dropped his hand by his side. "How sick is he?"

Lieutenant Gardiner sat forward in his chair and rested his arms on Billy's desk. "He's coming down off a high. It's bad, but it won't kill him. It may even soften him up some. He's a material witness in a murder investigation. That's all I'm going to say." He stood up.

"Well, I'm not through." Auntie Em also stood up. "When can I see him?"

"When we're done questioning him."

"He ask for an attorney?"

"Not yet."

Molly also stood up and put a hand on Auntie Em's arm. "Look, lieutenant, our quarrel isn't with you." Suddenly exhausted, Molly rubbed her tired brow. "It's just that we've never dealt with anything like this. We don't understand things like 'material witness' or how long you can hold him."

"Look, we think your brother," he said, gesturing toward Molly, "knows something about the death of Professor Davenport. We are simply questioning him and we're going to continue to question him until he gives us some answers. Besides, he violated his bail conditions so"—the lieutenant shrugged—"we can hold him."

"Will we be able to see him tonight?" Molly looked at her watch. "I mean today?"

"Probably not. He's in a cell right now. We're hoping it'll help him remember. We plan to question him again later."

"Well, we're getting an attorney," Auntie Em huffed. "I don't like the sound of this."

"Suit yourself." The officer shrugged. He walked toward the door. "You get him an attorney, if he's smart the attorney will tell him to answer our questions. Otherwise, that young man is going to jail for a while."

"Sounds like you plan to send him to jail regardless," Auntie Em said.

The officer looked at them and silently closed the door behind him.

"I don't like him. I like Billy. Billy would talk to Tommy." Auntie Em was fuming. "We need a lawyer." She pulled her jacket more tightly around her shoulders as she headed for the door. "Call Carolyn."

Molly frowned. "Carolyn? Why?"

"She's an attorney. She can help." Auntie Em looked at her as if she had asked the most stupid question on the planet.

Molly hesitated. "I don't want to get Carolyn involved."

"Fine, then I'll call her." Auntie Em marched in front of Molly, past the police desk and out the front door.

"Auntie Em, wait," Molly called as she caught up with her. "Let's just take this one step at a time. I'll call Joe Matthews. See what he can do for us first."

"Well, do something," Auntie Em sputtered furiously. Then her shoulders sagged and she put her hands over her face. When she looked up Molly could see the tears in her eyes. Molly pulled Auntie Em to her and held her tightly. "I'm scared for him." Auntie Em's words were muffled. "He's never been in this kind of trouble before."

"I know." Molly cleared her throat. "This could get worse before it gets better."

"How so?"

"I don't know. They're holding him as a material witness. Maybe that's just their way of holding him. Questioning him as much as they want. They might be thinking of charging him . . ."

"We need a lawyer." Auntie Em stepped back, resolute once again, and rubbed her sleeve against her face.

"I'll call Joe."

"Not Carolyn?"

"No," Molly said huskily. "I don't want to involve her in our problems."

"She'd want to help."

Molly clasped her hands together, her palms sweaty even though there was a smooth morning breeze. "Not now, Auntie Em. Right now this is our problem."

Auntie Em opened her mouth but said nothing.

"Come on. We're wasting time," Molly said as she held the truck door open for Auntie Em. "Let's drive over to Joe's office. If he's there, he can help right off."

Chapter Seventeen

Molly and Auntie Em spent more than an hour with Tommy's attorney. He agreed to go to the jail immediately and find out what evidence the police had. He confirmed what the detective had said; they could hold Tommy for as long as they liked, questioning him as often as they liked. Add to that the bail violation, he said, and Tommy would be in jail until the next Superior Court date.

Molly dropped Auntie Em off at her house and returned to her boat. Her aunt had wanted her to stay, but Molly felt jittery and apprehensive. All she could think about was her brother and what his role was in the professor's death. She could picture her brother, that sullen resolve he had when he was determined not to talk about something. Even playing with Cat did not offer the calm stability she was looking for.

When Auntie Em asked to see Tommy, Molly had secretly hoped the detective would say no. She didn't want to listen to how bad he looked or how sorry he was, all the things Auntie Em would dwell on once she had seen Tommy. She knew that the town's whisper mill had already begun, and her mood alternated between blinding rage and furious loathing, and now that her brother had unloaded his homophobia on her, she couldn't even muster familial compassion. She felt as though she was sinking into a hellish abyss.

She needed the peace and quiet of being out on the water. She had pulled out of the finger-pier, ignoring the questioning looks of her fellow lobstermen. She knew they wouldn't ask about her brother. At Roger's Island she cut the engine and let the boat float.

Molly leaned against the gunwale. She closed her eyes and could feel the rhythm of the waves, yet it did not soothe the rage inside, the scorching fury. All she wanted to do was put her clenched fist through a wall or better yet, she thought, into her brother's face.

She stepped into the pilothouse and revved up the engine faster than she ordinarily ran it. She wanted speed. She needed to feel as though she was forcing something beyond its limit. She wanted to take her anger out on the diesel engine that now erupted with an almost painful force. She thrust the throttle forward and the boat rammed against the waves and the bow plowed into a sandbar. The momentum threw her against the wheel. She rubbed her ribs where the engine wheel had hit, the pain searing. Shit, she thought, she probably broke a rib. She cut the engine and sat on the floor, the tears flowing out of her like spring water rushing to the sea. She did not know if it was the throbbing of her ribs, or her throbbing anger that had generated the tears. All she knew is she wanted to cry.

Molly leaned her head against the wall. She had a thumping headache and her face felt feverish. Her right side ached. Lately, she thought, she was a waterworks of tears.

The sound of a boat motor forced her to get off the floor of the pilothouse and look. Allan's boat was racing toward her. She stood motionless, staring at the white boat that grew larger as it approached her.

Allan finally slowed the boat and cut the engine. The small vessel seemed to just skim across the top of the waves. As he eased along-side, Allan reached out and grabbed the railing. She could see the muscles in his arm flex as he slowed the momentum of his boat down. "Permission to come aboard."

Molly shrugged. "You don't need permission. You're going to board whether I want you here or not," she snarled.

"You got it, hon," Allan said as he swung his leg over the railing, a task made more difficult because of the ocean swells. He tied his boat to the stern railing and turned to her. "Come here," he said gently.

Molly stepped into his arms. She buried her face in his chest and cried. Allan stroked her hair and rubbed her back. "How'd you know I was here?" she said, sobbing.

"Years of predictability. I just knew you'd be here."

"How'd you hear?"

"It's all over the college."

"What they saying?" Molly stood back and wiped her face on her sleeve. Her eyes felt puffy from crying.

"A wildfire of mixed messages. Some think your brother's been arrested and charged with murder, others know that he's been picked up for questioning."

"I am so angry at him." Molly turned her back on Allan. "I am so furious with him, I could split my spleen. What he has done to this family is . . ." Molly paused. "Unforgivable. Nothing but whispers and innuendo will be cascading down upon us for years. He—"

"Wait a minute, pet." Allan reached out and touched Molly's shoulder. "I'm sorry, but this isn't about you. This is about your brother and the problems he's facing. This isn't about the Bean name," he added more gently.

"How can you say that? Of course it's about me," Molly said louder than she had intended. She inhaled deeply, trying to keep the fury that was still raging inside from detonating. "I live in this town. I have to look at people every day. I—" Molly stared at Allan. "This is small-town America, Allan. People thrive on gossip that will tip between those people who want to believe the worst and those who just want to believe."

"I don't believe the worst," Allan said quietly. "I think your brother may know something connected to the murder, but I don't believe he had any part of it."

Molly stared at the water. "I don't know," she said, her voice hoarse from strain. "I just don't know."

"He's your brother."

"He's a stranger," Molly countered.

"Probably. I know you two haven't been close all these years, but it doesn't matter. He's blood and you have to stand with him."

"Why?" Molly whined. "Why do I have to stand by him? I wouldn't stand by a stranger who did something like this—"

"You'd stand by a friend," Allan interrupted. "You might not understand it, but you'd stand with your friend until you knew the facts and, knowing you, even afterwards because you wouldn't believe your friend was capable of doing something like that."

"I wouldn't have friends who would do something like this."

"Molly, Molly, this isn't about you," Allan said again with more emphasis. "You've got to put the 'me' in this aside. Right now your brother needs you and Auntie Em. He needs to know that you two are ready to catch him when he falls. You've got to know that he's scared. He's never ever been involved with something like this so he's got to be terrified."

"And what about me? Don't you think I'm scared?" Molly could feel her eyes brim with tears again. "Don't you know what people are saying right now? The innuendoes and veiled accusations. Some not so veiled. I went through this with my father. The indulgent smiles because he was drunk most every night. I swore I'd never go through it again and now this . . ." Molly began to pace back and forth on deck. She alternated clenching and unclenching her fists. "Can you imagine finding out that your brother hates the very spirit of your being? You don't just turn being a lesbian off with a switch. He acted as though I had a choice. I've tried to deal with this, I've tried to rationalize that it was the drugs talking, but I'm just so angry."

After a moment, Allan said, "Is that what this is about? I'm not sure your brother even knew what he was saying. He feels abandoned. Take all of that and throw in equal amounts of panic, anger and drugs and you have a person who would rather thrash about than solve issues. And in that thrashing, screw the feelings of others."

"Well, he broke a new record for penetrating remarks." As Molly turned to Allan, she couldn't keep the venom out of her voice. "And I'm supposed to forgive him. Never." She could hear the granite in her voice. "Never," she hissed to the sea.

Allan leaned against the gunwale. "Something else is going on here," he said.

Molly kicked over a bucket and sat down. "All my life I've been told 'he's your brother, he's family, you love him.' Allan, I don't love him. I don't know what it means to love a person you don't know. To love someone just because they are in your life or share the same blood. I don't understand that fake rite of passage when you decide you should love someone just because you happen to have the same parents. What does that mean?" Molly asked, suddenly deflated. "There are all kinds of people in my life that I think more about than I've ever thought about my brother. We never had that hang-together relationship or any kind of closeness. We lived under the same roof but, I don't know, it was as if we've always been strangers. I don't know if that separation was there before my mom died and it grew into a huge crater or it was always there because we were so far apart in age."

"I don't know how to answer that." Allan turned over another bucket and sat down next to her. He reached over and took her hand.

"And I wonder," Molly said, looking out across the ocean, "if now I'm just going through the motions of caring because it's what is expected of me." She paused and looked down at Allan's hand over hers. "The other night Auntie Em and I were talking and all of a sudden I felt this mental rush that turned absolutely physical—it took my breath away. What if Auntie Em died? Allan, I could feel the loss. I actually was overwhelmed with sadness. I don't feel that way about Tommy. I've been angry at myself because I want to feel and I can't. " Molly sighed, finally giving in to the pain that had been so palpable inside her. "If something happened to you or Charlie I would feel as if a part of my life had been cut away. I just don't feel that about my brother."

"I'm not good at this," Allen replied sadly. He rubbed Molly's hand with his. " I can't tell you what's the right or wrong way to feel about your brother. But it could be, sweetie, that you're so angry at him right now, you're throwing up all these defenses, to protect yourself from later pain. Maybe, just maybe," he said more quietly. "you're building walls."

"I don't know." Molly rubbed her hand against her forehead. She felt feverish and her side ached. "It's possible. I am so scared." Molly put her hand against her chest. "I'm so terrified that he had something to do with it that I can barely breathe when I think about it."

"Molly, right now you've got to believe that he isn't involved. You've got to talk with him."

"And if he doesn't want to see me?"

"Start by first asking to see him," he said reasonably. "Have you talked with Carolyn?"

"No, and I don't intend to."

"She didn't call?"

"Didn't check," Molly said huskily.

"So you're doing what?" he asked reprovingly.

"Nothing," she blurted.

"Are you telling me you're mad at her?"

"Allan, I am furious with everyone," she said in a tone that she hoped permitted no discussion.

Allan sat back as though she had attacked him. "Everyone, Molly?"

"No . . ." Somewhat mollified, she said, "Not you. Never you." She buried her face in her hands. "I just want this pain to go away."

Allan put his arm around her shoulder. "Let's go home."

"Not for a while. I'm stuck on a sandbar," Molly cried. "On top of everything else I stupidly beached myself."

Allan looked around. "Not so bad. I'll use my boat to pull you off. Tide's coming up, so it should pop right off," he said as he stood up and reached for the rope. He began to pull his boat alongside Molly's. "Come on, it'll give you something to focus on other than yourself. I'll pull and you put your boat in reverse and we'll go home."

He threw his leg over the railing of his boat, went inside his pilothouse and started the engine.

Molly stood up and walked to the pilothouse. She started the engine and put the gearshift in reverse. She could feel the bottom of the boat quake and quiver as Allan's boat pulled it away from the sandbar. She put the gearshift in neutral and stepped on deck. Allan eased his boat alongside hers.

"I wish I didn't have to go back," she said above the roar of the two engines. "For the first time I wished I didn't have to go home."

"I know, pet, but that's just delaying it. Come on, Charlie and I will be there with you." Allan smiled.

Molly nodded and turned back to the wheel.

Chapter Eighteen

Carolyn picked up the telephone in her office. It was six p.m. She was frustrated. She had tried to call Molly and now she was trying to reach Allan. After Auntie Em's call around noon, she had been frantic to talk with Molly. She could hear the telephone ring on the other end. Finally Allan answered.

"Hi, doll. You heard?" he asked.

"Auntie Em called earlier today."

"How'd she get your number?"

"I thought you'd given it to her."

"No, I haven't talked with her. Knowing her, though, she was determined to talk to you and she got it. She is one strong-headed woman."

"I like her." Carolyn hesitated. "I've tried to reach Molly several times, but no answer. I've been calling you and Charlie the rest of the time."

"Charlie's at a day-long conference. He was going to cancel when he heard about Molly's brother, but I told him there was nothing either of us could do."

"How is she?" Carolyn could sense Allan's hesitation. "Allen, how is she?"

"Dealing with it, but not very well."

"Is she at the jail with her brother?"

"Actually, right now she's with Auntie Em." Allan paused as he seemed to make up his mind about something. "Look, I may forever lose her friendship, but I think you should know. She's floundering right now. She's so angry at her brother she's questioning their relationship." He then told her about Tommy's comments about Molly's being a lesbian.

"Oh, no," Carolyn whispered, saddened. "No wonder she's not answering her telephone. I must have called her twenty times."

"She knows." Allan took a breath. "Carolyn, I don't know any easy way to say this. She doesn't want to talk to you."

"Why not?" Carolyn tried to keep her voice calm. "I don't understand."

"I'm not sure I do either. But if I were to make a guess, I think she's embarrassed. This problem with her brother, what happened between you, it's as though she's collapsing under the weight of it all. I'm worried about her."

"I've got to see her." Carolyn picked up her car keys and reached for her jacket. "I can be there in two hours. Is she at Auntie Em's? On her boat?"

"I left her with Auntie Em. I don't know if she's staying there or going to her boat. I tried to get her to come over here, but she didn't want to."

"If I can't find her, can I stay with you tonight?"

"Of course, love."

❧

Carolyn's nerves were jangled. She fiddled with her car radio and then turned it off. She had been driving for more than an hour. She reached for her Celine Dion CD. She popped it in and turned up the volume. Celine started to sing, "I drove all night to be with you." How appropriate, Carolyn thought.

She sighed. The usual enjoyment she felt when driving along Route One was not there. All she could think about was Molly and the what-ifs she had painted during the drive. "Quit it," she chastised herself.

Carolyn turned onto Route 189. She then headed down the long driveway to Auntie Em's house. She could see Auntie Em's porch light in the distance. She pulled around a curve and was disappointed when she didn't see Molly's truck. Carolyn parked. She was relieved—it was maybe nine o'clock, but the lights were still on.

Carolyn knocked softly.

"Land, yes, just the person I was hoping to see standing at my door," Auntie Em said as she opened the door and stepped out on the porch to give Carolyn a big hug.

Carolyn laughed. "Well, I'm glad to see you're happy to see me. I can't say that much for Molly."

"She'll be happy to see you. She's just stubborn. I gave her a talking-to tonight. Course it didn't do no good, but I felt better."

"About?"

"You. I asked her if she'd called you. She hadn't so I gave her a lecture. She just sat there saying nothing. She has that Bean stubborn streak, reaches a mile down to her toes."

"How is her brother?" Carolyn inquired.

"He still won't talk. His attorney called at suppertime, said he won't talk to him either. I tried to see him, but they wouldn't let me. I know I can talk some sense into that boy. I know he had nothing to do with this, but he's covering for Robbie." Auntie Em paused. "I told her I want you to be Tommy's lawyer. One he has is okay, but I know you'd be better."

203

Carolyn frowned. "Okay if I sit down?"

"Course, dear. How about a cup of coffee, some tea? I know just the thing, a nice glass of lemonade."

"Thank you." Carolyn watched as Auntie Em reached into the refrigerator. She took two glasses from the cupboard and poured lemonade into them. "I make this from real lemons, none of that powdery stuff for me." She sat a glass in front of Carolyn. "I saw that frown. What's the matter?"

Carolyn took a sip. "This is good. Thank you. Auntie Em . . ." Carolyn paused, uncertain how to start. "Something happened between Molly and me that makes it impossible for me to represent her brother. It would be a conflict of interest."

"You mean that stuff about what happened on the boat?"

"Molly talked about it?" Carolyn could hear the squeak in her voice.

"Heavens, no. But I could tell the minute I saw your faces when Allan and I came out to meet you."

Carolyn could feel the hot blush creep up her neck. She looked down at her drink. "I—"

"Don't be embarrassed, child," Auntie Em interrupted. "But why should that keep you from helping Tommy?"

"It has to do with ethics. Something like a doctor should never operate on a family member or close friend."

"But this is different."

"Not really. This is one of those no-win situations. But the reality is, I can't represent him." Carolyn could see the disappointment in Auntie Em's eyes. " I talked with his attorney before. He's good, someone who is close to the situation and can help Tommy. And I'll tell you, I think he genuinely cares."

"Well, if you can't help, you can't help." Auntie Em seemed uncomfortable.

"I really want to help," Carolyn said quickly. "But I can't. I know it sounds strange, but if I lost, neither you nor Molly would ever forgive me. So I would rather see the disappointment in your eyes now rather than later."

"But that's the point. I don't think he did it. So this isn't something you can lose."

"Aside from that"—Carolyn took another sip of lemonade—"I'm a stranger to him. There is no reason in the world for him to trust me and, quite frankly, I don't blame him. Now he has someone local, who knows the town politics, police, the judge." Carolyn tapped her finger against her palm as she emphasized each point. "I walk in, I don't know anyone."

"Maybe that's right, but how about you help his lawyer?"

"Auntie Em," Carolyn said as she took her hand, "it would be ethically wrong for me to get involved. I know that disappoints you, but I would rather tell you the truth now than lead you to believe I can make a difference."

Auntie Em slowly pulled her hand away and sat back. "Well, I didn't expect this," she said.

Carolyn folded her hands together. "I suspect Molly knows this and that's why she hasn't returned my telephone calls."

"Probably," Auntie Em said quietly. "But she's been spleeny lately."

Carolyn blinked. "Spleeny?"

"You know, out of sorts. Not herself." Auntie Em shrugged. "It happens to people. She's embarrassed. Right now she's more concerned about what people are saying than in getting her brother out of jail. She's dug a pit and bent over and put her head in it."

Carolyn smiled in spite of herself. "Well, it's a lot to take in and it is difficult. This is a small town and people are talking. I understand where she's coming from."

"True, but they'll get over it. Next week they'll be onto other juicy gossip."

"Probably." Carolyn stopped. "Is Molly on the boat?"

"That's where she said she was going."

"I'd like to see her." Carolyn stood up. "Look, Auntie Em, I will talk with Tommy's attorney see where things are going. I can do that much."

"I knew you'd help." Auntie Em smiled as she stood up and hugged Carolyn. "You're special."

"Don't get happy yet. I said I'd talk with his attorney. I didn't say I could make a difference."

"Don't matter. At least you're looking into it. That's what matters."

"We'll see." Carolyn looked at the clock on the wall. "I'd better get going."

"Course, you take care now."

"I will, Auntie Em," Carolyn said, hugging her one more time.

Carolyn thought about her conversation with Auntie Em as she drove toward the marina. She suspected that Molly wasn't going to ask her to be her brother's attorney. Molly was dealing with a lot more than who was representing her brother. Carolyn drove past the police station and down the ramp to the marina. She parked between a police car and Molly's truck. Carolyn felt a sense of dread as she looked at the police car. What more bad news, she wondered, could this family face?

She could see Molly's boat in the distance. Two people were in the pilothouse. As she got closer she saw that the woman with Molly was wearing a uniform. Molly had her face in her hands. Carolyn stepped quickly down the marina ramp toward the boat. Molly was evidently crying. Carolyn could feel her insides collapsing as she felt her lover's pain.

As she hurried down the ramp, she watched as if in slow motion as the police officer stepped toward Molly and took her in her arms. Carolyn stopped and stared. So this was Julie. Carolyn could see the woman rubbing Molly's back with her hand. She then tipped Molly's head back and kissed her. Carolyn swallowed and turned her back on the boat. Tears burned her eyes. She couldn't look. She walked back up the marina ramp and into the parking lot. She got in her car and slammed the door. *Well, why not,* she thought. *Who better to comfort Molly than her ex.* Carolyn turned the key in the switch and her Chevrolet SUV sprang to life. She pulled out of the driveway. *I gotta go home,* she thought. *I gotta go home.*

Chapter Nineteen

"What the hell are you doing?" Molly said as she pushed Julie away from her. "You come here to apologize and you kiss me?"

"I'm sorry, Molly. You just looked so sad, then you started to cry and you let me hold you and I just felt this desire to kiss you. You kissed me back."

"Old habits." Molly could feel her anger ramp up. True, she had kissed Julie back, but she had so wanted the lips to be Carolyn's. Molly turned from Julie, embarrassed that she had been so foolish.

Julie reached out and touched Molly's shoulder and Molly recoiled. "That wasn't old habits. You kissed me back." Julie stepped toward her.

Molly dropped her head and rubbed a hand across her forehead. She said softly, "I wasn't kissing you." She put even more distance between them. "I wasn't kissing you." She said in a stronger voice, "I'm sorry, I wasn't kissing you."

Julie's jaw tightened. "I don't believe that."

"Believe it, Julie. I don't love you anymore. I wasn't kissing you." Molly felt contentment cleanse her.

"Carolyn?"

Molly stepped to the wheel of her boat.

"Look, Molly, I said I was sorry that I lied to you about your brother being arrested. I was so jealous. I saw you coming from that boat and I just knew you'd been with that woman."

"That's none of your business," Molly said curtly. "I don't want you in my life. I'm sorry I let you hold me. I—" She stopped. She could feel her anger sharpening. "You know, Julie, you haven't read me right from the day we met. Then tonight you come in here apologizing and saying you're all sorry. Tell me my brother is still being stone-faced and when I start to cry out of fear and frustration, you take advantage of the situation. You have no feelings, lady. None whatsoever. I want you to leave."

"Look, Molly, I'm sorry. I screwed up. I'm still in love with you."

Molly could hear the uncertainty in Julie's voice. She said bluntly, "I'm not in love with you."

"Are you in love with Carolyn?"

Cat purred as it rubbed against Molly's legs. "That's also none of your business." She picked up Cat. "Julie, I don't know any other words to say it: I. Don't. Love. You. It's really that simple." Saying the words gave her a surge of power. "I'd like you to leave," she said as she opened the door to the pilothouse. "Julie, I will never ever again have a discussion with you about my brother. I don't want you to talk to me about him. I don't want updates from you about him. I don't want you in my life. If I need to know something, I want to hear it from Billy."

"Molly, I'm sorry—"

"It doesn't matter anymore how you feel. I really don't care if you're sorry or sad. I just don't care," Molly said emphatically. "Now, I'd like you to leave." Molly watched as Julie stepped through the door. She quietly closed it behind her. Julie turned and looked at

Molly through the window. Molly could see the tears in her eyes. *Funny, even the tears don't matter,* Molly thought. She watched as Julie headed up the ramp. "Well, Cat. it looks like it's just you and me." Molly set Cat on the bulkhead. "Come on, I'll feed you."

Just then her telephone rang. It was Allan.

"You sound better," he said.

"Well, not a whole lot better but somewhat better." She then told him about Julie kissing her.

"You sound relieved, pet."

"I am. After the breakup, I always thought if she came back into my life I might take her back. But not now and I am certain of that, Allan. I really am. I've got to call Carolyn."

"You'll probably get her on her cell phone. She called a little while ago, said she was going to Auntie Em's. She was really upset."

"Carolyn's here?" Molly was surprised. "She's upset? I don't understand."

"Molly, I love you dearly, but sometimes you are a swamp dog, and I mean that affectionately," he added quickly. "She was upset because she has called you more than a dozen times and you didn't return her calls. She was scared and lonely and upset."

"I'm an ass, pure and simple. I'm going to feed Cat and then go over to Auntie Em's to see Carolyn. I'm going to take her in my arms and beg her forgiveness. No, better yet, I'll get on my hands and knees and beg her forgiveness. Allan, I love her. I really, really love her. I've been riding this guilt trip about Tommy. It's not all gone, but it doesn't hurt as much. I've got to find her and tell her I love her."

"Welcome back to the world, girlfriend. We all knew you loved her."

Molly laughed. "So hit me on the head with a pumpkin."

"Naw, I won't do that. Just go get her, Molly. Grovel if you have to but get her back."

"I will, sweets," Molly said. "I'll call you later after I've spoken to her."

"Good. See ya, pet."

" 'Bye, darlin'." Molly flipped the cover on her cell phone and stuck it in her pocket. "Come on, Cat, time for your feed and time for me to get out of here," Molly said as she stepped down into the cabin.

Molly hummed as she drove toward Auntie Em's. She still had to deal with the problems with her brother, but at least she had her heart on straight when it came to Carolyn. She had promised Allan she would grovel—crawl was more like it—if she had to.

She turned into Auntie Em's driveway and frowned when she didn't see another car besides Auntie Em's.

Molly jumped out of her truck and ran up the porch steps. "Auntie Em," she called. "Is Carolyn here?"

"No, dear," Auntie Em said as she came from her bedroom. "She left more than thirty minutes ago. She was going to the boat to find you. You two must have missed each other by minutes."

Molly could feel her stomach drop. Not by minutes, she thought. Carolyn must have seen Julie kissing her and left. "Can I use your telephone?"

"Course, dear."

Molly dialed Allan's number. She drummed her fingers as it rang. "Hello, sweets. Look, is Carolyn there?" Molly frowned when he said no. "Do you have her cell phone number?" Molly picked up the pen that was on Auntie Em's telephone table and wrote down the number. "Look, something happened, but I'll tell you later. Right now I've got to talk to Carolyn." Molly rang off, looked at the piece of paper and punched in the numbers. She waited impatiently as the telephone rang and rang. She hung up when she heard the recorded message about the customer being away from the telephone. She looked at the number again and punched them into the telephone. Molly tapped her foot as the telephone continued to ring. "She's not answering."

"Seems to be a lot of that going around lately," Auntie Em scoffed.

"I've got to find her." Molly started toward the door but stopped when the telephone rang. It was Billy wanting her to come to the police station. "Can I bring Auntie Em?" Molly laughed. "Fat chance of leaving her home," she said as she hung up.

"Something happening with Tommy?" Molly could hear the anxiety in Auntie Em's voice.

"He wants to talk to me." Molly stared at the window. "Funny, at first that's all I wanted to do was talk with him, now I want to rush and find Carolyn. How many directions can one person be pulled in?" Molly wondered out loud.

"As many as it takes." Auntie Em grabbed Molly's arm. "Come on, let's get over there before he changes his mind. He wants to see us."

Molly dug her heels into the linoleum. "Wait just a minute. Now, you know Billy said Tommy only wants to talk to me."

"Don't matter," Auntie Em said, picking up her pocketbook. "I can be there, lend you some moral support. I know he'll feel the vibes once I'm there. Start to feel better."

Molly hesitated.

"I know you're thinking about her, but family comes first right now. Your brother needs you."

"I know, Auntie Em. I feel miserable. I should be going after her, instead I'm chasing after my brother's problems yet again."

Molly stood at the booking desk looking at the posters on the wall. Auntie Em was seated on a worn brown bench thumbing through a two-month-old copy of *National Geographic*. Molly decided she'd feel better if she paced back and forth in front of the desk. When they had first arrived, Fibber was at the desk. She had asked to speak with her brother and Fibber had gone into a back room. When he returned he had told Molly to wait, that the lieutenant wanted to speak with her first. Molly stopped pacing and again tried to read the posters.

"Miss Bean?" the lieutenant said from behind her.

"Yes." Molly turned.

"I'd like to speak to you before you speak with your brother." Lieutenant Gardiner gestured toward an office.

"I want to come." Auntie Em stood up.

"I'm sorry, I would rather speak with Ms. Bean."

"Too bad," Auntie Em huffed. "Where she goes, I go."

The lieutenant shrugged. Molly suppressed a smile. He had Auntie Em's back up and she wasn't about to back down.

Molly stepped aside to let Auntie Em enter the office first. Auntie Em sat down in a chair in front of the desk. Molly sat down next to her.

"You wanted to see me, lieutenant?"

"Yes," he said as he fiddled with the papers on the desk. He was studiously avoiding eye contact. She waited. "Your brother has asked for you. Ordinarily, in situations like this, I wouldn't let the perp— your brother . . . talk to you, but maybe it will help."

"Anything my brother tells me that he asks me to keep confidential, I'm not going to divulge. You can put me in a cell next to him, but if he says to keep it quiet, I will." Molly was surprised at her own matter-of-fact tone. She was mad at her brother but knew in her heart she wasn't going to help this cop.

The detective rubbed the back of his hand against his day-old beard. Molly could hear his hand as it scraped against the prickly stubble. "Why don't we just wait and see what he has to say before we get our backs up. Okay?" Molly could hear the tiredness in the lieutenant's voice.

"Agreed. Now when can I see him?"

"Now, just follow me." Lieutenant Gardner turned to Auntie Em. "I'm sorry, ma'am, he's just asking for his sister. Wouldn't be right if you go in there too." Molly braced herself for the explosion she knew was just behind Auntie Em's lips.

"I understand," Auntie Em said quietly. "I understand."

Molly reached out and put a hand on her shoulder. "It's okay, Auntie Em. Let me talk with him first, then you can go in and see him. Might be that he wants to tell me before he has to tell you. You know he loves you."

"I know." Auntie Em didn't look at her.

Molly followed the lieutenant down a hallway to another room. The door was closed. "You'll be alone in there with him. But my officers will be right outside this door. So if this is some kind of trick and your brother thinks he can get away, tell him to forget it."

Molly nodded as he opened the door. Two officers stepped outside and the lieutenant motioned for her to go in.

Molly was shocked as she looked closely at her brother's blotchy face. His eyes were almost as red as his hair. "Hi," she said quietly.

"Hi yourself."

Molly pulled out a chair opposite her brother. She sat down and waited.

Her brother traced a circle on the table with his finger. "I wanted to talk to you."

Molly nodded, afraid to test her voice.

"Look, I'm sorry, Molly, about that other stuff. I was coming down off a high that nearly killed me and I was angry and sad and scared . . ."

"It's okay." Molly could feel her throat tightening.

"No, it wasn't. It wasn't true, Molly. I've never really had a problem with your being a lesbian—not once I got older. I didn't understand it, but it didn't bother me. It was hard when I was a kid, I was teased a lot about my sister liking girls, other stuff that I don't want to repeat."

"I'm so sorry, Tommy. Honest, it wasn't something I planned."

"I know. I figured that out later, much later. This age difference between us has been a bummer. Ma always said it was because she

214

wanted one grown before she raised another, but we both know that was Ma's way of covering up the fact that I was an accident."

Molly smiled. "You figured that out."

"Actually, that's another one I was constantly teased about by the other kids. But I got over it. Hey, I figure an accident is better than not happening at all." Tommy tried but failed to muster a smile.

"If I'd known, Tommy, we could have talked about this sooner. Not now while you're sitting in jail."

"That's something else I wanted to tell you." Tommy reached across the table and took Molly's hands. "I didn't kill that professor," he said, his voice soft, almost inaudible. "It could have been me, Molly. We was doing drugs, talking about money. I was supposed to be there, but I did a lotta drugs that night. Anyway, I passed out. Probably the luckiest pass-out of my life."

"Thank God." Molly could feel the tension being stripped from her shoulders. "Have you told the police?"

"No, and I'm not going to. If I do it will implicate others. I can't do that."

"I don't understand. You're saying you know who murdered that woman."

"No, I'm not saying that either. I'm saying that I wasn't involved and, funny, since I've been sitting in here, I really wanted you to know that. I may be a lot of things, but I'm not a killer. No one was supposed to die. She was supposed to be away, then from what I been told she was there and things got out of hand."

"Tell the police," Molly said, rising from her chair.

"No." Tommy put a hand on Molly's arm and eased her back into the chair.

"Then tell me."

"Uh-huh," he said quietly. "But I just wanted you to know. You can tell Auntie Em, but no one else."

"I don't understand. You're going to go to jail for someone else's crime?"

"I don't think it'll come to that. I think the cops are going to solve it soon without any help from me. The lieutenant said they found a ski mask nearby and the hairs inside didn't belong to me. They've taken every bodily sample from me they could. They're pretty certain the ski mask is connected to the murder. I think they'll figure it out and I won't have to rat out my friends." Tommy stopped.

"That's crazy," Molly blurted. "Absolutely nutso."

"Probably." Tommy's smile was tired. His face was stressed to the maximum. "But I've got to keep my word. I told someone I wouldn't say anything and I ain't going to. But I wanted you and Auntie Em to know the truth. I didn't want to have Auntie Em see me now. I look like shit."

Molly smiled. "I'm not going to argue that one."

"Molly." Tommy reached across the table and took both her hands in his. "I've been a screwup my whole life, and this may seem strange, but somehow because I gave my word, regardless of the consequences, it's important I keep it." He looked at her, conviction in his eyes. "I've got to start being responsible somewhere."

"This lieutenant is going to put you in jail. Your lawyer said that by not telling, you're obstructing justice and can be sent to jail."

"I know. But this is something I've got to do. Not for anyone else but me. I've somehow got to get my integrity back. At night in the cell, I just lie there and think about my life, and I know Auntie Em raised me better than what I've become. I'm a drug addict, I'm going to have to face that. Right now, I feel strong, tired, but determined to get clean." He paused. "But once I get out, I may backslide, I'm going to need you and Auntie Em by my side. I know I'm going to need help."

"Of course." Molly could feel tears burning her eyes.

"Oh, don't do tears," Tommy whispered, stricken. "I can't have my big tough sister crying. How'd it look in front of the other lobstermen?"

"Well, you're not going to get a vote in this one, little brother," Molly said, wiping the tears on her sleeve. "Anything, Tommy, anything you need I'll do for you, know that. Somehow all these years we've been like two boats drifting side by side, now finally we're bumping into each other. You know I'll do anything to help you."

"I know." Tommy looked away but she could see the tears in his eyes. "Well." He cleared his throat. "Give Auntie Em a big hug for me, okay, and right now I need a big hug from my sister." He stood up.

Molly stood up and walked around the table. "Come here." She pulled her brother to her. She felt his large hands slide around her and he pulled her tightly against him. "I'm going to cry," Molly said against his shoulder.

"I know," Tommy said gently. "I know."

Molly returned to where she had left Auntie Em. When she opened the door, the lieutenant and Auntie Em were just where she had left them.

"How is he?" Auntie Em said, getting up.

"Fine." Molly put her arms around her aunt. She looked over her shoulder and said to the lieutenant, "He knows who did it."

"We figured. I had hoped that he would tell you."

"He did, indirectly. It's definitely Robbie. That's about the only friend on this earth he'd go through this for." Molly paused. "Actually, I think it's more than that. I think he's going through it for himself. These drugs have robbed him of so much. I think that by remaining loyal to Robbie, in his mind he's getting some of his self-respect back. A hell of a way to test his character, but I think it's a way for him to begin the healing process." Molly shook her head. "Of course, the only person who is being honorable here is my brother. Robbie certainly hasn't come forward to get Tommy off the hook."

"You know he's going to be charged once this is over with," the lieutenant said.

"Why?" Auntie Em, indignant, advanced upon the lieutenant. "He didn't do anything. He didn't kill that woman."

"Auntie Em," Molly said, grabbing her gently by the arm. "The lieutenant isn't the enemy here. How can we help?"

"I don't know," the lieutenant said wearily. "Your brother has been here for several days now and although we have a pretty good idea of who did it, we don't have anything solid enough to arrest anyone on."

"Why don't you question Robbie?" Molly asked.

"We have, several times. Claims he was with another man. Said they were doing drugs and passed out. We questioned the other guy. He claims he was with Robbie. They've rehearsed their stories. We split them up, hoping to get one to roll over on the other, but right now they're singing the same tune. Even told Robbie that someone had put him at the house. Robbie's one cool guy—he told us to arrest him."

"He knows that someone is Tommy and that's why he dared you to arrest him. He knows my brother won't say a thing against him."

"All we can do is just keep following leads."

"Not me," Auntie Em said. She squared her shoulders. "I'm going over to Robbie's and I'm not leaving until he tells me what he did."

"Whoa, tiger," Molly said. "You're not going anywhere. Robbie's dangerous, and if he's cornered, no telling what he'll do. You're not going over there, promise me." She gave Auntie Em a stern look. "Promise me."

Auntie Em dropped her head. "I promise."

"No way, old lady. Look me in the eye and promise."

"I promise," Auntie Em said, looking Molly in the eye.

After she dropped Auntie Em off, Molly returned to the boat. She tried Carolyn's cell phone again. She had called her repeatedly since she had returned to the boat. She had called her office, her home telephone and her cell phone. Finally she punched in Allan's telephone number and listened as it rang.

"Hello?" a groggy voice said.

"Allan? Oh, God, I woke you up. What time is it?" she said, looking at her wall clock for the first time since she'd been home.

"I was asleep, Molly. I don't usually keep track of the time in my sleep."

Molly sat down on the edge of her bed. "It's one o'clock in the morning. Allan, I'm so sorry. I didn't bother to look at the time after I got home. It's been a long night."

"That's okay, hon. Carolyn hasn't called. I tried calling her, but I didn't get an answer. Charlie tried also."

"Oh, man, I don't know what to do. First my brother, now this."

"What happened with your brother?"

"He's doing the strong silent type. Trouble is, he isn't the strong silent type." Molly sighed. "We talked, that was good. He seems all right with the lesbian thing. He also knows who killed the professor. Thank God he wasn't involved."

"Who?"

"Won't say. For some reason he's decided to walk the high moral ground. Says that he's not going to point the finger because he—" Molly took a deep breath. "Actually, while he was telling me it sounded logical, but now as I try to explain it, it all sounds like crap. He believes that morally, ethically, he can't rat out his friends."

"Wow, I don't know what to say." Allan cleared his throat. "Any idea who he's protecting?"

"Robbie. They were best friends growing up. They hung together all the time. Tommy wasn't part of any in-group and I think he and Robbie saw themselves as the outsiders, so they just hung together. Some other guy's also involved. I don't know who. I think Tommy knows, but he's not saying. He's just not talking."

"Any chance Robbie might do the honorable thing and turn himself in?"

"Not likely. I don't remember Robbie ever doing the honorable thing, even when they were kids. They got caught, seems to me Tommy always took the blame." Molly sat down on the side of the bed. "You know, I hadn't thought about that in years, but you know I'm right. They were playing baseball at the school one time where they weren't supposed to be playing—this was before my mother died. They broke a window at the school. Tommy got caught and was suspended for a couple of days. I learned later that Robbie was the one who hit the ball."

"Old habits."

"Yeah, and my brother's paying for it."

"What are you going to do?"

"Right now, let you go back to sleep. Go to bed. Get up, call Carolyn. Pull some traps, I haven't been out for several days. Then go over and talk to my brother again. Call Carolyn."

"Why don't you go to Bar Harbor and talk to her. Grovel if you must, but talk to her."

Molly felt a disembodied calm float over her. "I don't know what I would do without you. I'm so lousy at this falling-in-love stuff. I will go to Bar Harbor. I'll beg, grovel, whatever it takes." Molly paused. "God, why didn't I think of that?"

"Don't beat yourself up, love. You've got a lot to worry about with your brother."

"You're my best girlfriend."

"You say that to all your girls." Allan chuckled quietly. "Charlie sends his love."

"Love back. I'll talk to you tomorrow. You going to be at the university?"

"For part of the day. Tomorrow the countdown begins to the end of classes. Another two weeks, exams start, so it'll be squirrely over there, but we seem to get through."

Molly laughed. "Sorry I woke you. Get some sleep."

"You too, babe," Allan said softly.

Chapter Twenty

Molly cut the engine on her boat and stepped on deck. Kevin swung his long legs up on the pier and Molly tossed him first the sternline and then bowline. "We going out tomorrow?" Kevin asked as he secured the bowline.

"Don't know yet. I may go to Bar Harbor. I'll call you tonight, let you know."

Kevin nodded. "You expect Auntie Em be back with you soon?"

"I expect. She's been busy lately." Molly stopped. "That's not accurate. Actually she's been anxious lately what with all this stuff going on about my brother, but I think she wants to come back. This thing with my brother has knocked her sea legs out from under her. Why?"

"Just that I was thinking I need to get back helping Dad. My brother isn't happy doing the job that I love to do."

Molly nodded. "Of course, Kevin. I wasn't thinking. Your dad comes first."

"He said I should work with you as long as you need me, but I just wanted to know if I should make other plans."

Molly smiled. "I've not been at my best lately, Kevin. I'm sorry. Look, give me a couple more days. By then I'll know if Auntie Em's coming back. If not, then I'll make plans to hire another sternman."

Molly stopped when she heard the phone ring. Billy wanted her to come right over. Molly agreed then clicked the off button on her cell phone. She felt like she had stepped into the vortex of a storm again. "Look, Kevin . . ."

"It's all right, Molly. I expect you have more important things right now. Call me if you need me."

"Thanks." Molly was relieved Kevin hadn't asked.

Molly arrived at the police station, parked her car and ran up the stairs. If one more thing happened in her life, she thought, she would explode. They would find bits and pieces of her all over the town.

When she opened the door she saw several Gin Cove policemen talking near the front counter. She was relieved that Julie was not with them.

"Hi, Fibber." Molly cleared her throat. She nodded to the other police officers. "I understand you have Auntie Em here."

The other police officers turned away, but not before Molly saw the smirks on their faces. "We do, Molly," Fibber said.

"Is she in jail?"

"No, she's in with Billy. She had a bit of a tussle with Robbie."

Molly groaned. "What kind of a tussle?"

"Billy said he wanted to tell you." Fibber coughed.

"Is there something funny going on here?" Molly could feel her blood pressure rise.

"Look, why don't I let Billy know you're here?"

Molly ran both her hands through her hair. "Thanks." She watched as Fibber stepped through the door to Billy's office. He closed the door. The other police officers continued to avoid making eye contact with her. She was relieved when the door opened and Billy walked out. Fibber was just steps behind him.

"Molly, glad you're here. Why don't you come over here a minute. I want to talk with you before I let you see Auntie Em." Molly followed him outside.

"Billy, what's wrong? Have you arrested Auntie Em?"

"Well, not quite. Seems that she went looking for Robbie today."

Molly groaned. "Did he hurt her?" She tried to quell the panic rising inside her.

"Well, no." Billy bit his bottom lip to keep from smiling. "Actually, the one who got hurt was Robbie."

Molly scowled at him. "I don't understand."

"Well, it seems Auntie Em went looking for him and found him down on Main Street. When she tried to talk him, he—and I only have this from what she told me because Robbie was taken to the hospital—he supposedly pushed her away and called her an old bat. He then went to get in his truck, but Auntie Em was closer to her car, and she may be seventy years old but eyewitnesses said she hot-footed it to her car, got in and just rammed the side of his truck, pushed it into the curb. When he tried to back up to get away, she took that little car of hers and put it in reverse, got behind him and rammed it right up his exhaust pipe. I never seen anything like it." Billy couldn't hold back the laughter. "I got there, it looked like those two cars were joined together. A Ford truck with a tiny Chevrolet rear."

"Was she hurt?"

"Heavens, no. She had a seat belt on. Got out of the car, walked up to Robbie and told him he should have had his seat belt on. His face had hit the steering wheel and he was bleeding from the nose and mouth. Then she told him if he didn't tell her what happened that night, she was going to take a baseball bat to him. She grabbed him by the hair and pulled hard. By the time they pulled her off him, she had a chunk of hair and he was yelling he wanted the police."

"Did he confess?"

"That's the funny part. He said just enough that the Maine State Police are interested." Billy was still laughing. "I've never seen anything like it."

Molly started to laugh. "I can't believe her, and she promised me she'd not do anything."

"Well, she explained that one." Billy wiped his eyes. "She said she was at home and she was getting madder and madder. Said she just went to talk to him, but when he pushed her and called her an old bat, said she could feel the steam coming out of her ears and she let him have it."

"Tell me she didn't have a baseball bat."

"Not that we could find."

"Oh God, first my brother, now my aunt." Molly turned serious. "Wait a minute. Billy, you going to charge her?"

He scratched his head. "I don't know. I talked with the lieutenant. Seems if they get enough to charge Robbie for murder, then it's not likely he's going to have much to say about his truck because he won't be using it. Could be a civil suit, don't know. Right now, I'm looking for you to take her home. I gave her a good talking-to."

"What she say?"

"She'd do it again." Billy preceded Molly back up the stairs and into the police station. "Do me a favor. Right now she thinks I might charge her. I even demanded she hand over her driver's license. Of course she didn't know that she didn't have to turn it over, but she did. So let it be at that. I don't want her in some rental car running down anyone else who might be connected with the crime."

"I'll help. Anyway, I want to keep that senior citizen terminator off the highway. I can't believe she did it."

"Well, she did." Billy opened the door to his office. "Auntie Em, Molly's here."

"Don't start." Auntie Em was in a rage.

"Could I give you a hug first and tell you I'm glad you're not hurt?" Molly said as she took Auntie Em in her arms and held her tightly against her. "Can we start with that?"

"Okay, but don't start with the lecture. I've been listening to this junior cop for the past hour, and by the way"—Auntie Em stepped back and pointed her finger at the chief—"I did change your diapers once."

Molly watched as Billy turned away and put his hand over his mouth to keep from smiling.

"What you did was wrong," Molly said to her. "You could have killed someone."

"Nonsense. I didn't hit him that hard. Cheap cars nowadays. Metal crumples, always looks worse than it is. He wouldn't've been hurt either, he'd been wearing a seat belt." Auntie Em turned on Billy. "You charging him for not wearing a seat belt? It's the law in this state, you know. I had mine on."

"Right now, Auntie Em, all I want is for you to get out of here. I think the best place for you is at home, making some apple pies or something."

"Don't you patronize me." Auntie Em was getting her back up again.

Molly grabbed her by the arm. "Come on, Arnold Schwarzenegger, let's get out of here before they throw you in a cell next to Tommy."

"Wouldn't bother me a bit," Auntie Em yelled as Molly dragged her out the door. "Jail don't scare me a bit."

"Well, it scares the hell out of me," Molly said as she pulled Auntie Em out of the police station and toward her car. "What the hell were you thinking? He could have killed you. We're going to the boat, I'm going to feed Cat and then we're going to your house and you're going to stay put."

"You can't guard me every minute."

"No, but I sure can try. Tomorrow, you're going on the boat with me. You got way too much time on your hands."

Molly started up her truck. She looked over at Auntie Em, whose jaw was set as tight as a bear trap.

"You could have been hurt," Molly said softly.

"I couldn't just sit there and not do anything. It was driving me crazy, what with Robbie running around and Tommy sitting in jail. I had to do something."

"They could charge you."

"Don't matter. I wanted Robbie to know I meant business. I think I got his attention. He sure was hollering when I grabbed hold of his hair." Auntie Em paused. "Funny, the police took the hair from me."

"Probably to throw away. What?" Molly looked over at her. "You going to keep it as a souvenir?"

"Possibly. I want Carolyn as my attorney. I need good representation," Auntie Em said matter-of-factly. "Before, she said something about not being able to help Tommy 'cause she was involved with you. Well, she can help me as I'm not direct family."

"I don't think it works like that. Besides"—Molly could feel her depression growing as she thought about Carolyn—"she isn't answering her telephone."

"That's because she's gone away for a few days."

"How'd you know that?" Molly asked, surprised.

"I called her office. Her secretary said she taken a couple of days off. Said she'd be back on Monday."

Molly shook her head. So much for going to Bar Harbor. "I called her office. I didn't get any answer."

"Probably didn't call at the right time. I called several times, finally got an answer. That's what the secretary said. I left my name and number and asked her to call me. I expect she will. I told her I had some legal issues."

"You're amazing."

"You just figure that out?" Auntie Em shook her head.

"No, I've known that most of my life." Molly reached over and squeezed her hand. "I love you, Auntie Em."

"Course ya do. Now let's stop with all this nonsense, get Cat fed and go home. I'm hungry."

Chapter Twenty-One

Molly threw the rope over the snatch block and listened as it whirred. She reached down and grabbed the trap and shoved it across the gunwale to Auntie Em. For the past several days she had kept Auntie Em close to her. She couldn't keep her mind from drifting to the demolition derby scene her aunt had been a part of. After they had returned to Auntie Em's that night, Molly prepared supper and then Auntie Em had gone to bed. Molly smiled to herself as she remembered Auntie Em's words—that she'd had a busy day and was tired. Molly had gone out and sat on the swing where she and Carolyn had sat. How much nicer the swing had felt that night. Now all she could think about was Carolyn. She felt apprehensive, restless. What if Carolyn had gone back to the woman in California? Molly felt her stomach tighten again. She had a brother in jail, an aunt headed for jail and the woman she loved back with her former lover. All in all it had been a pretty good year, she thought cynically.

Molly looked up when Auntie Em tapped her on the arm. She was pointing toward a boat that was headed toward them. Molly's heart skipped a beat. She looked at the boat as it came closer and was disappointed when the boat turned out to be Allan's and not Carolyn's.

"Wonder what he's doing out here?" Auntie Em said.

"Don't know." Molly pushed the trap into the water and turned her boat toward Allan's advancing boat.

Allan drew alongside. Charlie stepped out on deck and threw her a line.

"What you doing out here?" Molly asked as Allen cut the engine on his boat.

"You sure are hard to find. We've been to every one of your trap sites, finally found you here," Charlie said.

"Why didn't you radio me? I'd've told you where I was."

" 'Cause we wanted to tell you face to face," Allan said. "Robbie's been arrested. It's all over the radio. He's been charged with murder."

"I knew it," Auntie Em said with a smile.

Molly felt the melancholy she'd been under for weeks lift. "When, where, what happened?"

"Well, he was picked up last night, charged with murder today. The radio said that charges were pending against another individual," Charlie said with a broad smile.

"There's more," Allan added. "The word on campus is that Auntie Em's lock of hair from Robbie's head helped unravel the case. They tested it and all that stuff. I don't know the details, but it's enough to get Tommy out of jail."

Auntie Em smiled mischievously at Molly. "See, I told you."

"Don't start, Ms. Terminator," Molly chided her.

"We heard all about it." Allan laughed. "It's all over town. Everybody's been over to Smith's Garage to take a picture of Auntie Em's car coupled with Robbie's."

"I like that." Auntie Em arched her eyebrow. "My car coupled with Robbie's. Has a bit of a ring to it."

"Stop," Molly said to Allan and Charlie. "Don't encourage her. Next thing you know she'll start running others off the road if she gets her mind set."

"Anyway, this calls for a celebration. I expect you'll go over to the jail to see your brother and after that it's dinner at our house."

"You inviting Carolyn?" Auntie Em asked.

Charlie shrugged. "I am going to try a couple of places where we used to hang out, but I don't know. She's just not answering her cell phone."

Molly felt her spirits fall. "I had hoped you'd heard from her by now."

"Sorry, kitten. We haven't," Allan said kindly.

"Let's just call this a little celebration," Charlie said. "We'll have a big celebration when she gets back. Right now, we're having dinner with you, Auntie Em and a few other friends and Tommy, of course. You up for that, Auntie Em?"

"Absolutely." She reached over and touched Molly's hand. "And so is Molly. It'd be better if Carolyn was there, but we have lots to celebrate tonight."

"Maybe we're being a little premature, calling it a celebration," Molly said reflectively. "I want my brother out of jail. He doesn't have much to celebrate."

"Well, let's go get him," Auntie Em said. "I expect they already told him. That's a huge weight off that boy's shoulders. Besides, if that clump of hair helped, then that should mean something toward helping Tommy. It's my clump of hair."

Molly laughed. "God, you are impossible. I'll head in now. Stop by the jail. We'll be over after that."

"Great," Charlie said and held out his hands. Molly tossed him the bow rope. "See you tonight, and bring a smile and your brother," he yelled as Allan started up the engine on his boat.

"Golly, my stomach's churning," Auntie Em said. "I feel like my butterflies have butterflies."

"Me too. Come on, we can haul the rest of these tomorrow. I want to get to the jail and find out what's happening with Tommy."

Molly and Auntie Em waited next to the desk in the police department. As soon as they arrived, they asked for Lieutenant Gardiner. Once again they waited.

Molly looked up when the lieutenant opened the door. "I expected to see you two today." He did not smile as he gestured for them to come into the office.

"Well, I heard you finally did the right thing and arrested Robbie. When can Tommy go home? Can we take him now? I understand I helped break the case. Should mean something toward getting him out," Auntie Em said in a rapid-fire barrage.

"Hold on there," the lieutenant said. "Yes, we are going to release Tommy, but he's been charged."

Molly looked up. "Charged? With what?"

"Obstruction of justice. This case would have been behind us a lot quicker if he'd told us what he knew."

"What? That he got high with a couple of guys and they went out and killed a woman?" Auntie Em asked. Clearly she was angry. "So you've charged him. Well, uncharge him."

"Look—" The lieutenant held up his hand as if to stop another onslaught of Auntie Em's questions. "He's been charged, but I don't expect he'll see any jail time. There are extenuating circumstances here." Molly noticed a brief smile dance on the edge of his mouth. "The hair sample helped. We were able to match hair samples we found near the scene."

"Humph. Seems to me that counts for a lot, since you folks weren't getting anywhere."

Molly placed her hand on Auntie Em's arm. "What about Auntie Em, she going to be charged with anything?"

"Not by us, and I don't think the local boys are going to charge her either. Although we don't encourage civilian help in solving a case, in this instance it did help."

"Course it helped." Auntie Em was unrelenting.

"Can we take Tommy home?" Molly asked, to change the subject.

"You can pick him up in a few minutes at the jail."

"'Bout time." Auntie Em said.

"Anything else?"

"I understand from the radio that another guy may be charged."

"Yes, but I'm not saying anything else until he's been arrested."

Molly nodded. "You going to need Auntie Em or me for anything else?"

"Well, if Robbie decides to take this to trial, Auntie Em will be called to testify."

"Her? Why?" Molly said, alarmed.

"We don't want his attorney making a case that the police put Auntie Em up to crashing into the car and getting some of his hair."

"Well, you didn't," Auntie Em huffed.

"Exactly. More than likely, it won't happen. I suspect Robbie's going to try to plea bargain this down, get himself a lighter sentence. He says he's not the one who killed the woman." The lieutenant nodded toward the door. "Now, that's all I'm going to say about this case. Do me a favor," he said to Molly, "get your aunt and your brother out of here. I've had enough Beans in my life."

"Finest kind," Auntie Em said. "We had enough of you."

Molly stood up and grabbed her aunt by the arm. "We're going," she said as she pushed Auntie Em out the door. "Thanks for all your help, lieutenant."

Déjà vu, Molly thought as she reflected on the weeks before when she and Auntie Em had waited for Tommy to come out of the jail. But this time, unlike the sullen brother who had emerged from jail the last time, Tommy grabbed first Molly and then Auntie Em and hugged them.

"Freedom feels wonderful," Tommy said.

Molly pulled Tommy to her a second time. "Welcome back, little brother," she said quietly.

"Thanks."

Auntie Em put her arms through his. "We're all invited to Allan and Charlie's tonight for dinner, and you're the guest of honor. They want to celebrate. We want to celebrate."

Molly braced herself, waiting for her brother to wiggle out of the invitation.

"I would love to see them," he said.

"And they would love to see you," Molly said softly.

"This *is* a celebration," he said as he linked his arm through Molly's. "I know I'm probably going back to jail, but you know what? I don't care."

"Well, I do," Auntie Em groused.

Tommy looked quizzically at Molly.

"Auntie Em feels," Molly said quickly, "that because of what she did, you shouldn't have to spend any time in jail."

Tommy grinned. "Auntie Em, you're famous—no, I would say infamous. That story was all over the jail. You're a hero. There are probably forty men in there who wished they had an Auntie Em."

Embarrassment was etched on Auntie Em's face. "Well, it wasn't nothing. He just got my temper churning like hurricane seas and I had to do something about it. Imagine pushing a seventy-year-old woman."

"I wouldn't think of doing something like that," Tommy said as he clasped her hand. "I understand he's still smarting from where you yanked his hair out."

"Come on, you two," Molly said, as she held the door open to her truck. "Get in and let's get back to life."

"I was thinking, Molly," Tommy said as Molly started up the engine. "If you're looking for a sternman, I'd like to volunteer. I got rehab to go through, but I was talking to the counselor at the jail. That's going to take some time, but a lot of it I can do right here in

Gin Cove. I know I've got some jail time facing me, but I'd like to be out there with you."

"Well . . ." Molly glanced at Auntie Em. "The job does belong to Auntie Em."

"Lord, don't think I want the job." Auntie Em patted Molly on the arm. "I enjoyed it and occasionally I'd like to go out with you, maybe give Tommy a Saturday off, but I'd like it if you'd hire your brother."

"It's a deal. The job's yours for as long or as short as you want it. You want to find something else? Tommy, do it."

"Thanks."

For the first time in weeks, Molly felt good about going to the boat. She had dropped her brother and aunt off at Auntie Em's house and now she was headed toward the marina. At last, she thought, she could concentrate on pulling traps. Well, almost concentrate. She wanted to change her clothes before going over to Allan's and Charlie's. Carolyn was out of her life, and that biting pain would not go away. She pulled up to the marina and parked. She reached in the bed of her truck for her gear. She tossed the bag over her shoulder and walked toward her boat.

"Hey, Molly," Kevin yelled. "Glad about your brother." He strode toward her.

"Thanks, Kevin. Looks like you can get back to working with your dad."

"Awesome. I know he'll be glad. My brother just don't care about lobstering like I do. Dad said he's going to loan me the money for a small boat. I'm going to start my own business."

"That's great, Kevin," Molly said. "You've got the heart of a lob-sterman."

Kevin looked away and blushed. "Say, glad to see Carolyn's back."

Molly almost dropped her gear. "I beg your pardon?"

"Yeah, her boat's right over there. She got here about an hour ago."

Molly looked to where Kevin was pointing. The *Carolyn S.* was moving gently on the waves. "She there?"

"No, I saw her go on your boat. I expect she's still there."

Molly swallowed, her throat tightening. "Thanks, Kevin."

"Sure thing, Molly. Well, glad your brother's back. We was all pulling for you, Molly, you know that."

"I do," Molly said distractedly. "Thanks again," she said as she walked toward her boat.

She tossed her gear on deck and stepped on board. The door to the cabin was open. She stepped inside the pilothouse and for the first time Cat didn't come running to greet her.

Molly walked down the steps to the cabin. Carolyn was sitting up on her bed, her back propped against the wall. Cat was curled up on her lap. "Hi, you," she said quietly.

"Hi yourself." Molly felt as though her legs were frozen.

Carolyn gently picked Cat up and put her on the bed and got up. She walked toward Molly and slipped her arms around her neck. She rested her head against Molly's shoulder.

"How—"

"Charlie figured out how to get hold of me. He told me what happened. I'm sorry, Molly. I should have stayed behind and confronted the situation. But when I saw her kiss you, it just brought back all the anger I'd felt when I caught my ex cheating on me."

Molly tipped Carolyn's head back and saw her expression, an image of hope and desire. "I'm just so glad you're here. I thought I'd lost you." Molly pulled Carolyn to her.

"I love you." Carolyn sighed.

Molly saw the raw, naked want in Carolyn's eyes. "I love you," Molly said as she kissed her. She backed Carolyn onto the bed. "You are my love," she said as she kissed her neck. She knew they were going to be late getting to Allan and Charlie's. But then, she thought, they had a lifetime to get to Allan and Charlie's.